Jan Costin Wagner was born in 1972 in Langen/Hesse near Frankfurt. After studying German language, literature and history at Frankfurt University, he went on to work as a journalist and freelance writer. He divides his time between Germany and Finland (the home country of his wife).

# SILENCE

In Finland a young girl disappears while cycling to volleyball practice. Her abandoned bike is found in exactly the same place that another girl was assaulted and murdered thirty-three years previously. The perpetrator was never brought to justice and the authorities suspect the same killer has struck again. An unsettling crime — particularly for someone who's carried a burden of guilt for years . . . Investigating, Detective Kimmo Joentaa is helped by his colleague Ketola, who worked on the original murder. As the ripples from the impact of the new disappearance spread, Kimmo discovers that the truth is not always what you expect.

JAN COSTIN WAGNER

# SILENCE

TRANSLATED
FROM THE GERMAN
BY
## ANTHEA BELL

*Complete and Unabridged*

## ULVERSCROFT
*Leicester*

First published in Great Britain in 2010 by
Harvill Secker
The Random House Group Limited, London

First Large Print Edition
published 2011
by arrangement with
The Random House Group Limited, London

First published with the title *Das Schweigen* in 2007
by Eichwen AG, Frankfurt am Main

British Library CIP Data

Wagner, Jan Costin, *1972* –
  Silence.
  1. Missing children- -Finland- -Fiction.
  2. Missing persons- - Investigation- -Finland- -Fiction.
  3. Police- -Fiction. 4. Detective and mystery stories.
  5. Large type books.
  I. Title
  833.9'2–dc22

ISBN 978–1–4448–0819–3

Published by
F. A. Thorpe (Publishing)
Anstey, Leicestershire

Set by Words & Graphics Ltd.
Anstey, Leicestershire
Printed and bound in Great Britain by
T. J. International Ltd., Padstow, Cornwall

This book is printed on acid-free paper

For Niina, Venla, Ninne and my parents

# PROLOGUE

Summer 1974

The time came when they got into the little red car and drove away. Before that, they'd sat in the shade inside the small flat for a long time. For hours, days, weeks.

At first Pärssinen had had to entice him, spend time persuading him to come in. Later he himself used to knock at the door, then Pärssinen would open it and he would sit in Pärssinen's flat looking at the dappled sunlight on the floor, concentrating on Pärssinen's voice. A soft, monotonous voice that suddenly cracked now and then, only to go on, barely audibly, next moment.

Sometimes he had raised his head to try meeting Pärssinen's eyes, but he couldn't, because Pärssinen had been looking past him, speaking to the wall. Then he would lower his head again, close his eyes and go on concentrating on Pärssinen's voice.

After a while Pärssinen would take a roll of film out of one of the containers, switch on the projector and, while the film ran, Pärssinen would at last fall silent.

While Pärssinen sat in silence he himself had stared at the screen, moving his hand

3

slowly up and down in his trouser pocket, and out of the corner of his eye he sensed that Pärssinen noticed, but that became less and less important, and first Pärssinen had laughed, then, a little later, he had joined in and the moment came, after a few weeks, when they drove off.

Pärssinen had said, 'We'll be off now,' and he had not replied. Pärssinen had placed the film in its container, put the container away on the shelf unit, then he had stood up and said again, 'We'll be off now.'

He thought he remembered that for a brief time — he didn't know just how long but it couldn't have been more than seconds — he went on sitting there. He even thought he remembered a flicker in Pärssinen's eyes, a moment of uncertainty. Briefly, Pärssinen had doubted him. But then he too had got to his feet, feeling an ache in his lower body as he followed Pärssinen out of doors.

The sun had been hot and Pärssinen's small red car was grubby with the dirt accumulated over months, maybe years. They had got in.

In his memory he saw Pärssinen sitting at the wheel. He didn't see himself in the passenger seat. During the drive Pärssinen started talking again. Hectically, insistently. He had run quickly through the plan once more, summing it all up, while he thought about the film and a certain particular scene, a specific situation in that film, then he had felt that it would soon be over, it was only just beginning but it would soon be over. And Pärssinen had said they were going to go through with all that shit now, at the same time taking his eyes off the road to look fixedly at him. For a moment, the moment he might have used to wriggle out of it, Pärssinen's eyes met his.

After that he had looked through the windscreen at the dry road, with the sun baking down on their red car, and he'd thought of that particular scene in the film, seeing it in his mind's eye, imagining what it would be like to act it out for real, and Pärssinen had slowed down, muttering to himself when he saw something out there at the roadside, muttering, then shaking his head and saying, 'No, that won't do,' without any further explanation of why it wouldn't do.

Then Pärssinen had begun cursing to himself, had driven right out of the city, and he had felt that Pärssinen knew what he was doing, although Pärssinen had assured him he'd never done such a thing before and only their friendship, their meeting, their finding their way to each other, as he had once put it at the very end, had shown him that it must be done, it damn well had to be done some time, there was no point in denying that, they'd do it, they'd do it together. And while Pärssinen drove along the country road he had felt that the time had come, it was going to happen now, whatever *it* was, and he had imprinted the scene from a film he'd just seen on his brain, until he realized that nothing else played a part in this, and any kind of explosion would come as a relief.

Pärssinen had turned off the road, clapped him on the shoulder and signed to him to look a certain way, through the window on the driver's side.

He had seen what Pärssinen wanted to show him and Pärssinen had slowed down, moaning. Humming to himself or moaning, he didn't exactly know which, hadn't known at the time, but anyway Pärssinen had slowed down, looking alternately ahead and in the rear-view mirror, then finally stopped the car, put his hand on the door handle and said, 'Ready?'

Then — he remembered this very well — he had replied, 'What do you mean?'

Pärssinen hadn't reacted to that, except to say again, 'Now!'

Pärssinen got out of the car and he had seen him walking off, calmly and purpose-fully, and at that moment he'd understood that it was over, that it was all over, even as it was just beginning, and Pärssinen had pushed the girl off her bicycle, dragged her into the field, and he hadn't seen either of them any more, only the bicycle lying on the path with its handlebars wrenched round the wrong way.

He too had got out of the car, and he must have walked twenty or thirty metres to the bicycle path and the bicycle lying on the ground, although he couldn't remember the seconds he had spent walking those few metres.

First he picked up the bicycle.

He straightened the handlebars.

Then he went a few steps into the field and looked at Pärssinen, who was lying on top of the girl. He saw Pärssinen's bare buttocks and the girl's legs. Pärssinen was saying, 'It doesn't matter, go on, go on, go on, mmm . . . ' The girl said nothing, probably because Pärssinen was holding her mouth shut. Pärssinen was strong. Small but strong.

He stood for a while waiting for it to be over. And then it was over. It was all over.

'N . . . no. Please . . . no, no, don't, don't do that,' he said after a moment.

A little later Pärssinen got to his feet and pulled up his trousers. 'Shit,' he said. He was sweating.

The girl lay perfectly still, staring at Pärssinen.

'Shit,' said Pärssinen and as he was trying to work out from Pärssinen's face what Pärssinen meant by that, he was thinking that it was over, and Pärssinen bent over the girl and closed his hands round her throat.

The girl hardly reacted.

When he took a step in Pärssinen's direction, Pärssinen was standing up again and he said, 'Shit, now we'll have to get rid of her,' and, when he didn't reply, Pärssinen specified, 'Make sure she disappears. We have to get rid of her, understand? Give me a hand, you arsehole.'

He stood there watching Pärssinen as he dragged the girl along the bicycle path.

'Help me, can't you?' said Pärssinen and, when he didn't move, because he couldn't, Pärssinen laid the girl down, went to the car and drove it closer to the place where the girl was lying and he himself was standing.

Pärssinen got out of the car, crouched down, seemed to concentrate for a moment, then hauled the girl upright with a jolt, letting her drop into the boot. He closed the boot, threw the bicycle into the field and said, 'Let's get out of here!'

He stood there looking at the bicycle in the field.

'Are you just going to stay here, or what?' called Pärssinen from the car, hammering and kicking at the passenger door.

He went to the car.

He got in.

Pärssinen started the car. They drove for a while in silence. The sun was shining brightly. Not another car in sight.

After a while Pärssinen turned off down a woodland path. 'I know this place,' he muttered. The girl. He thought of the girl's legs. She had still had her shoes on, she was lying in the boot. 'I know this place, there's a lake over there,' Pärssinen had said, steering the car through the woods along increasingly narrow paths.

On the way home Pärssinen said nothing, and sweated. He had smelt the sweat, he could still remember the smell. Pärssinen was sweating as he'd never seen anyone sweat before, his grey shirt was drenched and sticking to his body. He himself hadn't been sweating. He'd been shaking. He'd felt cold. Anyone looking attentively at them would have been sure to notice the remarkable difference, one of them sweating and one freezing, although they were driving in the same car, but they met no one, so there was no one to notice them and feel surprised.

He had sat beside Pärssinen in the car, had

begun to recognize the buildings moving swiftly past, the streets they were driving down, and he had thought of the girl. Of the moment when Pärssinen let her drop into the water and sink, and of a scene from Pärssinen's film that had nothing to do with it, but he simply couldn't get it out of his head, although it was all over now and he hadn't done anything, because he hadn't touched the girl, hadn't even touched her, he was sure of that, he'd refused to lift a finger to help Pärssinen.

Pärssinen had driven on and he had seen a summer's day on the other side of the windscreen.

When they finally arrived, when Pärssinen had stopped the car in the car park next to the big concrete building among the trees, he had got out, leaving the sweating Pärssinen sitting there, he had gone up to his own flat and immediately began flinging everything lying around into his travelling bag, as well as all the stuff from the cupboards and drawers.

He looked at the time, gave himself twenty minutes, put everything that wouldn't fit into the travelling bag into bin bags, emptied the fridge, threw away the food, it was all going into the garbage container in several bin bags, which he lined up beside his travelling bag; he stripped the bed and stuffed the bedclothes into another bin bag, and then he went down. He had had to make three journeys, down into the sunlight and up again to the shade of the flat; he'd been freezing in sun and shade alike, and as if from a great distance he had seen Pärssinen hosing down the tyres of his car, so intent on his task that he didn't even notice him.

He had watched Pärssinen working away in the flickering sunlight while, with deliberate movements, he dropped the bin bags one by one into the big container.

There were some people about by now, they'd passed him coming and going, had stood around somewhere, not wanting anything special from him: the old lady, the lush who lived next door to him, carrying her shopping and talking to herself, and Susanna, the girl from the building opposite — he'd often thought about her and sometimes dreamed of her — she had passed him with two other girls. The three of them had said a cheerful hello to him, the kind of greeting you'd expect on a fine summer's day.

The girls were giggling and said they were just back from the lake — a different lake, and not far away — Pärssinen had been scrubbing the boot of his car and polishing it all up, without raising his head.

He had gone back into the building after

the girls, who had been wearing swimsuits and had wet hair and were barefoot, although there were often broken bits of beer bottles lying about on the asphalt, he'd thought of that as he went upstairs step by step. Then he closed the front door of the flat behind him, went to the phone book and called a firm to come and take away the bed and the rest of the furniture, and dispose of it.

It hadn't been easy to get the man to understand that no, he wasn't moving house, he just wanted to get rid of furniture he couldn't use any more, but after a while the man got the idea and assured him he'd be there first thing next morning.

After that he'd looked out of the window at the trees and the sky for a bit, and through the glass he could faintly hear the vacuum cleaner that Pärssinen was using to clean his car.

He went round the little flat again, filling a final bin bag with what was still lying around. He did it several times to make sure it was really empty. Then he had gone out into the white corridor, closed the door, heard it latch shut, left the key for the removal men and went down into the sun.

He'd thrown the bin bag into the container. Pärssinen had been crouching on the back seat of his car, removing stains that weren't there, couldn't be there because the girl had been lying in the boot, nowhere else. But there'd been no stopping Pärssinen, and he had gone up to the car and said, 'I'm leaving now.'

Pärssinen had straightened up and stared at him. 'She bled. Shit. The boot's all over bloodstains, and I think the back seat . . . '

'I'm leaving now,' he had repeated, seeing surprise spread over Pärssinen's face, the surprise he was feeling himself, astonished as he was by the total calm surrounding him. His travelling bag was slung lightly over his shoulder, the sun was warm and he hardly heard what Pärssinen said.

'I'm leaving now. We won't be seeing each other again,' he had said and looked briefly at Pärssinen's open mouth. Then he'd turned away and gone to the bus stop. The bus came after a few minutes, he bought a ticket and sat at the back.

The grey building that was nothing to do with him soon disappeared from his field of vision and, as the bus turned into the main road, giving him another glimpse of the car park, the small red car looked like a toy.

And he never had seen Pärssinen again.

# THIRTY-THREE YEARS LATER

## LATER

January

# 1

On the day of his retirement Ketola rose at six in the morning. He took a cold shower and put on the clothes he'd laid out beside his bed the evening before. A dark green jacket and the black trousers that went with it.

He ate two slices of bread with a scraping of butter, read the leader in the daily paper, drank a cup of coffee, a shot of vodka and a glass of water to take away the taste of the alcohol.

He washed up the glass and cup, put them both back in the china cupboard, folded the newspaper and sat at the table for another five minutes, looking through the darkness beyond the kitchen window at the snow-covered trees in the garden next door.

When those five minutes were over he got to his feet, took his coat off the hook, put it on, and went out to his car. The car had a roof over it by way of shelter, but it had been very cold last night and the windows were iced up.

He scraped the ice off, got in, switched on the blower and waited until he could see clearly enough. Then he drove the car through the thick snow towards Turku.

Warmth slowly filled the vehicle and Ketola began to feel his exhaustion. He hadn't slept all night. Now and then he'd got up and tried to keep busy. He had read a book for a while, but now he couldn't remember a single page of it, or what the words on the page had said. He had switched the TV set on and off again, and after that he'd spent the final hours of the night staring at the ceiling and waiting for the shrill note of the alarm clock.

Now he switched on the CD player to keep himself awake, choosing the tune he'd kept playing as he drove to work recently. He had little idea of music, but he liked this piece, a duet for flutes. He didn't know the composer. The CD was a present from his son Tapani, who had given it to him on his birthday a few years ago.

Tapani had given him the CD without any sleeve notes. Typical of Tapani. Ketola had been pleased with the present, but it was typical for the sleeve notes to be missing and now it was too late to ask Tapani who had composed the music, even if he made up his mind to try asking next time they met.

He liked the piece. The melancholy of the music was really unusual and so pronounced that over the last few weeks Ketola had always felt a little better every time he listened to it.

He had to force himself to keep his eyes open and laughed out loud twice within a few seconds, because two thoughts that amused him, or at least made him laugh, had occurred to him in swift succession.

One was that it would be a pity to die on his last day at work, and in an accident that was his own fault at that. The other was that later, when Nurmela launched into his speech, which they were all agog to hear, perhaps he would finally fall asleep. Nurmela couldn't hold it against him, not today.

Ketola chuckled to himself for quite a while, then the tune began to make him feel sad. He switched off the CD player.

The rush of warm air from the blower filled the car. It was hot inside by now. Ketola felt the heat, and fancied that this was the first time he'd directly noticed the difference between the warmth of the interior and the cold darkness beyond the windscreen.

His eyes kept closing, nothing to be done about that, but he'd be there in a moment, he was already in the slow traffic of the city centre, which he knew looked worse than it was. His drive would be over in a few more minutes.

The snow mingled with exhaust fumes, yellow headlights and red brake lights to form a curious picture. He had the impression that he was seeing it for the first time, or for the first time in this way. That was nonsense, of course, and he began doing exactly what he had not in any circumstances meant to do: he began trying to work out what was special about this winter day, which in reality was exactly like all the others.

At last he turned left and drove down the less crowded, narrower street to the big building where he worked.

His glance went, as it had done for years, to the third floor CID offices and the window of his own room. There was no light on yet, he'd be the first in today, which was only right. After all, he'd been the first in for decades.

Only over the last two years, since Kimmo Joentaa lost his wife, had the light in his office very often been on first and Kimmo was to be found sitting at his desk in front of his gently humming computer when Ketola came in. Today Ketola had deliberately set off slightly earlier than usual, so as to win this silly little contest, although he suspected, or rather was sure, that Kimmo didn't see it as a contest at all, but simply came into the office early when he couldn't stand being at home any more.

Anyway, Ketola understood Kimmo's reasons for coming into the office early better than his own. In his first years in the police it must have been ambition, an attempt to make his mark, and ultimately he had done just that. But latterly that reason wouldn't wash, because Ketola had achieved the senior position he'd wanted, so now he had no idea why he still had to be first in at work, day after day.

However that might be, he was sure that Kimmo would take care not to arrive too early today. Indeed, if he knew Kimmo, he'd be in particularly late, just to give Ketola the space on his last day to do whatever he needed to in the empty office, maybe compose his mind, think quietly.

Ketola chuckled softly as he strode through the snow, which was falling more thickly now. He liked Kimmo, the man's integrity or whatever you liked to call it was rather overpowering, the way he took everything so damn seriously . . . but he really did like him and over two whole years now he had toyed with the thought of talking to Kimmo at greater length, some time, about his wife's death, because he couldn't shake off the feeling that, calm as he might seem, the death of his wife was sending him crazy. And Ketola knew his way around with crazy people, particularly young ones.

He greeted the man at the gate, as he did every morning, with a nod, and the man behind the glass pane nodded back. If he wasn't very much mistaken, he and the man behind the pane had greeted each other daily in the same way for years, without ever exchanging a word. He'd have to think some more about that later, but for now he really couldn't remember a single conversation.

Ketola took the lift up to the third floor and went along the dark corridor to his office. He switched on the light, sat down at his desk and started the computer. A brand-new machine, state of the art, although its predecessors had worked perfectly well and, above all, after much practice, Ketola had been able to use its operating system.

However, management had been so proud of their investment that they had placed a long article in the daily paper. Nurmela had posed readily and quite convincingly in front of one of the new machines, although he was the only member of the team who understood even less about modern technology than Ketola himself. And Tuomas Heinonen had shown the impressed woman journalist what you could do with these computers and this perfectly interlinking system, because Heinonen was very knowledgeable about such things and had often come to the rescue when Ketola's screen blacked out, or error messages came up, and had been remarkably patient about it.

For Nurmela's sake, Ketola had joined the training sessions given by self-important IT experts, although everyone knew that he wouldn't be working with the new computers for more than a few weeks. He chuckled again as he remembered those training seminars, because he had let himself go a little there, sometimes cracking jokes like a child in lessons at school, and once he had even rocked his chair back and forth for so long that he fell rather heavily to the floor.

Heinonen, who had been sitting beside him, had jumped, Petri Grönholm had roared with laughter, even the ever-serious Kimmo had grinned, and finally the speaker had shut up for a couple of seconds and stared at him as if he were an extraterrestrial.

At his age you could allow yourself these little flights of fancy, thought Ketola. After all, he didn't want to know all this stuff and he felt almost a little dizzy at the idea of what was being said about him in the corridors of this building.

All the little symbols were now lighting up on the screen against a deep blue background, the manufacturer's default setting. All the others had found different screen savers for their new monitors. Heinonen had a sunny beach, Grönholm had a picture of the Finnish ice hockey star who played successfully in the North American professional league and Kimmo Joentaa had a picture of a red church in front of blue water.

Whenever Ketola saw this picture he felt a pang, and to be honest it seemed almost an imposition to have to look at it more or less deliberately every day. Kimmo's wife was buried in the graveyard between the red church and the sea. Ketola had been there on the day of the funeral. The fact that Kimmo had chosen a picture of that church as his screen saver brought up certain questions. For instance, what was really going on inside the man? How was anyone to get over an experience like that if he sat facing it day after day? Ketola couldn't make it out.

He sat there leaning back for a while, looking out of the window. It was as dark as ever and snowflakes were settling on the pane, visibly blurring into a soft, white mass.

When Ketola looked at the situation properly, he didn't have much business here any more. He had cleared his desk last week, taking away what he wished to keep and throwing out the rest. He had wanted to avoid spending his last day in a burst of frantic activity and winding up in a gloomy or irritated mood. There hadn't been much anyway, strictly speaking only a shoebox full of stuff, which he couldn't claim had any deep meaning for him.

And of course Ketola wasn't planning to work today. He had spent most of the last few weeks showing his successor the ropes. Paavo Sundström was a colleague from Helsinki whom Ketola by now considered a very difficult but not unlikeable man, with qualities that, he hoped, would yet come to light. If he'd only been one of the ambitious careerist kind — but no, Sundström was only ten years younger than Ketola himself and his most striking characteristic was a sense of humour that could at the very least be called odd, bordering as it did on cynicism and sometimes going too far even for Ketola. Sundström was a tall, angular man with hair receding at the temples, a man of outwardly impressive appearance, and Ketola suspected that certain philistines had already interpreted that as a talent for leadership. And Ketola had to admit that Sundström did seem to have taken a certain amount of trouble with the results he had delivered in the first few weeks. The rest of it was only Ketola's initial and perhaps slightly prejudiced impression.

Ketola stood up, or rather suddenly jumped up, he had no idea why. To shake off his thoughts about Sundström, or just because he felt a little restless. Perhaps it had been a mistake to come in even earlier than usual today. He'd have done better to come in around midday, or even not until Nurmela was beginning his speech. He would have listened for fifteen minutes, said goodbye and made off.

He wondered whether to do just that. He still had plenty of time to drive home, go back to bed — he really was tired now — and considerably later, when the occasion was almost over, he'd thank Nurmela for his kind words and say his final goodbyes in short order.

But he decided against that, and the reason was an idea that took shape instantly. A good deal later Ketola kept wondering why that distant idea had come into his mind just then. It must have been something to do with the shoebox and the stuff in it, or the snow settling on the dark windowpane that he was staring at when the thought occurred to him. A thought about something he had forgotten long ago, and that was the moment when Kimmo Joentaa came into the office.

'Hello,' Ketola heard him say.

He raised his arm, studied Kimmo's questioning glance and said, 'There's something I have to look for.'

He set off, leaving Kimmo where he was.

'Can I help you?' Kimmo called after him, and at first Ketola wasn't going to answer the question, but then he turned and said, 'Yes, maybe you could. Come along. I want to find something.'

They went downstairs quickly, in silence, and Ketola muttered, more to himself than to Kimmo, 'It was before your time, ages ago . . .'

Out of the corner of his eye he saw Kimmo nod and quickened his pace, because this was something that he wanted to get over and done with now that he'd thought of it. It was a case that had been waiting to be cleared up . . . oh, for almost exactly thirty years.

'Must be thirty years ago,' he murmured. 'No, thirty-two . . . thirty-three years.'

Kimmo nodded.

'Crazy . . .' said Ketola.

The Central Archive of the department was on the first floor and filled three large, interconnecting rooms furnished with extreme austerity. At the white desk in the first room sat a young man whom Ketola had never seen before, presumably a temporary assistant.

'We're looking for something,' said Ketola and appeared to be waiting for the man to hand it to them.

'Yes, what is it?' asked the young archivist.

'A . . . well, a kind of model.'

The young man nodded vaguely.

'A model. From a case dating back thirty-three years.'

The young man nodded again.

'It was 1974. The time of the football World Cup, so it must have been 1974.'

'That's quite a while ago,' said the young man.

'Tell me, do you work here?' asked Ketola.

'I . . .'

'I mean do you have a regular job here or are you just temping? Because if so you may not know where we can find it in the archives.'

'No, no, I've been working here for . . . oh, three weeks now. It's my probationary period.'

'Hm, well,' muttered Ketola. 'Where's Päivi? She's usually in charge here.'

'Yes, that's why I . . . Päivi's on holiday, so this is my first week on my own.'

'I see,' said Ketola. 'Right, listen carefully. The case was thirty-three years ago, and back then the technicians made a model, a kind of . . . well, a kind of model railway without the railway.' Having managed to come up with this explanation, Ketola breathed a sigh of relief, but the young man was no use at all and just sat there looking gormless.

'Understand? We're looking for a model, a rectangular plastic model. Where might a thing like that be?'

At least the lad appeared to be thinking about it now.

'Any idea?' asked Ketola.

'Well, thirty-three years, that's . . . '

'A long time ago?' Ketola helped him out.

'Yes, we don't really have anything much up here, certainly not a model, anything like that. Downstairs there just might be . . . '

'Yes?'

'There's a room down there full of all sorts of stuff, Päivi hates the place, it's kind of our lumber room . . . '

'Oh yes?'

'Because it's all jumbled up and none of it means anything any more.'

'Then let's go down there now.'

'Well . . . but I can't leave the archives here.'

'What's your name?' asked Ketola.

'Er, Antti. Antti Lappeenranta.'

Ketola was suddenly in high good humour, he almost felt like joking. He took out his official ID — perhaps for the last time ever, it occurred to him — held it in front of the lad's nose and said, 'Antti Lappeenranta, I'm arresting you on suspicion of who cares what? Anyway, you're in custody. Follow me.' Then he went ahead, glancing back over his shoulder to make sure that Kimmo and the baffled youth were following him.

They took the lift down to the basement, which couldn't be reached in any other way, because the stairs ended at a door to which no one ever seemed to have had a key.

'After you,' said Ketola when they were down in the basement, and the young archivist led them to a room that really was remote, even in this basement storey, and was in fact large, but in relation to the quantity of stuff it contained it was decidedly small.

Ketola stared in amazement and Kimmo said, 'Hm.'

'Yes, well,' the young man agreed.

The room was stacked high with several strata of cardboard cartons, some of them open and showing that they contained file folders in varying states of grubbiness and assorted fading colours. Similar folders stood or lay on shelves, old office machines were crammed close together along the walls of the room: copiers, printers, overhead projectors. Ketola could smell the dust that had settled everywhere and, still in a mood for joking, he suggested, 'Päivi might clear up in here when she gets a moment.'

'Mm, well, it's only for the time being because we . . . I mean the archives . . . well, I wasn't there at the time, but Päivi told me they had to make space, so they took stuff down here that wasn't so important any more. Soon a lot of it's going to be thrown out entirely.'

'Of course. So where's my model?'

'Er . . . well, if it's anywhere at all, it would be here.'

Kimmo was already forging a path through the cardboard cartons. He stopped in the middle of the room and asked, 'How big is it, then? I mean, how long and how wide?'

Ketola thought about it. 'I'd say it was about the size of a small table. And it's on wheels.'

'Wheels?' asked the young archivist.

'Yes, we kept pushing it from the office to the conference room and back. It's on wheels. A table on wheels.'

Kimmo went over to the machinery pushed back against the walls, some of the items covered with white cloths. Ketola followed him and stumbled over a carton as Kimmo called, 'Here!'

'What?'

'I think this is it.' Kimmo stepped aside to give Ketola a view of the model he had been looking for. Ketola was still standing on the carton, half dazed. He straightened up and saw the plastic rectangle. Ketola sighed at the

31

sight before him; he merely heard himself sighing, although he didn't know where inside him the sound came from and couldn't interpret its meaning.

'Yes, that's it,' he said and went closer. He stood there for a while and was consciously trying to absorb every detail. He still didn't understand why he had suddenly been so keen to find this model, because he had forgotten the case long ago.

'That's it,' he repeated. By now the young archivist had joined them. They looked at the model in silence for a while. It depicted a yellow field, an avenue of trees carefully glued in position and a grey bicycle path fenced off from the two-lane road, which was also grey. The whole thing was made of cardboard and plastic, even the fences beside the road had been marked in and, although the sun was missing, the model showed that it was intended to capture a moment in a summer's day. A plastic bicycle lay in the plastic field and a red car stood at the roadside. The model was as detailed as Ketola had remembered it.

'What is it?' asked the archivist.

'A model,' said Ketola without looking up. But out of the corner of his eye he saw the young man nod vaguely. Kimmo stood there motionless.

'It was a murder case. The murder of a girl,' said Ketola. 'I'd only just started here when it happened. She was raped and murdered in that field, very close to her parents' house. We never caught the murderer.'

The young man nodded again. Kimmo still didn't move.

The girl was not in the picture. They hadn't found her until a good deal later when she wasn't a girl any more.

'I'd really forgotten the case. I've no idea why I thought of it today of all days. A few months later, just after we'd finally found the girl, the CID officer leading the enquiries insisted on having this model made. He thought it would help us to see the full picture. We were getting nowhere and it sent him half out of his mind.'

'So the case was never solved?' asked the archivist.

Ketola nodded. 'The man in charge at the time is dead now,' he said.

'What make of car is it?' asked the archivist, pointing to the small red car.

'Hmm . . . ' said Ketola. The small red car that they'd never found. The most important part of the picture. It caught your eye at once. By now the small car must be a lump of scrap metal, or even less. In fact that was for sure.

Maybe it had never existed anyway, because the witness who saw the car was a little boy who had been cycling along the parallel bicycle path on the other side of the road at around noon on that day thirty-three years ago.

No, they had never found the small red car. On the other hand they had found the girl; they'd fished her out of a lake. One of the divers threw up immediately after they pulled her out, and Ketola and a colleague had broken the news to the girl's mother.

It wasn't the first time he'd spoken to the families of murder victims, but he had never seen the life go right out of someone's eyes before. Like everyone else, Ketola had expected that the girl would be found dead some time, and the mother too must have taken her daughter's death for granted, but during the seconds when his late colleague spoke the words Ketola had seen the woman's life end in a way that he could never have described to anyone.

'I see,' said the archivist, when Ketola's silence had lasted a long time.

'I'd like to take it with me,' said Ketola. 'Give me a hand, would you?'

They carried the model through the basement to the lift and, once on the next floor up, they carried it past the intrigued doorman

34

and out into the driving snow. With some difficulty they got it into the boot of Ketola's car. As they turned back to the building, Ketola realized that he hadn't answered the archivist's question about the red car, but as the young man didn't ask again, Ketola left it unanswered. He didn't want to discuss the subject. The important thing was that he had just stowed the plastic and cardboard model away in his boot, and as for why he had done it, he'd have plenty of time to think about that later, when today was over.

'Okay, then,' said the archivist, when the lift door opened on the first floor.

'Thanks for your help,' said Ketola.

'You're welcome,' replied the archivist, sketching a clumsy goodbye wave and returning to his work station, while Ketola and Joentaa went up to the third floor.

Ketola sat down at his desk and resumed looking alternately at the clear blue of his screen, which to his mind was the best kind of background image, and the snow-covered pane of the window. Kimmo sat opposite him and kept his mouth shut, presumably either out of consideration or because his mind was hard at work wondering what on earth was the matter with him, Ketola.

'Chatty today, aren't you?' Ketola remarked, realizing that he had never felt so relaxed and in such a humorous mood on any other working day as he did now, on this last day of all.

'I noticed that you didn't answer that question about the red car, so I thought maybe you didn't want to talk about it.'

Of course. Finger on the sore spot right away. And still considerate about it. He was going to miss Kimmo.

'We never found the car. A witness saw it, a little boy. Back then, I mean. Today he'd be . . . oh, in his forties. It was odd, somehow. But the whole thing didn't really mean much . . . I don't know what put me in mind of it. I haven't thought of that girl for decades. Or the mother either.'

'The murdered girl's mother?'

'Yes, it was . . . it was a strange experience, you might say, breaking that news to the woman. I'd started work here only a few months before.'

Kimmo nodded, and Ketola ended the conversation with a dismissive gesture. He didn't want to start getting loquacious at the last minute. 'Do you know what's happening today?' he asked instead.

Kimmo looked enquiringly at him.

'I mean the goodbyes. It's my last day, see?' Perhaps the jokes were getting out of hand, he thought.

'Oh, we've got this and that ready,' said Kimmo.

'Come on.'

'Let it be a surprise,' said Kimmo and he actually smiled.

Then they went on sitting there in silence. Kimmo was sorting papers that had nothing to do with Ketola any more. Ketola was looking out of the window after brushing the snow off the pane. So now he was watching the snow start to cover the pane again, and trying for the last time to find a good way of mentioning Kimmo's wife and asking how he was doing these days, but of course he didn't, because it would just have been ridiculous, and then Tuomas Heinonen came into the room anyway and asked Kimmo to come with him, they had something ready. Winking. Obviously Heinonen had also gone off his rocker.

So he sat there without thinking of anything in particular; now and then he took phone calls, which proved to be not very important, and around midday Nurmela knocked on the door and came in wearing a chef's hat and an apron, and balancing an enormous tray.

Nurmela was followed by the entire team, they really were all there, even Petri Grönholm had come to Ketola's goodbye party, although Petri Grönholm had been off sick with flu for several days.

There were little sausages in tomato sauce, Ketola's favourite. Nurmela served the lunch in cheerful mood. Kari Niemi, head of forensics, poured champagne, also in cheerful mood, but that was nothing unusual in Niemi. Ketola's successor Sundström shone with a number of particularly pointless puns and the entire team sang the Finnish hit that Ketola must have hummed quite often over the last few years — 'Oh, all the time, my dear fellow, all the time,' Nurmela insisted — when he was thinking, or when he gave the impression of thinking.

The performance was very good, his colleagues had obviously worked hard on it, and just as Ketola was wondering when they could have rehearsed, Nurmela wound things up by launching into his eagerly awaited speech, and instead of dropping off to sleep as he had originally intended, Ketola stood there feeling the words take shape before his eyes, come together in a blur and concentrate into a feeling, the feeling that Nurmela was making a very well prepared speech, a speech praising him from the heart and, if he was honest, a positively touching speech, but it was no more than a feeling, because when Nurmela had finally spoken the last sentence Ketola couldn't have repeated a word of it. The one thing Ketola still had to say in these circumstances was, 'Thank you.' And as they stood there and seemed to be waiting for more, he said again, making it rather more specific, 'Thank you all.'

A little later Ketola set off. Kimmo, Niemi and Tuomas Heinonen had driven away to investigate the death of an old lady found at the foot of the cellar steps in her building. Ketola left with Grönholm, who was on his way back to his sickbed.

'Good of you to come,' said Ketola. He felt dizzy. It was snowing as hard as ever.

'Well, of course I did,' said Petri Grönholm. And when they had reached Ketola's car, he added, 'We expect you to come and see us regularly.'

Ketola nodded. 'Get well soon,' he said, climbed in and started the car. He really did feel dizzy, but of course he'd drunk a fair bit of champagne and it had made him a little tipsy, which was surprising, because it was a long time since vodka and whisky had been able to do that.

Ketola went the long way home. To his surprise, he could still remember the road precisely, a road with very little traffic on it even today, a road he hadn't driven along for many years. There was a cross at the place where they had found the girl's bicycle all that time ago. It had been standing there for some thirty-three years.

As Ketola got out of the car and walked towards the cross, he was trying to remember that day, to bring the whole thing back, the image of the woman in whose eyes he had seen something extinguished and who had then suddenly walked away, carrying the cross, which had been waiting as if ready for her in a corner of the coat stand, like an umbrella. He and his boss had followed the girl's mother, and after a while the woman had started running until she reached this very place, hardly five minutes from the house where she had lived with her daughter and her husband. The man didn't often put in an appearance. What Ketola remembered about him chiefly was that he had left his wife a few months after their daughter's body was found.

So the cross was still there. Carefully, Ketola brushed aside the snow and read the name. Pia Lehtinen. Exactly, that had been her name. He had been thinking about it briefly in the car and could come up only with the surname. Yet her first name was very simple and easily remembered, and it had been a common one at the time. Pia Lehtinen, murdered 1974, said the wording on the cross.

And five minutes from here, five minutes'

walk from the place where they had found the bicycle at that time, the girl's mother lived. Or rather she had lived there, because very likely she didn't live there any more; how could she still be living there after that . . . ? But now Ketola even remembered talking to her briefly on that subject at the time, in the months when the investigation was still in full swing and they'd assumed that their enquiries would be successful. The woman had told him she had no intention of moving, she would leave this house, at the earliest, after the murderer was caught. And he never had been caught, so maybe the woman was still living there. For a moment Ketola wondered whether to visit her, tell her that this was the day of his retirement from the police, and for reasons he didn't understand today, of all days, he had been thinking of her and her daughter.

Of course he rejected the idea and instead went straight back to his car. If the woman did still live here he didn't want her seeing him.

He drove home. It was still afternoon, but beginning to get dark. The snowfall was slackening.

He left the car under the projecting roof, took the newer of his two shovels and dug the snow out of his entrance.

41

He greeted the married couple from the house next door, who were walking past him, in a clearly audible voice. They both looked surprised, presumably because Ketola sometimes forgot to say good day at all. The couple's daughter, so Ketola thought, would be about the same age now as the dead girl had been back then.

After finishing his work, Ketola put the shovel back in its place and went up to the house. Unlocked the door, knocked the snow off his shoes and went in. He headed straight for the kitchen and made coffee, adding a shot of cognac.

Then he sat down on the living room sofa, switched on the TV set, put his cup on the table and, for the first time in a very long while, and with a sense of decided relief, began shedding tears.

# 8 JUNE

# 1

Timo Korvensuo felt the evening sun resting on him, warm and high overhead.

He quickened his pace, took the three wooden steps up to the front door in a single stride, and gave the woman another smile before he opened it.

'I thought you might like this,' he said, and left the view to do its work.

The woman stayed in the doorway, because even from here she could see the sun over the lake through the living room window and Timo Korvensuo knew that during these weeks of the year, in this weather and at this time of day, it always stood at an unusual angle, flooding the lake with almost improbably beautiful light.

He had shown the house to eight potential buyers so far and, although none of them had yet decided to clinch the deal, this image never failed to impress clients. Korvensuo stood beside the woman as she admired the view and thought that he liked this house, and in spite of its structural deficiencies might perhaps have wanted to buy it himself except that, as it happened, he already had a weekend house on this same lake, only a few minutes' drive away. Later, after this last appointment of the day was over, he would go there at his leisure and have a little while to himself before Marjatta, the children and their guests arrived. He might even manage a sauna and a swim.

'Shall we take a look inside this gem?' he asked the woman.

'Yes, let's,' she said. 'I think I really like it.'

Korvensuo nodded and took her round the rooms, which as usual he had had cleaned and furnished in a style that was bound to appeal to viewers.

In the course of his guided tour he never failed to mention every single flaw in the house to interested parties, but at the same time he took care that the properties he was selling showed their best side. And if the owners of a house themselves were not in a position to make sure of that, he would lend a hand himself. No sellers had ever yet complained.

'It's . . . yes, attractive, in spite of the drawbacks. I'll think about it,' the woman finally said and Korvensuo nodded.

They shook hands, and he waited for her to get into her car and drive away before seating himself in his own. He was satisfied. He lingered for a little while, looking at the house

46

in the red glow of sunset. It would soon find a new owner.

Then he started the car and drove round to his own place on the other side of the lake. As he had hoped, he still had a little time left before all the noise and racket started. The kids would be in high spirits today, the first day of the long summer holidays.

He was looking forward to a family weekend together, the first in a long time — he'd been travelling a great deal these last few weeks. But yesterday he had finally found takers for two properties that were really beginning to feel like a burden on him, and now he felt liberated. He decided not even to go indoors first, or take a sauna, he would just jump straight into the lake.

He got out of the car and went down to the landing stage, stripped off his clothes, put them all together in a neat rectangular pile, left his shoes at a right angle to it, put his watch in his left shoe, then decided on the right shoe after all, and jumped into the water. He let himself sink to the bottom, catapulted himself back to the surface and swam far out to the middle of the lake.

Only now did he really feel how those two properties had been weighing on his mind, and what a great relief it was not to have to drive to that Helsinki suburb again at long last, to offer two more flats in dire need of renovation, as if tempting someone to have a sour beer. It had been a mistake to take on those properties in the first place, particularly as the seller had expressed unrealistic ideas of the price he could get and had been a prickly character in general, but in view of the present financial situation Korvensuo hadn't had much choice. And ultimately it had been worth while, because thanks to a builder who would undertake to renovate the two flats himself and was obviously glad of the job, those properties were off his hands.

He swam back to the bank, swung himself up on to the landing stage and dressed. In half an hour's time Marjatta and the children would be arriving. And another half an hour later so would their guests. Johanna and Arvi Mustonen with their two daughters. And Pekka, his young colleague, a man he really liked. Pekka did good work, he was a quiet, decent man.

It was going to be a fine evening. He draped his jacket and tie over his arm; he had a T-shirt in the car boot. He felt good. He turned round once and after a few seconds turned again in the opposite direction. Then he ran up the slope to his car.

# 2

The children were chasing back and forth between the sauna and the lake, never tiring. Aku, Laura and the Mustonens' daughters. Timo Korvensuo watched them, and felt nothing but pleasure, relief and a sense of agreeable emptiness after several days of hard work.

The Mustonens' younger daughter was wearing a pink bathing suit, the older girl wore red bathing trunks with a green and white striped bikini top. He liked the look of that, it didn't trouble him, he talked to his guests in relaxed mood and merely took in the details out of the corner of his eye. The drops of water on the girls' skin, the older girl running her hand through her hair in a certain way, the water spraying on his arm when the girls ran round the table.

They were playing Catch, and Aku was always It and had to be caught. The girls got him down, swarmed over him and tickled him, and Aku laughed, otherwise not bothered, and was already jumping back into the water. The girls followed. They swam far out, their laughter dying away in the distance.

'Please take care!' Marjatta called.

'They'll be all right,' said Arvi.

'Anyone like a second helping of meat?' asked Korvensuo.

Johanna and Marjatta waved the offer aside. Arvi raised a hand.

'You too, Pekka?' asked Korvensuo.

'Well, yes, just a little more,' murmured Pekka. Korvensuo was mildly amused by his young colleague. When it came to selling houses, Pekka Rantanen wasn't half as diffident as now, sitting carefully motionless on his chair, saying hardly a word and eating little. People acted so differently in various situations.

Korvensuo served meat on to the guests' plates, turned round, which the others didn't seem to notice, sat down, began eating heartily and let Arvi muse on the state of the national Finnish football team.

'They have good players, but they just don't make the best use of them. You can bet we'll be left nowhere again,' he said, and Korvensuo nodded as the children's laughter came closer again.

'Terrible luck with injuries,' murmured Pekka.

'While we're talking about football, why not switch on the box? The Under-21s have a game today.'

'Sure, if the ladies don't mind,' said Timo Korvensuo, but the ladies were deep in discussion of second-hand shops. Korvensuo smiled to himself as he carried the little portable TV set out on to the terrace. He placed it on a chair, switched it on and fiddled around to find the best position for the aerial.

'You even watch the juniors playing?' asked Pekka somewhere in the background.

'We won't ever really be up with the best if we don't have promising youngsters coming through,' replied Arvi.

The picture wasn't particularly good, but it would just about do.

'You might get yourselves a new set some time,' said Arvi. 'This one's out of the Ark.'

'We don't really watch TV much here ... and look, it's okay,' said Korvensuo, pointing to the screen. Sure enough, the picture was clearer now and the Finns had possession of the ball.

Korvensuo turned away and looked at the lake. The girls were standing in the evening sunlight, jostling one another about until Laura, screeching, fell into the water. Aku had put his clothes on again now and came running towards them shouting that he wanted ice cream.

'Coming in a moment,' called Marjatta.

Korvensuo sat down and let Arvi's ramblings about the Finnish team lull him almost to sleep. From time to time Pekka added a comment. The game on the screen was soporific too, and the warmth of the evening enveloped him like a blanket. Now and then his eyes closed.

Marjatta brought out ice cream, the children chattered to each other and reached for the dishes that she was handing them. The sun had gone down now, but he almost felt the air was getting warmer and warmer. He saw a newsreader on the screen. He was about to ask Arvi whether the game was over or if this was half-time, but Marjatta asked him a question that he heard only indistinctly, because he was looking at something that had caught his attention.

'What?'

'I asked if you'd like ice cream too, or what little they've left,' Marjatta repeated, holding the dish in front of his face, but he couldn't take his eyes off the picture he was looking at, the picture that ... And the girls were chattering away all round him, and Aku had started to cry.

'I'll just go and get another pack out of the fridge, then everyone will be happy including our little Aku,' he heard Marjatta say, and he realized that he had risen to his feet and was on the move. 'What's going on there?' he asked Arvi as he went past, but Arvi, deep in animated discussion with Pekka, didn't hear him.

Aku had stopped crying.

'I want some more ice cream too,' said Laura.

Korvensuo knelt down in front of the TV, never taking his eyes off the screen, and tried to concentrate on the words coming out of the set. He groped for the volume button.

'Anything special?' he heard Marjatta ask. She was standing right behind his back as he carefully turned up the sound.

Marjatta put a hand on his shoulder.

He listened to the newsreader's matter-of-fact voice.

'Turn it up a bit louder, sounds like something's happened,' said Arvi.

There was a bicycle on the screen. A field. A field in the sunlight. Korvensuo made out a cross beside the bicycle. A cross standing just outside the field, and beyond it, in the field itself, was a bicycle. The bicycle lay there in the sun. The newsreader's voice spoke of the cross and a similar case that was now thirty-three years in the past. A girl's photograph came up on screen. The voice gave her name and age, and said the girl had been murdered thirty-three years ago.

'How awful,' he heard Johanna saying and then he saw a red car on the screen, not a photograph but a drawing of a small red car. He sat up abruptly. Something was trickling through his body. A warm feeling. Dry. Like sand. He moved past the others and back to the chair where he had been sitting, The rest of them were standing around the TV set talking, but he heard only Arvi's voice as the dry, warm sand trickled through his body.

'You wonder what kind of bastard would do a thing like that again,' said Arvi. And when no one replied he added, 'Enough to stop anyone wanting to have children.'

After that no one said anything for a while. The children were hovering about in front of the TV, eating small spoonfuls of ice cream. Marjatta suggested making coffee and Johanna followed her in. Aku took advantage of his mother's absence to pile another helping of ice cream on to his plate.

'Can I?' he asked.

Korvensuo nodded.

Arvi and Pekka went back to where they had been sitting before and watched the screen. The second half of the football match was beginning. The girls went down the slope to the landing stage with a pack of cards.

Korvensuo saw everything very clearly. His body was full of sand.

Marjatta poured coffee.

Arvi and Pekka were cheering a Finnish goal.

'People somehow don't think such things happen in Finland,' said Marjatta. Johanna nodded. Arvi and Pekka were concentrating on the game. Korvensuo nodded. Nodded to himself and looked at the screen. He raised the cup to his mouth.

'Do you see what I mean?' asked Marjatta.

'Of course,' said Johanna.

'You get bastards everywhere,' said Arvi, without taking his eyes off the screen.

'That was offside,' said Pekka.

Korvensuo felt his wife's gaze resting on him. 'Sure,' he said. 'Sure.' He raised the cup to his mouth again. A shot in slow motion flickered before his eyes. A foul.

'They were saying on the news there was a girl murdered on that very same spot thirty years ago,' said Johanna.

'Thirty-three years ago,' Pekka said.

'On that very same spot. The cross beside the bicycle is in memory of the dead girl,' said Johanna.

'Really weird,' said Arvi. 'Whoever murdered the girl back then must be drawing his old-age pension by now.'

'That depends,' said Pekka.

'I expect it was the girl's family put the

cross up there,' said Marjatta. 'And now the place has been . . . well, kind of desecrated again.'

'Hm, desecrated . . . ' said Arvi.

'Did you say her family?' Korvensuo asked.

'Yes. Well, I suppose it was them, anyway, the report didn't say that in so many words, but it mentioned that the girl lived only a few minutes away from the place. I mean the girl who was murdered all that time ago.'

'Did anyone say how old she was?' asked Korvensuo.

'The girl back then?'

'Yes.'

'Thirteen,' said Pekka.

Korvensuo nodded. Nodded to himself.

'There's one good thing about it, maybe they'll catch the man now. Maybe this time he slipped up, made a mistake,' said Arvi.

'But it can't be the same man. Not after thirty-three years,' said Pekka.

'Who else would it be?' asked Arvi.

Korvensuo reached for his cup. The flickering in front of his eyes was getting worse. He heard the children laughing. He felt curiously light. The game on TV seemed endless. Marjatta poured more coffee and handed round chocolate biscuits.

'Do you think . . . ' Korvensuo began. He met Marjatta's eyes.

'Think what?' asked Marjatta.

'Oh, nothing.' He couldn't remember what he had been going to say. Presumably he'd intended to change the subject, start talking about Finnish football again, but he couldn't get the words out. He seemed to weigh light, very light, and he had a queasy feeling in his stomach. Marjatta's gaze was resting on him, and Arvi and Pekka were talking about the missing girl who hadn't yet been found.

'They'll find her in the same lake as the other girl all that time ago,' Arvi was just saying.

'I expect so,' said Pekka.

'But it's still odd. I've never heard of something like that happening all over again thirty years later, just like that,' said Arvi.

Pekka murmured something that Korvensuo couldn't make out. The footballers on the screen were crowding around the referee.

'Did he blow for a penalty or what?' asked Arvi.

'Looks like it,' said Pekka.

They both leaned forward to hear the commentator's opinion. Korvensuo watched the screen, saw the penalty kick. The man taking it tricked the goalkeeper, the ball flew low into the left-hand corner of the net. The players celebrated and Arvi said, 'That's how these stupid games always go. Three minutes

57

before the final whistle.'

'What's the score?' That was his own voice. 'What's the score now?'

'One-all. I can see you've been concentrating!' said Arvi.

'That's okay, then,' said Korvensuo.

'How do you mean, that's okay? It's not good enough. When it comes to the crunch that'll only get them third or fourth place in the group.'

The children were laughing down on the landing stage. To his right, Marjatta and Johanna now seemed to be talking about the murdered girl. Yes, they were saying how scared it made them feel. Korvensuo raised his cup to his mouth again and ate a chocolate biscuit. A player was being interviewed on the TV screen.

'Do you know . . . ' Korvensuo began again.

'What?' asked Arvi.

'How many matches are there still to go?'

'How do you mean?'

'Well, how many games in the qualifying period? For the A team.'

'No idea. Three, is it?'

'Five,' said Pekka.

'But they still won't make it,' Arvi opined.

Korvensuo nodded to himself and concentrated on the children's laughter as they played cards on the landing stage. The flickering in front of his eyes was wearing off now, but sand was trickling through his body again, a slight but steady sensation. Arvi switched off the TV. Marjatta picked up the empty coffee jug.

'Let me do that,' said Korvensuo. He had risen quickly and was fighting off mild nausea as he went into the house. In the kitchen he switched on the coffee machine and watched coffee dripping into the jug. He'd have to sort out his mind later. When their guests had gone. When Marjatta and the children were asleep. He would think certain things over then, perfectly calmly.

Through the window he saw Arvi walking down the slope. He probably wanted to use the sauna again. Johanna and Marjatta were deep in lively but relaxed conversation, certainly no longer about what they'd seen on the news. Pekka was leaning back slightly with his face turned up to the sky. Korvensuo took the coffee jug and went outside.

'Anything else? We have chilled drinks too. Lemonade, anyone?' he asked when he had reached the table.

'Sounds good,' said Pekka.

He went back into the house, into the kitchen, and took a bottle of lemonade out of the fridge. It felt cold in his hand, and in his head a vein burst. Or that was what it felt like. A hot sensation spreading from his forehead over his cheeks and down into his body.

He went back out and handed Pekka the bottle. Pekka thanked him. Korvensuo nodded. He too felt thirsty. He went back into the house and helped himself to a lemonade from the fridge. He drank greedily, draining it in a single draught, then he felt himself swinging back his arm and bringing the bottle down on the sink with all his might. The bottle shattered in his hand. Through the window he saw them all jumping up outside.

'It's all right! I'll clear it up. I just dropped a bottle,' he called.

Marjatta was running to the house.

'It's all right,' he repeated when she reached the doorway. He turned his back to her and felt about in the cupboard for a dustpan and brush. 'It won't take me a moment to sweep it up. It's all right.'

'Do be careful with the broken glass,' warned Marjatta.

Korvensuo nodded. 'No problem,' he said.

Most of the shards were in the sink. A few were clinging to his T-shirt and his arms. A little blood was flowing from one finger, but it was only a scratch. He stopped the blood with a handkerchief and tipped the broken glass into a bin bag.

He looked through the window. Outside, Arvi was running out of the sauna and down to the lake where, to the children's great amusement, he jumped into the water stark naked.

# 3

The lake lay calm and still in bright daylight, although it was nearly eleven p.m.

Nights of no night, Sanna always used to call them, adding that these long nights were more beautiful in Finland than anywhere else. Once, when they were staggering back through Turku after a midsummer party, she had fallen into the river, hopelessly tipsy. Kimmo, panic-stricken, had jumped in after her and Sanna had laughed at his clumsy attempts to pull her out.

'Nothing!' called one of the divers. 'We're not finding anything.'

'Carry on!' called Sundström, who was standing on the bank beside the motionless Petri Grönholm, rocking vigorously back and forth on the balls of his feet. He turned and came over to Kimmo. 'No sign of her,' he said. 'I don't think we're going to find the poor soul in this lake.'

Kimmo nodded. If so, the curious parallels would probably end here. When the discovery of the bicycle was reported at midday, no one had made the connection at first. A couple of officers on patrol had gone to take a closer look, and reported back that the bicycle was lying near a cross erected in memory of a girl murdered in 1974. They said they had also found traces of blood and a sports bag containing gear that presumably belonged to a teenage girl.

While Niemi and his team were driving out to the scene, Kimmo had gone in search of the files. He had immediately remembered the day of Ketola's retirement, the case that Ketola had described, the model they had carried out to Ketola's car in the sleet and snow.

With Päivi Holmquist, the head archivist, he had gone back down to the big basement room where long-forgotten items were stored. Päivi had gone straight to the right folder, taken it out and, presumably noticing his amazement, pointed out, with emphasis, that she did know what files were to be found in this room.

There were dozens of file folders, faded yellow folders containing a wealth of carefully compiled material. Joentaa had thought of Ketola putting that particular folder down there so long ago.

He had thanked Päivi, taken the folder up to the third floor in an old cardboard box and had a first quick look at it before driving out with Sundström to the place where the bicycle had been found.

The site as reported was the same as the crime scene of the old case, and the name on the cross was indeed the name of the girl in the files dating back to that time. Niemi and his colleagues had been hard at work. Joentaa, feeling the sun on the back of his neck, had read the inscription on the cross. Pia Lehtinen. Murdered 1974.

'Take a look at this, will you?' Sundström had said, indicating the place where Niemi was standing a few metres away. They had approached cautiously, and Niemi had pointed to the spot where the soil joined the asphalt bicycle path and the thin trail of blood there.

'It's as if someone had been dragged along the ground to the bicycle path. That's where the trail ends,' Niemi had said.

Kimmo had nodded, remembering the reconstruction of the old crime in the files. There had been a trickle of blood then too and the reconstruction suggested that the murderer had put Pia Lehtinen in his car before sinking her body in the lake, where she was found months later. Sundström, Grönholm and he were now standing on its bank, while divers searched the bottom for the corpse of a still anonymous girl.

'Could be the girl doesn't exist,' Grönholm

was just saying. 'Could be the whole thing will turn out to be just a joke.'

Kimmo nodded.

'Funny sort of joke, of course,' Grönholm added. 'But to date all we have is a bike found by chance beside this cross and the sports bag.'

'And traces of a struggle. And a trail of blood, my young friend,' said Sundström.

'Yes, well,' said Grönholm.

Kimmo Joentaa wasn't really listening. He was thinking what it would mean if the parallels between then and now ended here. Beside this lake. There were dozens of other lakes around here. Lakes they'd have to search. Ultimately, Grönholm had a point, but at the same time Joentaa thought the idea of a joke was ridiculous. What kind of joke would that be? What was all this about, anyway? Had the same murderer come back after thirty-three years to commit the same crime at the same place? If so, what on earth had got into the man?

'I . . . ' he began.

'Yes?' asked Sundström.

'I don't understand any of this,' said Kimmo.

'Well, congratulations!' said Sundström.

Joentaa wasn't sure what Sundström meant by that, and Sundström went on, 'What we need now, my friends, is that damn body.'

Grönholm and Joentaa exchanged a brief glance.

'Or alternatively, how about the girl herself, uninjured and in perfect health?' asked Grönholm, but Sundström didn't even seem to notice that Grönholm was alluding to his remarks.

The divers went down and came up again. Unsuccessfully. By agreement with Nurmela, Sundström had already informed the media that afternoon. Joentaa thought this was the right thing to do. And the decision to carry out a thorough and immediate search of the lake where Pia Lehtinen had been found so long ago was the obvious course to take, even though Kimmo was beginning to wonder if there was any point in searching this lake for a body, when there was a chance that the missing girl was still alive somewhere else. If, indeed, there was a missing girl.

The ringtone of his mobile brought him out of his thoughts. 'Tuomas here,' said Heinonen. 'I've located the girl.'

Kimmo's stomach lurched. 'Oh no, that's . . . '

'No, sorry. I mean I probably know who she is,' said Heinonen.

'Ah. I see,' said Kimmo.

'Guy called Kalevi Vehkasalo rang to say the bike on the news belongs to his daughter

66

and his daughter hasn't come home today.'

'Was he absolutely sure about the bike?'

'Yes, that's why I think it's important. I mean, it was shown in close-up on the news and he's perfectly certain it's his daughter's bicycle; he recognized the green sticker on the bell and he says his daughter's bike had one just like it, a sticker with strong language on it — well, it said Fucking Bitch — and he'd always wanted to take that sticker off, he said, but she wouldn't let him. And the sticker really does say Fucking Bitch.'

'How did you leave things?' asked Joentaa.

'I said we'd come right over to see him. And his wife, they're both at home. I thought maybe Sundström would do that.'

'I'll have a word with him. Give me the address.'

'Sodankylänkatu 12. That's in Halinen, quite a way from where the bicycle was found.'

'Right, thanks. See you later,' said Joentaa.

He spoke to Sundström, who narrowed his eyes, began rocking back and forth again and said, 'Ah, so now we're seeing some action.'

# 4

Ketola saw the bicycle beside the cross in the field on the late news.

His son Tapani had dropped in early that evening. Unannounced and out of the blue as usual. Ketola didn't hear from him for weeks, sometimes months, then there would be Tapani standing in the doorway, smiling and looking at him with that expression of his, which might conceal some unfathomable world, or an empty world, or a world full of something or other, but anyway a world that Ketola didn't understand.

Tapani sat on the sofa, facing him, and talked about things he had done, or rather said he had done. Meetings with people who didn't exist. Couldn't exist. Although it was sometimes difficult to keep reality and fantasy apart with him.

About a year ago Tapani had been arrested in northern Finland for simply walking out of a shop with a DVD player, obviously hoping the theft would be so conspicuous that no one would notice. Legal proceedings against him had been dropped, partly through Ketola's influence, and yet again Tapani had spent some time in a psychiatric hospital. Ketola had visited him every week and they sat in his room. Tapani had talked, Ketola had kept quiet.

It was the same now. Tapani talked about men who went into the woods and never came out again, dwelling on the fact that he, Tapani, had warned them but no one listened to him, no one took him seriously.

'I take you very seriously,' said Ketola.

'Yes, but the others — I mean, the others don't understand anything. I'd like some water,' said Tapani.

Ketola nodded and fetched a bottle of water and two glasses. Tapani drank greedily and said he'd been thinking of learning to do flip-flops in the next few days.

'What?' asked Ketola.

'Flip-flops. Lots of backward somersaults like the gymnasts do. Then I could get about very fast. It would be much quicker than walking. I just have to find someone who can teach me how to do them.'

Ketola poured water into his glass and topped up Tapani's as well, and when he looked up he thought, for a moment, that he saw a flash in Tapani's eyes. Then Tapani laughed and Ketola laughed too.

'Didn't mean it seriously,' said Tapani.

These were the best moments for Ketola,

the times when Tapani was the way he used to be for a few seconds. So far no one had been able to give an adequate explanation of what had really happened to Tapani. No doctor, no psychologist. Ketola could have worked out what such people said for himself. Drugs. Obviously a wild, haphazard mixture. Obviously consumed to excess. Ketola had known that for a long time, and he also knew that it couldn't all be explained nearly so simply.

About ten years before, Tapani had told him and Oona, on the evening before the party celebrating the end of the final school exams, that he had passed only with the aid of certain substances, that he probably didn't tolerate those substances well and he was telling them because he intended to kick the habit. Because he had a feeling that it wouldn't be good for him in the long run. Tapani had been sitting on this same sofa, putting his parents in the picture very objectively, infuriatingly objectively. Ketola had shouted at him, slapped his face and stayed away from the ceremony next day when the exam certificates were handed out.

Now Ketola was thinking of that, of his own appalling failure, while Tapani, very serious again, talked about a villa he had bought in Spain, where he intended to spend the next few years.

He knew now that Tapani had not stopped taking drugs, but instead had massively increased his consumption. He had gone to study mechanical engineering in Joensuu, although he hadn't had the faintest interest in mechanical engineering, and all the time he had been taking cocaine and synthetic drugs in a weird and wonderful mixture.

Meanwhile, Ketola had separated from Oona, his wife and Tapani's mother, because he didn't get along with her any more, for reasons that he couldn't have specified today, and he had taken very little interest in Tapani during those years. For instance, it had never entered his head to ask why on earth he was studying mechanical engineering, of all subjects.

Joensuu was hundreds of kilometres away; Ketola hoped his son was all right and suppressed any other ideas. About two years ago, just when his young colleague Kimmo Joentaa had lost his wife, Tapani too had had a nervous breakdown. He had appeared at the door one evening, saying what a nice, mild wind was blowing and looking at his father with an expression that went right to Ketola's guts.

A little later a woman from some official department had got in touch and told him, with many bureaucratic turns of phrase, that

Tapani Ketola had been picked up on the runway at Helsinki airport and taken to a psychiatric hospital for two weeks. Couldn't Ketola, she asked, or the young man's mother, Oona Ketola née Vaisänen, now living in Tampere, do something to help their son?

After that Tapani had spent a week with Ketola and then the three of them — Oona too had come to visit for several days — furnished a flat for him in a high-rise building on the outskirts of Turku. That had been a good time, but it passed quickly, it was too fragile to last, although Ketola, looking back, was not really sure why.

Anyway, he had not seen Oona since, or heard from her, and month by month Tapani had descended further into a strange world to which Ketola no longer had any access, and which in his opinion could not be plausibly explained by either drugs or anything else.

His son had become a puzzle to him, and now that puzzle, resurfacing after a considerable time, was sitting on his sofa again, and Ketola was both glad of that and at the same time, as always, felt absolutely desperate.

'Do you have anything to eat?' Tapani was just asking.

'Of course.' Ketola jumped up, relieved to be able to do something. He stood in the kitchen and heard more voices. Tapani had switched on the TV set.

'Bloody TV mafia,' Tapani was muttering as Ketola came back. He immediately began stuffing bread rolls into himself, returning to the subject of the house he had bought in Spain. 'You don't need things there, for instance you don't need any towels because it's so warm,' he said, and Ketola looked at the TV screen and saw a bicycle lying in a field, and a cross beside the bicycle.

'You know what they've done, they've . . . ' said Tapani and Ketola felt the ground give way under him. He wanted to stand up, but he just slumped even further back in his chair and stared at the TV.

Tapani followed his gaze. 'A bicycle . . . yes, that's it, I must buy a new bicycle too,' he said, and the face of Pia Lehtinen came on screen, the photograph from his files — he remembered the photograph vividly. A similar case, they were saying. A newspaper report of the time came up on the screen, with a drawing of the small car at the centre of it, the small red car that they had never found. Then came an interview with Nurmela on the steps leading up to the entrance of the police building. He was saying that nothing had been found yet, but they were taking it very seriously, still hoping that the whole thing would turn out much less grave than had been assumed at first. When asked what he thought the connection with this case from the distant past could be, Nurmela said it was too early to speculate.

'Will you give me a bicycle for my birthday?' asked Tapani.

'What? What was that . . . ?' said Ketola.

'I was asking if you'd give me a bicycle.'

'Yes, yes,' said Ketola.

'Is it a promise, then?' Tapani went on.

'No — yes,' said Ketola, without taking his eyes off the screen. A different news item had come on now; it might have been from another world. Soon after that came the weather forecast, then the sports news. Ketola watched it all without taking in any of it, and what Tapani said also echoed in a void. A feature film starring Alain Delon was just beginning on the TV screen.

'I like him,' said Tapani. 'I like the film, but about that bicycle . . . '

'What? Oh, yes, for your birthday. Let's talk about it another time.'

'I mean the bicycle they've found in the field in Naantali.'

'Yes.' Ketola straightened up.

'What I was thinking,' said Tapani, 'is if that girl, the one they showed in that photo . . . '

74

'Yes?' asked Ketola. Pia Lehtinen, he thought; they had just shown the photo of Pia Lehtinen on television, his photo, the photo that the girl's mother had given him at the time.

'If she was thirteen years old then, she'd be forty-six today,' said Tapani. 'Do you see what I mean?'

'What?' asked Ketola.

'Well, she'd be an old woman now.'

'I'm over sixty myself,' said Ketola automatically.

'You know what I mean. That girl would be old today, older than me,' said Tapani and Ketola looked at him, his son who looked like a child, and wondered what on earth was going on; and at that moment he felt that something he couldn't define was entering his body and making him laugh. He laughed, first chuckling quietly, then out loud, roaring with laughter. He couldn't stop, and what was particularly funny was that Tapani asked in all seriousness if he, Ketola, had gone crazy, before at last he too joined in.

It was a long time since they'd laughed together so heartily — it must be decades — if indeed they had ever laughed together like this. They laughed until Tapani suddenly stood up and said he'd have to go now, because he had an important appointment, but he was afraid he couldn't tell Ketola any more about it.

Ketola nodded. Of course, he thought, naturally. He went to the front door with Tapani, gave him a brief hug and waited until his son had disappeared into the side street, walking with springy, confident steps.

Slowly, Ketola went back into the house and into the living room. Tapani had been in a good mood. Ketola had felt, several times that evening, how much he loved his son. Now he felt drained and empty. So he'd give Tapani a bicycle for his birthday. A really good one, a bicycle that would take him anywhere fast, and at least then he wouldn't feel he had to learn to do flip-flops.

He shook his head. Those flip-flops, what a daft idea, but rather splendid in a way, he thought.

The television was still on, showing the French film that Tapani liked.

Ketola shook his head, went on and on shaking it, although the rest of him stood there motionless as he stared at the TV screen.

# 5

As they approached the large, pale green clapboard house, Joentaa saw a woman's face behind one of the windows, and even before they had gone the last few metres the door was opened. A powerful-looking man came towards them, greeted them with a vigorous handshake and said, just a little too loudly, 'Kalevi Vehkasalo. I think we spoke on the phone. Good that you could come at once.'

He still doesn't want to accept what's happened, thought Joentaa.

'Paavo Sundström. This is my colleague Kimmo Joentaa,' said Sundström, all of a sudden strictly matter-of-fact. In the car just now he had been singing along to an old Finnish Grand Prix song, amused to think that a few years ago, as far as he remembered, he had driven in the race and had come in last.

'Come on in,' said Vehkasalo, walking purposefully ahead. He led them into the house and a spacious living room, with large abstract paintings in glaring colours on the walls. A woman was standing in the middle of the room. The TV was on, with the sound

77

muted, and a box of tissues lay on the glass-topped table.

'My wife, Ruth,' said Vehkasalo.

The woman's eyes were small and reddened, her handshake almost too limp to be felt. But Joentaa got the impression that the appearance of Sundström in itself gave her some hope. Tall, athletic-looking Sundström, with his rugged features, radiated a certain air of confidence without having to say a word.

'Most of all, of course, we want to know what's really going on,' said Vehkasalo. Where outward appearance was concerned, he was in no way inferior to Sundström. Another tall, dynamic man who looked as if he could get things done. He wore a casual but elegant jacket and made Joentaa feel, with every word and every gesture, that he would like to take control of the situation. Which made it clear to Joentaa that control was just what Vehkasalo must have lost as soon as he saw the news.

'But let's sit down first,' said Vehkasalo and waited until they were all seated before he went on, 'Right, to keep it short; that was Sinikka's bicycle on TV. No doubt about it. Naturally, my wife is anxious. Sinikka is always coming home late, but — well, we'd like you to tell us what's happened.'

'I can understand . . . I quite understand

78

your anxiety,' Sundström began.

Vehkasalo interrupted, with a different tone in his voice all of a sudden. 'No. Forgive me, but please don't try that one with us. I don't like it at all. Tell us what's going on. It's simple enough. Our daughter hasn't come home and the police have found her bicycle. What happened?'

'First of all, I'd like to . . . '

'Are you deaf? I want a plain answer to my question!' Vehkasalo slammed the flat of his hand down on the table, jumped up, stood still for a moment, then strode over to the TV set and switched it off.

'Kalevi,' Ruth Vehkasalo whispered.

'I have photographs here,' said Sundström, 'and first of all I'd like you to tell me whether that is your daughter's sports bag and whether those items of clothing are hers.'

He handed one photograph to Vehkasalo, who had come back to the table, the other to his wife, who immediately nodded and said, 'Yes, I'm certain of it. She got the tracksuit for her birthday two weeks ago. I'm absolutely certain. Kalevi, it's the tracksuit that I bought her . . . '

She passed the photo to her husband.

'And that's her sports bag. At least she has one like it,' Vehkasalo murmured. 'And a bicycle with the same sticker, just as I said.'

'I see,' said Sundström. 'We have to make absolutely sure about this point, of course. We'll have to show you the bicycle again tomorrow, but meanwhile I think we can now assume that it is indeed your daughter's.'

'You can leave out that last empty phrase,' Vehkasalo interrupted him.

'There's something else that I'd like to tell you before we discuss this further, something very important. I'd like to say that we will do everything in our power to find your daughter. At this moment we don't know any more than you do. Your daughter disappeared a few hours ago and we've only just ascertained that the missing girl concerned is, in all probability, your daughter . . . '

'You can leave that one out too,' Vehkasalo interrupted again.

'All I mean is that . . . '

'Leave out the 'in all probability' bit. It *is* Sinikka. This is about our daughter Sinikka.'

'All I mean is that we're only just beginning on our enquiries. Your daughter is missing. We have found her bicycle and her sports bag. She didn't come home. We're investigating the place where those things were found at the moment and at the same time we've begun looking for your daughter herself. There's much to suggest that she will come home safe and sound, and . . . '

'You can leave out *all* the empty phrases. The bicycle was lying beside that cross.' Vehkasalo was speaking with studied calm and objectivity now, as if describing some other, random incident. 'We all know what happened to that girl in the old case. They made it very clear on the news. A girl dragged off her bicycle and murdered. I heard what they said, after all. So why was our daughter's bike lying beside that particular cross? And why is the whole thing making the headlines if our daughter is as safe and sound as you say?'

'I only want to make it clear to you that we are in the early stages,' said Sundström. 'I would like to ask you — and I know this is difficult — but I would like to ask you to keep calm.'

'I am calm. My wife is calm too,' said Vehkasalo, putting an arm round her.

There was silence for a few seconds.

'Did your daughter often go that way? Past the cross?' asked Joentaa as the silence lengthened. Husband and wife exchanged glances.

'I don't know. Where was she going?' Vehkasalo asked his wife.

'To volleyball. She's been playing volleyball for several months, that's why I bought her the new things . . . '

'She's always branching out into something new. After a while we lose sight of what she's up to,' said Vehkasalo, trying for a smile.

'So she always cycled that way going to play volleyball?' asked Joentaa.

'I think so,' said Ruth Vehkasalo. 'I don't know for certain because I was never with her when she went there. But I think so, yes.'

'How often did she play volleyball?'

'She went to training twice a week and there were usually games at the weekend.'

'She's very fond of sports,' said Vehkasalo. 'Unfortunately she has no staying power. She does this and that, she's always starting something new and never sticks with it. But I suppose that may be perfectly normal these days, I . . . well, it doesn't matter now.' He fell silent.

'Did she ever mention the cross?' asked Joentaa.

Both parents looked enquiringly at him.

'I mean, did she speak of passing the cross? Did she mention the inscription?'

'No,' said Vehkasalo, and his wife too shook her head. 'No, never. Why would she? Why would Sinikka be interested in something that happened thirty years ago? She wasn't even born then. Anyway, I'm wondering what all this stuff is in aid of. The same psychopath coming back thirty years later to kill our daughter? Is that your theory, or what have you found out so far?'

'Nothing,' said Sundström. 'Nothing yet. We're only just beginning. Of course the place where the bicycle was found is significant and there are striking parallels to that case, which does indeed lie far back in the past. But to be perfectly honest, I have to tell you that I've never heard of anything similar. For now we know no more than you do.'

Vehkasalo nodded, obviously mollified by Sundström's honesty, and his wife suddenly asked if she should make some coffee. She was already on her feet.

'No, thanks very much, not for us,' said Sundström. 'When did your daughter set out for volleyball training? Did you say anything to her before she started?'

'Yes, of course. Kalevi was at the office, but I was here, we had lunch together, then Sinikka went to her training session and I met my sister in town in the afternoon.'

'What did you talk about during lunch?' asked Kimmo Joentaa. 'Is there anything that seems unusual to you now, in the light of Sinikka's disappearance? Anything she said?'

Sinikka's mother considered the question for a little while, then thoughtfully shook her head. 'No, she really didn't. We — today was the last day of school term, so that was why . . . ' Her voice broke and she began crying, but went on, 'Of course we quarrelled over her report and I expect I raised my voice because — well, because we were really quarrelling all the time.' She suddenly began screaming. Joentaa felt Sundström flinch beside him. 'Because it was downright impossible not to quarrel with Sinikka!' she screamed. 'Because she always wants everything and never gives anything back! And now she's gone! Now she's gone away! Far, far away!' She hit out at her husband, who was sitting there as stiff as a poker. Then she jumped up and ran out of the room. Soon afterwards a door slammed. Vehkasalo stared after his wife, his mouth half open. 'I'm very sorry, that's to say — I'm terribly sorry,' he said. 'I'd better go and see how she is.'

'Of course,' Sundström agreed.

Vehkasalo went out of the room, as if in a trance.

'Of course,' Sundström repeated after a while, deep in thought, and he helped himself to a chocolate from a silver dish. 'Want one?' he asked.

Joentaa shook his head. He felt tired, and powerless to help the missing girl's parents. He thought about Sundström and how to some extent he understood Sundström even less than his predecessor Ketola. He had often thought about Sundström and his curious way of making a joke of everything. At the same time he could be very efficient in concrete situations, however difficult, and not at all inclined to joke about them.

Kimmo's reflections led him nowhere and after a while he found himself thinking of Sanna, who had always been amused by his constant wish to probe into anything and everything, to understand it down to the smallest detail.

He could faintly hear the voice of Kalevi Vehkasalo, obviously talking to his wife in a room at the other end of the house. Sundström, sitting next to him, was munching his chocolate, and Kimmo found his thoughts beginning to circle around Sanna.

An idea came into his mind, one that had often occurred to him since Sanna's death, one that frequently obsessed him and then, suddenly, seemed wrong and entirely meaningless. It was the idea that he was free of everything that tormented other people. In similar situations he had often felt the same as he did now. He sensed the fear and desperate anxiety of the parents, who didn't know what had become of their daughter, and at the same time felt sure that he himself would never have to fear anything at all, would have no more anxieties of any kind. Because unlike the missing girl's parents, he had that phase behind him; because he had long ago lost Sanna, the most important part of his life.

The idea began to feel vague and uncomfortable, and he obviously made some physical move in the effort to shake it off, because Sundström asked, 'Everything okay?'

'Hm?'

'Are you okay? You sort of suddenly twitched,' explained Sundström.

'No, I'm okay. It was nothing.'

Sundström nodded and surreptitiously, as if doing something wrong, took another chocolate from the dish. He choked on it when the door opened behind their backs.

'Forgive me,' said Vehkasalo. 'I'm very sorry; my wife, well, of course she's very worried. I think . . . if possible could you speak to her tomorrow? I'm entirely at your disposal myself.'

'Of course. I understand perfectly. I hope your wife will feel a little calmer in the morning. I'd like to clear up just a couple more points and then we'll be on our way.'

Vehkasalo nodded and sat down opposite them again.

'What we urgently need is a photograph of your daughter. A recent one if possible. We'll probably be distributing it to the media as well. A photo that's . . . well, as good a likeness as possible, I mean showing her as she looks today. An up-to-date passport photograph would be ideal.'

Vehkasalo nodded and thought for a moment. He stood up, left the room and soon came back with several photograph albums.

'My wife always puts them straight into albums,' he murmured, leafing through one of them. 'They sometimes have group photographs at her school, they take portrait photos as well . . . yes, here, for instance.' He handed them a picture showing a girl looking gravely at the camera lens.

Sundström turned it over. 'Taken only recently, good,' he said. 'Many thanks. We'll take this away with us, if we may.'

'Of course,' said Vehkasalo.

'We can talk about everything else tomorrow,' said Sundström, rising from the sofa.

They stood there in silence for a few seconds, then Vehkasalo went ahead of them to the door. 'I hope you'll — you'll find her,' he said, when they were in the doorway.

'We'll do our best,' said Sundström.

They drove along the urban motorway towards the city centre. Sundström nodded off to sleep several times, waking with a jolt after a few seconds. 'Terrible,' he muttered.

Joentaa didn't know whether he meant their conversation with the missing girl's parents, or his exhaustion, or something else entirely, and he was too tired himself to ask. They parted at the car park outside the police building.

'See you tomorrow,' said Sundström, clapping him on the shoulder.

'See you tomorrow,' Kimmo agreed, and got into his car and drove home.

# 6

It was just after one when he parked his car beside the apple tree outside the little house. Sanna's house. It was and always would be Sanna's house, and that thought was there every time, waiting for him, evening after evening when he came home. Sometimes it was strongly present, sometimes less so, sometimes it was a good thought, sometimes a painful one, sometimes just a thought, coming and going.

His house was Sanna's house. He had lost Sanna for ever. Sanna would be here for ever. It was as simple as that and he couldn't understand why some people didn't understand it. What was so odd about the idea?

He didn't talk to many people about Sanna and he had never really opened up to anyone, because it was no use. Because he felt he was unable to open up, and didn't want to either, and it would do him no good. How could he talk to other people about feelings that at heart, and to this day, he himself couldn't really understand?

As for the few who were close enough to him to try probing now and then, after a while he left them feeling they were talking to a brick wall. Because he had to indicate that such a conversation would soon come up against barriers that, with the best will in the world, he couldn't cross. He would suffer a near-allergic reaction when they said things like: you have to look to the future, life must go on some time, it's all in the past now, that's what Sanna would have wanted.

He was indeed looking to the future and life *was* going on, and he knew what Sanna would have wanted much better than any clever counsellor. It wasn't his problem if other people wouldn't believe that, and if they thought looking to the future meant removing everything to do with Sanna from his life they were very much mistaken. He had removed nothing. That had been his first reaction; he had thought he couldn't live in this house any longer, he had thought he must clear away everything that reminded him of Sanna from cupboards and drawers, but a moment came when he realized that no such plan would ever work.

He had put everything back in its old place, had spent a weekend restoring everything to the way it used to be when Sanna was alive, and when he sat there in the evening and looked around, he had known that was the right thing to do, and he would come to terms with her death, if he ever did, only in Sanna's presence.

His best conversations had been with Kari Niemi, head of forensics. Niemi was in his mid thirties, only a little older than Kimmo himself. They'd never really had much to do with each other in the past, but Kimmo had appreciated Niemi's very precise and careful work, and liked his unshakeable good humour, even if he also found it irritating.

Sundström told jokes without ever really laughing, and Kari Niemi was laughing all the time without, so far as Kimmo could remember, ever telling a joke. Behind Niemi's eternal smile, in Joentaa's opinion, there was a thoughtful, warm-hearted human being, and Kimmo could talk to him more easily than to anyone else about Sanna. Perhaps because apart from Sanna herself he had never met anyone with whom silence came so easily and who was so good at remaining silent himself. Conversations about Sanna, about her death, about his own life afterwards frequently consisted of silences.

Joentaa looked at the house. A sunny morning seemed about to dawn behind it, although it was only one thirty and still night. He pulled himself together, got out of the car and walked the short way to the house. He had had to fight off his drowsiness during the drive home, but now he felt wide awake again, and had a sense that he needed to think about several things at the same time. As if he still had something very important to clear up before morning came.

He went into the kitchen, poured cold milk into a glass, sat down in the living room and stared through the wide window at the lake.

They hadn't found anything in that other lake, about an hour's drive from here at the far end of Turku. Not yet; the divers would go on looking in the morning. Only recently Kimmo had been standing there on the bank of the other lake with Sundström and Grönholm, waiting for the divers to find the body of someone whose name they now knew. Presumably.

Kimmo put down his glass and realized what was keeping him awake. For the first time that day he found the time to think hard about what had happened. He'd have to talk to Ketola about it in the morning. Ketola might be able to help them. As usual.

A little while ago, when Grönholm mentioned the possibility of a joke, he had silently agreed. In one way a joke, or whatever you liked to call it, seemed absurd, but in another it was even more absurd to think of a murderer returning to the scene of his crime thirty years later, to commit the same crime again.

Now that Sinikka Vehkasalo's disappearance had been confirmed, the joke idea didn't work. The most likely thing seemed to Joentaa a copycat murderer, whatever the motives of this new murderer thirty-three years on might have been. Maybe he had come upon the idea of the cross, the way it persistently called Pia Lehtinen to mind, and that cross had set something off in him . . .

If the murderer really did intend the incidents of the past to run their course again, it would be months before they found the body of Sinikka Vehkasalo, because the search for Pia Lehtinen had also gone on for months. But there the parallel ended, simply on pragmatic grounds: today's murderer would know that sooner or later they would search the lake that had featured in the old crime, so he had hidden the body somewhere else, in a place that the investigating team wouldn't find until considerably later.

On the other hand, if for whatever reason the murderer wanted to repeat the course of events, reproducing exactly what had happened then, that meant there was a noticeable divergence in one crucial point — always assuming that they didn't find the corpse in the lake next morning after all.

Joentaa rose abruptly. His own speculations, leading nowhere, were getting on his nerves, while Ruth and Kalevi Vehkasalo, in their pale green house in Halinen, couldn't sleep for anxiety about their daughter.

He turned away from the lake beyond the window, and his eye fell on the two photographs on the bookshelves. They had always stood there, ever since he and Sanna moved in. In the weeks after Sanna's death Joentaa had removed them, then put them back in their old place a little later.

Standing in front of them, he looked closely at the photos. One was of Sanna as a small child; the date on the back showed that she had been two years old at the time. Sanna had just knocked a biscuit out of her mother Merja's hand and the biscuit was flying through the air towards the camera. Merja's mouth was wide open and Sanna was looking really furious, probably because her mother had told her she couldn't eat the biscuit without giving her, Merja, a bite. Jussi, Sanna's father, must have jumped just as he was taking the photo, because the picture was slightly blurred. A wonderful picture. Kimmo felt a smile spreading over his face.

The other picture had been taken a few months, perhaps only a few weeks, before she was diagnosed with cancer. When everything was still fine. Sanna had just begun working as an architect. The photo showed her standing in front of her desk. Kimmo remembered that she had particularly wanted to have that picture taken and they had sent a print to her parents. Her face showed pride and satisfaction. And the certainty that everything would go on just as well in the future. Kimmo's glance wandered from one picture to the other, then settled on the little girl knocking a biscuit out of her mother's hand.

Sanna.

Sanna just a metre tall, running, red-cheeked.

He went into the bathroom, washed, then lay awake on his back for a long time, his eyes open.

# 7

Timo Korvensuo heard Marjatta's slow, regular breathing as she lay beside him. She had clutched the quilt firmly round her. What a nice evening that had been, she'd said just before dropping off to sleep.

For a while, Timo Korvensuo had listened to the soft giggling of his children through the open window. Aku and Laura were sleeping in their tent down by the lake. Now their voices, too, had died away and all he could hear was the whining of the gnats.

He still felt curiously light. Weightless. The guests had stayed a long time. They had enjoyed the evening: the warmth, the clear night, the children had played games. Arvi had told stories, Marjatta, Johanna and even Pekka had talked loudly, having a very good time.

Maybe the news item about the missing girl in Turku had actually contributed to their good mood; maybe, after a while, discussing it had made them all feel more acutely how well off they were, living in safety — something of that kind.

Timo Korvensuo felt a vague satisfaction in

seeing through the others. But of course that was of no importance. He was digressing, wandering away from something he had not yet really confronted, although all the time he had been trying to concentrate exclusively on that one subject.

Of course it was important.

Something important had happened.

It was difficult for him to formulate it in his mind, to see exactly what it was.

He had drunk too much, he didn't have a strong head, usually he never drank. He felt tired and at the same time wide awake; he could hardly keep his eyes open, yet he couldn't close them either, because as soon as he did a torrent of vertigo streamed into his brain, instantly filling him with almost uncontrollable nausea.

He thought of going into the bathroom to throw up; he was sure he'd feel better afterwards. Above all he'd have a clear head again, and he needed a clear head.

He stayed lying there. He worked out how often he had thrown up in his life. Not many times. He couldn't do it, never had been able to. He had truly vomited only once, as a child, bringing up everything until the carpet was covered with the contents of his stomach. He remembered all about it; a rice dish, rice and curry, which had tasted very good.

Oh, and a second time, he remembered that now. The memory had been buried until a second ago, but now it was before his eyes. He had been on a bicycle tour with some friends and one of them kept pouring cheap red wine into cardboard cups, and quite early in the evening he had lost consciousness, the only time in his life he had blacked out. So he hadn't actually known what he was doing, but in the morning he had smelt the vomit on his sleeping bag and felt how wet it was.

That had never happened to him again, and it wasn't going to happen now, because he would stay lying here, he wouldn't move an inch. Wouldn't move. A few gnats were whining.

Marjatta was sleeping peacefully, almost inaudibly; she had certainly drunk less than anyone else, just the amount that she could tolerate.

Korvensuo tried to concentrate, but it was impossible. His thoughts were going round in circles, and his brain was made of cotton wool.

He had a headache, a bad one, worse than he'd had in a long time. So now he would have to get up after all, he needed tablets, several all at once, to get rid of this pain that had suddenly begun digging into what seemed to him his fluffy, cotton-wool brain. Get up.

He felt himself staggering as he walked. Marjatta's voice in the background, he couldn't hear what she was saying, all he heard was himself grunting something. 'Go back to sleep!' probably. 'Go back to sleep!'

He was standing in front of the fridge, holding the door open, propping himself on the work surface with his other arm and staring at the bottle full of ice-cold water that he was going to drink in one fast, endless draught. Just as soon as he found the strength to do it, and above all as soon as he found the tablets.

He turned away and rummaged in a drawer. The vertigo got worse again. His hands were shaking. He found a packet and spent some time trying, unsuccessfully, to get the tablets out.

When he straightened up his nausea returned. He stared at the tap. He pulled and tore at the packet until at last there were three tablets in his hands. He let them dissolve slightly in his mouth before picking up the bottle and pouring cold water down his throat. He felt as if his head were about to burst.

'Feeling bad?' he heard Marjatta's voice asking behind his back.

He turned and saw her standing in the doorway, hair untidy, eyes tired.

'Bit of a headache,' he said.

'Pour me a glass of water too, will you?' asked Marjatta.

'Sure.'

He took a glass out of the cupboard and tried hard to control his hands as he poured the water, but they were shaking worse than ever.

'You're drunk, darling,' said Marjatta.

He saw her smile and nodded. 'Yes, probably,' he said.

'Is it very bad?'

He shook his head. 'No . . . you go back to bed.'

'Very bad, then,' said Marjatta.

'Please go back to bed.' He let himself drop on to one of the wooden chairs, and with blurred eyes saw Marjatta coming over to the table, pulling out a chair and sitting down beside him. He felt her hand on his, and stared at the tabletop.

'But you — you don't have any worries, do you?'

There were letters scratched into the tabletop. Words. He'd never noticed before. *Laura loves Saku* they said, and a little stick man beside them was laughing his head off. Probably Aku's handiwork.

'Have you . . . '

'Timo, I asked you a question.'

'Have you seen this written on the table?' he asked.

Marjatta lowered her eyes. 'Yes, Aku did it. He doesn't like it when Laura looks at other men.'

'I see,' he said and saw Marjatta smile again.

'Everything went smoothly, then?' she asked.

'Hm?'

'The flats in Helsinki. You said they were off your hands.'

'Yes . . . yes, they are. That's great . . . the week couldn't have ended better.'

'Then everything's all right?'

'Yes, of course. I probably celebrated a bit too much. Really, it's not so bad . . . I'm feeling better already.'

He felt her hand on his. 'Too much to drink doesn't agree with me, that's all,' he said. 'Go back to bed. I'll join you soon.'

Marjatta stroked his hand for a while, and then, at last, she stood up and left the kitchen.

'I'm feeling better,' he said again.

'Then come back to bed soon, and if I'm still awake I can massage your head.'

He nodded and heard her echoing

footsteps growing fainter as she walked away over the wooden floorboards.

He actually was feeling a little better. The sense of vertigo was wearing off. The pain still throbbed behind his forehead, but the mists were beginning to clear slightly. Soon he would have the strength to think about it calmly.

Think about it calmly.

He looked at the words that Aku had scratched into the table. The little stick man looked comical. Aku and Laura. Aku and Laura were sleeping outside in the tent. Aku eight and Laura thirteen years old. Marjatta would soon be asleep again as well, perhaps she was asleep now, if not at this moment then she would be in a few minutes' time. Marjatta usually fell asleep quickly, soon after getting into bed she was asleep, and he would lie beside her hearing her quiet breathing.

His headache had eased. That was how it had always been; given a large enough dose, the tablets acted like a sponge sucking up everything, leaving a pleasantly woozy sensation where the pain had been.

The others were asleep and he would soon be able to think. To make connections.

He must have had some kind of shock, it couldn't be anything else. A state of shock was normal. Nothing for him to worry about.

He remembered the perfect sun beyond the windows of the house that he had shown a potential buyer that afternoon. A nice woman, she had been friendly, they'd had a pleasant conversation between equals, people talking to one another, understanding each other. That was how these things worked. It had been late in the afternoon. The woman had said a friendly goodbye, said she liked the house and he had driven to the lake, jumped into the water and swum right out, as far as his strength would take him, and he'd felt very strong.

He controlled the pain behind his eyes by holding his breath, by concentrating entirely on not breathing.

The other man's name had been Pärssinen.

Pärssinen. A surname. He didn't know the man's first name. He never had known his first name.

Pärssinen.

Later, he had kept meeting people with the same surname. Only a few months ago he'd sold a property belonging to a Pärssinen, a nice house in Vantaa, very close to Helsinki airport, but there was no problem with air traffic noise. A wonderful house, and the name Pärssinen had been nothing but a marginal note in his files.

Marjatta. Laura and Aku. They were close

to him, it would take him only seconds to be with them, and it was good to know that; the knowledge calmed him slightly.

The name had been Pärssinen.

He couldn't remember what the man looked like; in the following days and weeks he had spent a lot of time trying to erase Pärssinen from his memory in a way that would leave no trace behind. It had been clear to him right at the start that Pärssinen was the key, for once that man seemed never to have existed, none of the rest of it was real. That had worked. It had worked because he had wanted it to work. Because he had realized there was no other option.

Once the link was broken, none of it was real. If you made up your mind, if you really made it up, there was nothing left. He had known that ever since; he knew it better than anyone else.

It had worked, and now it wouldn't work any more. As simple as that. It could all be reduced to that so simply, and for a moment he felt a kind of satisfaction, because he had finally managed it, because he was alone at last and able to think.

He closed his eyes and felt Pärssinen coming back to life in his mind. Everything that Pärssinen had been. He let it happen, because there was no avoiding it. He leaned back and let it happen.

Pärssinen. A stocky, powerful man with a round face and sparse hair. He had been living in the grey block of flats on the outskirts of the city for several months when Pärssinen came to act as caretaker, and moved into the flat on the ground floor.

For some time they had said hello in passing; it was summer and university vacation. He used to sit on his balcony with his books, reading a little, watching the children playing a little, and Pärssinen had clipped hedges and mowed the lawn round the block of flats.

Then, on one of those summer days, Pärssinen had spoken to him. He said he had been watching him, he had an eye for certain things that other people didn't notice. He remembered. He remembered perfectly; it was all coming back now. He felt it flood into him. Not just the memory of that conversation, but also the memory of what he had felt like. Pärssinen hadn't needed to say any more, because he had understood at once. He had seen himself reflected in Pärssinen's eyes, had seen what no one knew, what no one could know, not Pärssinen and least of all himself, and he had understood that, against all logic, Pärssinen had simply seen it, and he had felt the moment of understanding and the moment directly after it as a huge and deeply alarming relief.

Pärssinen had smiled in a calm, even friendly way, and invited him into his flat.

That was how it had begun, and now the memory came back, now everything came back. He looked at what his son had scratched into the wood of the table, and once again he saw the flickering projector, the venetian blinds pulled down, the dappled sunlight on the floor, the films . . . Pärssinen taking the rolls of film off a shelving unit, that particular film, the one he had wanted to watch again and again, his favourite scene in that film, his hand on his thighs, and Pärssinen laughed when he saw that; then he had laughed too and felt free for the first time in his life, entirely free, and Pärssinen had wound the film back until the girl was sitting on the edge of the bed again with her head bowed, her hand moving up and down a fat penis; then the girl had raised her head to look at the camera and he had seen a strange, beautiful face; he had straightened up slightly, his trousers fully open now, let out a soft cry and ejaculated on Pärssinen's floor.

Pärssinen had laughed.

He heard himself groan. He was sweating. He felt dizzy.

'Papa, I feel sick. It was the ice cream,' said Aku.

He opened his eyes. Aku was standing in the doorway.

'I . . . '

He saw Aku at the door. He wanted to stand up and go over to him, but it was no use. He felt himself staring at his son, he saw pain and something like fear in the boy's face, he wanted to say something, he wanted . . .

'Did the ice cream make you feel sick too?' asked Aku.

# 9 JUNE

# 1

In the morning Kimmo Joentaa went to see Ketola. He had thought about calling first to say he was coming, but then he simply set out. He had never been to Ketola's place before, but he knew the address: number 18 Oravankatu.

The house was on a rise, in a well-tended, quiet residential area at the other side of Turku. The path up to the house was carefully raked, with flowers in bloom to right and left of it. Kimmo was surprised, without knowing what he had really expected.

It was some time before Ketola opened the door. He smiled at Kimmo as if he'd been expecting him to arrive. 'Hello,' he said. 'Come along in.'

He looked different, changed in a way that Kimmo couldn't pin down at once. He seemed calm, but at the same time as if he were concentrating. In any case, he didn't seem to have slept any more than Kimmo had himself. Kimmo caught the faint smell of liquor on Ketola's breath.

'Your weekend cancelled, right?' said

Ketola. 'Sit down.'

'Thanks. I'm sure you . . . ' Kimmo stopped short when he saw the model standing on the table in the middle of the living room. The field, the road, the avenue of trees, the little bicycle, the bright red car. Ketola had taken the whole thing off its wheels and put it on the table. It really did look like part of a model railway set.

'I'm sure you've . . . ' Kimmo said.

'Heard about it, yes, of course,' said Ketola. 'I have. I saw the news, and I was surprised. My old case from right back then . . . '

'That's why I'm here,' said Kimmo. 'I thought of you at once, on the day you retired.'

'And the model we found down in that lumber room. I brought it up from the cellar again last night, my own cellar this time.'

'Yes.' Kimmo looked at the model on the table and wasn't sure what to say.

'Do you know any more details?' asked Ketola.

'No. Or rather yes, we probably know who the missing girl is.'

'So someone really has gone missing?' Ketola had straightened up. Kimmo heard the excitement in his voice.

'Looks like it. A girl about the same age as Pia Lehtinen in the old case. Her parents recognized their daughter's bicycle and sports bag when they saw them on the news.'

Ketola stared at him. 'I see,' he murmured. 'That's . . . ' He began chuckling quietly. 'Sorry, that's downright, oh, just amazing . . . excuse me, please.'

'Of course I thought of you straight away. It mattered to me to hear how you see it, ask what you think about it.'

'Nothing simpler,' said Ketola. His voice was suddenly clear and penetrating, just as it used to be when he was still Kimmo's superior officer. 'Nothing simpler. It's the same man. For some reason or other he's come back. He must be out of his mind, but then he was already out of his mind thirty-three years ago, and now he's lost control again after thirty-three years. That's it. I don't know what set it off, but I feel perfectly sure that's the answer.'

'All the same, I can't understand . . . '

'It's not a case of understanding! One can't understand such people, Kimmo! Don't let anything lead you astray. I let myself be led astray back then, I did something wrong, to this day I don't know what, but you — all of you — you must put that right now,

113

understand? It's really important that you don't make the same mistake we made all those years ago.'

Kimmo nodded and avoided Ketola's piercing gaze. He did understand. Of course. He also understood Ketola's excitement. He understood how badly shaken Ketola, a younger Ketola, had been by the death of Pia Lehtinen and the failure of the CID's enquiries into the case. And how he could never quite put that failure out of his mind.

All the same . . .

'All the same, the idea of a copycat murderer strikes me as more plausible, don't you think?' he said.

'Nonsense!' Ketola had jumped up, stopped halfway across the room and sat down again. 'No, that's garbage. It's important for you to concentrate on what we found out at the time. Or at least you ought to bear it in mind. It has to be the same murderer, you have to keep your eye on that, anything else is nonsense.' He was speaking calmly again, but with conviction. 'I'll offer Sundström my assistance. In looking through the old files.'

Kimmo nodded. He thought that was a good idea, even though he didn't share Ketola's opinion. Not without further evidence. He simply did not know what had happened. All he knew was that Kalevi and Ruth Vehkasalo would not have slept a wink last night, and he was afraid that their daughter was no longer alive.

'How are you going to proceed? I assume you'll soon be searching that lake, the one where we found Pia Lehtinen.'

'We already have, although — well, I was going to say unsuccessfully, but successfully would be better, because we didn't find her. Not yet. We'll go on searching.'

'Hm, yes, you reacted quickly. That's surprising. Even before you'd identified the missing person.'

'The bicycle was lying right beside the cross erected in Pia Lehtinen's memory. I told Sundström about the connection and he ordered the search at once. He always reacts pretty fast, sometimes just on instinct. And very often he entirely forgets to discuss it with Nurmela.'

Ketola hardly seemed to be listening, for his smile was a long time coming. Then he said, 'Good man.'

'I'm going straight out to see the missing girl's parents. Her mother collapsed yesterday evening. I got Niemi to give me the sports bag we found before coming here. I want to show it to the parents. Maybe it's not their daughter's after all . . .'

115

'Mm, collapsed . . . ' murmured Ketola. 'I'll come too.'

'What do you mean?'

'I'll come too. To see the parents. Of course I won't go into the house with you, but I'd like to come along, I'm sure you won't mind; I'll wait outside. And then I'd like a word with Sundström anyway. I want to do my bit at this point. I'm sure you can understand that.'

Kimmo nodded. 'Yes, of course.'

'Give me five minutes,' said Ketola, standing up before Joentaa had any chance to object. A little later Ketola was at the door, ready to go. He had put on the green jacket he used to wear to work so often, whatever the time of year. Very likely Grönholm had been right in suspecting that he had ten to twenty identical jackets hanging in his wardrobe.

They went out of the house. It was going to be a hot day. A girl was jumping into a swimming pool in the garden next door.

'I'll drive my own car,' said Ketola.

Kimmo nodded.

'And by the way . . . ' said Ketola.

'Yes?'

'What's the missing girl's name?'

'Sinikka Vehkasalo,' said Joentaa.

Ketola looked at him for a while, nodding

to himself. 'Sinikka Vehkasalo. Ah, yes, right.' Kimmo had a feeling that he had been about to say something very definite, but then he just smiled faintly and waved it away. 'Pia Lehtinen, and now Sinikka Vehkasalo. I'll follow you,' he said, getting into his car.

# 2

The pale green house looked deserted.

Joentaa glanced over his shoulder, and saw that Ketola had parked some way off and was sitting in his car. During the drive he had been wondering whether he should ask Ketola to be present at his interview with the parents after all, and had decided against it. Now, on impulse, he waved to him, signalling that he wanted him to come into the house. Ketola got out of his car, looked enquiringly at him and strode to meet him.

There was nothing against it, thought Joentaa, and a good deal in favour. No doubt he ought to have discussed it in advance with Sundström, but there was no time for that now.

Ketola had been one of the CID investigators of the old case and, even if they didn't know just what had happened then, it was already clear that there was some connection. Knowing as he did about the earlier investigation, Ketola might be able to dredge up from his memory something that other people wouldn't notice. It was good to have him here.

'You want me to come in too?' asked Ketola.

'I think that would be a good idea. If you don't mind, I'll say a word or so — how you were head of the department for a long time and involved in enquiries into the Pia Lehtinen case back then.'

'Of course.' Ketola looked for a moment at the house outside which they were standing. 'I wonder if there's anyone at home?'

'I rang this morning and told them I'd be coming,' said Joentaa and pressed the doorbell.

A few seconds later the door was opened, as if Kalevi Vehkasalo had been waiting for them to ring the bell. 'Good morning,' he said, shaking hands with them both, and asked them in. Joentaa noticed that he was dressed for the office or a business meeting. He had shaved and there was a fresh smell of aftershave about him.

Everything has to be the same as usual, thought Joentaa. The less it really is the same, the more it has to be. Then he thought of Sanna and didn't hear what Kalevi Vehkasalo was saying. 'I'm sorry, what was that?'

'My wife. She's better, or a little better, I think. She'll be here in a moment,' Vehkasalo repeated.

'Good.' Joentaa nodded.

Kalevi Vehkasalo avoided looking at the sports bag in its plastic container, now lying heavy in Joentaa's hand.

'Do sit down,' said Vehkasalo and Joentaa sat where he had the night before. The dish of chocolates was on the table, with five still in it. Joentaa had counted them the previous evening while Sundström was eating them. There had been seven, Sundström had eaten two, leaving five in the dish, and they were still there. Of course. What would have made Ruth or Kalevi Vehkasalo feel like eating a chocolate? Maybe Sinikka had liked chocolates. Sanna for one could sometimes positively stuff herself with chocolates, looking cross when he laughed at her.

He dismissed that thought and turned to Kalevi Vehkasalo, who sat there in his formal office suit, trying to make himself seem normal.

Carefully, Joentaa put the sports bag on the table. 'I'd like to . . . ' he began.

'I'll just go and find my wife,' said Vehkasalo, rising again, but he stopped in mid movement. Joentaa, turning, got to his feet to shake hands with Ruth Vehkasalo.

Again, the pressure of her hand was barely perceptible, and Kimmo Joentaa remembered Sanna's mother Merja Sihvonen. In the days after Sanna's death she had looked just the way Ruth Vehkasalo did at this moment. She shook hands with Ketola as well.

'That's Sinikka's bag,' she said tonelessly.

Joentaa nodded and was going to take the bag off the table, but Vehkasalo stopped him. 'Wait a moment.' He bent over the bag and looked at it hard. 'Yes . . . yes, but we knew that anyway,' he said, leaning back again abruptly. Ruth Vehkasalo stood there beside Joentaa, staring at the bag and crying without a sound.

'We knew it, Ruth, after all. Now do — do please . . . ' said Vehkasalo.

Joentaa carefully put the bag down beside the chair he was sitting in. Ruth Vehkasalo went on staring at the table where it had been.

'Ruth, do please come and sit down beside me,' said Kalevi Vehkasalo.

After a while Ruth Vehkasalo came out of her trance-like state and sat down on the sofa beside her husband. 'There's no news,' she said. It sounded like a statement, not a question.

'No, not yet,' Joentaa confirmed. 'Well, first I'd like to say that I've asked Antsi Ketola to be present at our conversation. He was head of our department until a few months ago, and he's the only one left of the team who carried out enquiries into the case of Pia

Lehtinen. So I asked him to be here.'

'Of course,' said Vehkasalo absently. 'It's certainly good to know that you're doing all you can to . . . to find Sinikka.'

Ruth Vehkasalo cast an appealing glance at Ketola, as if looking for help, but Ketola just sat there beside Joentaa, curiously motionless, saying nothing.

'And I'll just go back over the course of events yesterday until the point when Sinikka went to volleyball training,' said Joentaa.

'She went to school,' said Ruth Vehkasalo. She spoke in a low, monotonous voice, as if she had already said that over and over again, maybe in her thoughts. 'She came home about one o'clock and of course she was in a good mood, because the holidays had begun. She was going straight out again, but I wanted to talk to her about her report because . . . because her class teacher had told us a few days ago, at parents' evening, that she was often truanting, and we hadn't known that. So I tried talking to her again, but it was no good, it was impossible. In the end I couldn't stand it any more and I shouted at her. She went to her room. She was perfectly calm, but she wouldn't look at me. She was going to see a girlfriend and on to volleyball . . . ' She stopped short and looked at her husband before going on.

'Magdalena plays in the volleyball team too, that's how they met. If only I'd let Sinikka leave when she wanted to, they'd have gone to training together and everything would have turned out differently!' She had straightened up and screamed rather than spoke those last few words.

Ketola still sat motionless, but Kimmo could hear him breathing heavily now and then.

'Can you give me the friend's name and address?' asked Joentaa.

Kalevi Vehkasalo shook his head.

'Magdalena Nieminen. She lives not far away, on Helmenkatu. I don't know what number,' said Ruth Vehkasalo.

'Which school did your daughter attend?' asked Joentaa.

'The Hermanni Grammar School,' said Kalevi Vehkasalo.

Joentaa nodded. 'So then she went to training. Did you say anything else to each other before she left?'

'No.' Ruth Vehkasalo looked at the chocolates in the dish. 'No, Sinikka was playing music, she turned up the volume and shut her door. I knocked a couple of times, but she didn't come out until she set off for the training session. We didn't really say anything else, not exactly, she just said she'd be off now and looked at me in a way . . . I think she was testing me to see if I'd try forbidding her to go, and if I had she'd have gone all the same.'

'Do you know exactly what the time was?'

'About two thirty. The training session began at three thirty, she had a little way to go first and she had to change when she got there. She always set off an hour before it began.'

'And that's what she did yesterday?'

Ruth Vehkasalo nodded.

'What exactly was she wearing?' asked Joentaa.

Ruth Vehkasalo thought for a while. 'Red shorts and a pale green T-shirt. And green shoes, trainers, or kind of halfway between trainers and street shoes. Yes, that's what she was wearing, and she had her sports bag with her . . . but they've already found that.'

'Did she say anything, either yesterday or in the last few weeks, maybe even the last few months, that seems to you significant in retrospect? Anything that surprised you, or simply something that stuck in your minds?'

Both the Vehkasalos shook their heads.

'I'd still like you to go on thinking about that. Something might occur to you. Does she have a boyfriend?'

'A boyfriend?' Kalevi Vehkasalo laughed

and a moment later Joentaa saw in his face all the desperation he was trying to cover up. He cleared his throat. 'She's very . . . well, so far as that's concerned I haven't really understood her for quite some time,' he added.

'She's only just fourteen,' said Ruth Vehkasalo. 'She's often had, well, relationships, but she's never introduced anyone to us and I think they were always brief episodes. I did try talking to her about . . . about that subject once, but she laughed and said she didn't think there was much I could tell her.'

Vehkasalo leaned forward. 'Forgive me, but what are you implying? What does that have to do with this situation?'

'Could we see her room?' asked Joentaa.

Vehkasalo seemed about to reply, but then just nodded. He led them downstairs to the lower ground floor, which turned out to have been extended into a separate flat.

'Sinikka has this floor to herself. Except for the laundry room, of course,' said Vehkasalo. 'And this is her own room.' He cautiously opened the door, as if Sinikka might be there and feel they were disturbing her.

The room was empty and quiet. Vehkasalo made an awkwardly inviting gesture and took several steps back.

Joentaa stopped in the doorway. A tidy

room. Not meticulously neat, but the first thing Joentaa thought was that every object was exactly where Sinikka wanted it to be. At least, that was his impression. As if everything was arranged and organized in a certain way. His second thought was that there was not a single shelf; everything, with the exception of a computer on a wooden desk, stood on the pale blue carpet, which looked both faded and pleasantly clean and fresh in the sunlight.

At the front of the room a glazed door led out to a terrace. On the left a small music system stood on the floor against a bare wall, with CDs stacked beside it pell-mell, but even this chaos looked tidy in a way that he couldn't quite grasp. To the right only a mattress covered with pale blue bedlinen lay against the wall.

'Yes, that mattress . . . Sinikka didn't want a bed,' said Vehkasalo, who had followed the direction of Joentaa's glance. 'She liked this better, just a mattress. Her bed is up in the loft. She preferred — prefers — she likes things to be simple. Recently she has, at least. Or clear, or whatever you like to call it. I have just this one daughter, so I don't have much practice at dealing with puberty. I can't remember my own . . . sorry, I'm probably talking nonsense.'

'No,' said Joentaa.

'And she had her hair cut like that. Well, you have the photo. She used to have very thick hair, it looked prettier . . . but I think she was going through a phase.'

Joentaa approached the mattress. Impressions left on the bedlinen showed that Sinikka had been lying on it. The day before, when she shut herself into her room so as not to have to talk to her mother.

A strange-looking soft toy animal lay under the quilt. Joentaa bent over it, but with the best will in the world couldn't say what kind of animal it was meant to be. A hybrid between a bear, a cat and a mouse, he thought. Anyway, Sinikka had carefully put the animal to bed before going out.

'Hm,' murmured Vehkasalo.

Joentaa looked at the soft toy and remembered the photo that Vehkasalo had given them the previous evening. Sinikka had been looking gravely, almost angrily, into the camera, but Kimmo had imagined that somewhere in her features a very wide, attractive smile lurked. He must look more closely at the photo again later. Though what use that would be — maybe they were finding Sinikka's body at this minute.

'Have you seen all you want to?' asked Vehkasalo.

'Er . . . no. Sorry.'

Beside the desk with the computer standing on it, Joentaa saw something else, something he couldn't identify at first glance. 'What's that?'

'That? It's a mini-trampoline,' said Vehkasalo.

'A . . . ?' asked Kimmo.

'For jumping on,' said Vehkasalo. 'Upstairs we always hear a springy, creaking sound when Sinikka's jumping up and down on it. We gave it to her for her birthday; it was the only thing she'd told us she wanted.'

Joentaa looked at the little trampoline for a while, then turned away. His eyes met Ketola's. Ketola was standing perfectly still in the doorway; apart from the few usual greetings, he hadn't said a word the whole time since they arrived. Joentaa saw that Ketola was sweating, and had the impression that it was painful for him to be there. Maybe memories of the past were coming back, of his first interview with Pia Lehtinen's parents. Or perhaps it was something completely different, nothing to do with their presence here. Kimmo avoided Ketola's glance and turned back to Vehkasalo, who was now standing beside him and looking around the room as if he were seeing it all for the first time.

'You know, the crazy thing is . . . ' he said.

128

He seemed to have lost the thread of what he was saying, but then went on, 'The crazy thing is, I have this incredible ... well, longing for Sinikka. It would be so wonderful if she was just back here sitting on her mattress. Now of all times I want to see her, just when I can't, whereas yesterday it meant nothing to me ... do you understand what I mean?'

'Thank you,' said Joentaa. 'We'll be in touch when we have any news.'

Vehkasalo stared at him, and nodded. 'Right,' he murmured.

They went back to the living room. Ruth Vehkasalo was sitting in front of the TV set reading the news on teletext. One new item was the missing girl's name. Sinikka V. The report had moved yet further up in the headlines since yesterday evening and was now among the main subjects of home news. Kimmo wasn't surprised; a child's disappearance always made the front pages of the popular press, at least, and the mysterious connection in this case with an unsolved crime in the distant past increased public interest.

Ruth Vehkasalo took her eyes off the screen only briefly when he and Ketola said goodbye.

'Come back whenever you like,' said

Vehkasalo, holding Joentaa's hand firmly. Joentaa nodded and went out into the sunlight with the still silent Ketola.

Ketola walked fast, keeping a step ahead of Joentaa, and said a brief goodbye to him. 'A good thing I'm retired. This thing really got to me just now.'

'Yes,' said Kimmo. He would have liked to pursue the subject, but he wasn't sure how to begin, and Ketola was already on the way to his car, swaying slightly.

'See you later,' he called back before getting in.

Kimmo Joentaa watched him drive off. He was still trying to make eye contact, but Ketola stared past him at the road.

Sundström had left a message on his mobile. Kimmo felt an uncomfortable tingling sensation. Perhaps they'd found Sinikka Vehkasalo's body. He closed his eyes and listened to Sundström's voice, but it was only telling him about a team conference at two that afternoon.

He put the mobile in his pocket and spent a little while looking at the pale green house in the sunlight.

He saw Ruth Vehkasalo inside the window. She was just pulling the venetian blinds down.

# 3

What monstrous energy, thought Timo
Korvensuo. He couldn't get the word out of
his head.

Energy. Everything consisted of energy.

He was sitting in the shadow of the house,
watching his children running around. They
seemed indestructible, they ran and jumped
and swam and laughed and called and
shouted, and Timo Korvensuo had been
watching them with a pleasantly hazy feeling,
until at some point the word 'energy' entered
his mind and wouldn't go away, and his
headache had come back.

Energy, energy. Power, monstrous power, it
had been stronger than he was. He had
watched himself. A spectator of his own destruc-
tion. It was inevitable. Quietly, very lightly,
struck down with indescribable feather-
weight force . . . and then he had gone to
Naantali beach with a towel and his
textbooks. Children's mouths, children's
bodies, naked children's bodies, limbs
stretched out . . . boats in the warm breeze,
laughter around him, women eating ices
and asking him now and then, in friendly

tones, what time it was, and his books, probability calculus or algebra, on a towel, a little sand on the paper, numbers and letters half hidden, his eyes veiled . . . young bodies brown from the sun, leaping about, jumping head first into clear, cold water from a wet wooden landing stage, not far away, a cool breeze on his skin. And the feeling of being drawn gently, carefully, deeper and deeper into a beautiful nightmare.

Marjatta came out of the sauna, put down her towel and jumped into the water.

He had been thrown on his own resources, alone — worse than alone.

Until Pärssinen came along and asked him into his flat. Everything was energy, nothing was chance. Nothing simply happened. He had sensed that when he first crossed the threshold of Pärssinen's flat.

Venetian blinds drawn down. Dappled sunlight on the floor. Pärssinen had poured plum schnapps into shot glasses, put a film into the projector and unrolled the screen. While the film was running Pärssinen kept quiet, he always did then.

Aku came towards him. He ran, stumbled, slipped and ran on. Armed with a pistol. He laughed, sprayed water in Korvensuo's face, asked if he'd like to play with their ball with them.

'Let your old man get a bit of rest,' said Timo Korvensuo.

Aku ran back to the landing stage, where Laura and Marjatta were kicking a brightly coloured ball about. Aku shouted that he was goalie now.

Korvensuo felt the water on his skin. Pleasantly cool. Marjatta didn't seem to notice anything, thought he just had a hangover. He did, too. It happened rarely enough.

Aku saved a shot and clutched the ball like a trophy. Laura snatched it from his hands and kicked it back to Marjatta. Laura was a pretty girl. He loved her.

Pia Lehtinen. So that had been her name. It made no difference. He had never known her name, and he had seen her face for the first time the previous evening, in a photo on the news. An old photo.

Pärssinen had been lying on top of her, had covered her face, and it had also been Pärssinen who dragged her to the boot of the car. He had stood to one side, looking at the bicycle the whole time. He had straightened the handlebars.

He would call Pekka and tell Marjatta his plans. It would be a little difficult, he'd have to make a great effort to lie to her, but there was no help for it. He had to do something, he didn't know what, but something . . . it would be best to stay on this chair, not moving . . . but he had to call Pekka, go into the house and call Pekka while the three of them were playing down there. Pekka might be annoyed. Maybe he'd wonder what was up, or maybe not.

He stood up. Turned round, then round the other way, and went indoors. He stood at the window, practising in the silence the words he was going to say.

Then he dialled the number. Pekka answered. His voice sounded young and relaxed.

'Hello, Timo here,' said Korvensuo.

'Hi, how are you doing? Still out there by the lake?'

'Yes. Yes, we are.'

'I was going to call you anyway and say thanks for yesterday. It was a great evening.'

'Thank you, I'll pass that on to Marjatta. I . . . listen, I thought of something I'd totally forgotten. I have to be in Turku at the beginning of the week. There's a major project in the offing, some properties in Helsinki, but the potential buyer lives in Turku and I'd fixed to meet him.'

'I see . . . did you mention this before?'

'No, I didn't.'

'Well, that's a relief, because I don't

remember anything about it. A major project, you said?'

'That's right, but we're only in the early stages. That's why I didn't want to make a big thing of it.'

'What properties are they?'

'Well . . . an estate of terraced houses. We'd be handling all the sales for the housing estate, but it's still at the construction stage. I'll know more when I've talked to the potential client.'

'Right, that's no problem. I'll hold the fort at the office. I'll call Kati, maybe she can help out a bit. How long are you going to be away?'

'I'll . . . oh, not long. I don't know exactly. I'll call on Monday.'

'Fine. Enjoy your trip. And my regards and thanks to Marjatta.'

'I'll tell her. See you soon.'

Korvensuo broke the connection. He was sweating all over. Marjatta was there in the doorway.

'Anything in particular?' she asked.

'No, no — or, well, yes, I entirely forgot an appointment. Almost entirely, anyway. I have to go to Turku, today would be best because I have a date to meet the man sponsoring the construction tomorrow. It's about several terraced houses.'

'In Turku?'

'No, no, the houses are here in Helsinki, but the man happens to live in Turku and he can't get away just now.'

'And the two of you agreed to meet on a Sunday?'

'That's right . . . yes, he could only make Sunday. Pressure of work, apparently.' He took a step towards her and caressed her face. He felt her wet hair in his hand. 'I think I ought really to leave this evening.'

'But you can't, we're all spending tonight here!' said Aku, who was suddenly standing beside Marjatta. Korvensuo saw the disappointment in his face.

'Some other time we can . . . '

'You said you'd be here this weekend! You said so! You said so!'

'Yes, I . . . I won't leave till first thing tomorrow, okay?'

Aku hugged him. Marjatta smiled and, soundlessly, formed the word 'Thanks!' with her lips. Korvensuo held Aku tight, as tight as he could, until after a while, half laughing, half scared, Aku cried out, 'Ow, that hurts, Papa!'

'Sorry,' muttered Korvensuo, as his son ran down to the lake again.

# 4

That evening, looking through his kitchen window, Kimmo Joentaa saw Pasi and Liisa Laaksonen, the elderly couple who lived next door to him. Pasi was carrying his fishing rod over his shoulder, the basket for fish dangled from Liisa's hand.

It had been like that the morning after Sanna's death. Kimmo often saw the two of them, and every time he did he thought of Sanna, because the picture of Pasi and Liisa with the fishing rod and the basket was engraved on his mind.

Paso and Liisa had seen him through the windowpane that day and waved to him, and they did the same now. This time Kimmo waved back; then, he had stood there motionless. This time they were coming away from the lake; then they were going down to it. And they had come by in the evening to give him and Sanna some of the fish they had caught. Kimmo had felt the fish, wrapped in foil, lying cold in his hands, had seen Pasi and Liisa smiling expectantly, and told the couple that Sanna had died in the night. He hadn't forgotten that moment either, the moment when what he said had sunk in to the husband and wife.

A few months ago Pasi Laaksonen had suffered a slight heart attack. Liisa had come in to see Joentaa that evening and they had talked for a while. Liisa had been in tears, and Kimmo hadn't known what to do, how to comfort her, but when she left Liisa had thanked him for their conversation. A few days later Pasi was going fishing again.

Kimmo stared out of the window. Very likely Pasi would soon be ringing the doorbell to bring him some fish.

For a little while he looked at the rather battered cardboard carton standing in the front hall. The files on the old case. He had taken the carton home because he felt he wouldn't be able to sleep anyway. Sundström had frowned, but said nothing.

They hadn't found the body of Sinikka Vehkasalo either that day. They had had two team conferences, they had decided on areas of operation, allotted various tasks to various officers and had already carried out some of them.

By now about thirty investigators were working on the case. Most of them were officers on patrol or temporarily conscripted from other departments. Sundström had coordinated this comparatively large group well, and had said a few clear, self-confident words, creating an effective working atmosphere.

Most of the officers were presumably still out and about seeing people connected with the Vehkasalos — neighbours, friends, relations, acquaintances — interviewing them or taking statements, reading their statements back to them. As yet, so far as could be seen at present, none of these people had been able to give them any useful leads.

Sundström had delivered a final address of some length to the core group of investigators, Heinonen, Grönholm and Joentaa, with a touch of emotion about it, or perhaps of irony, or then again maybe he was perfectly serious; then he told them to go home and have a relaxing evening. Kimmo Joentaa had taken the cardboard box when he left. He had already spent most of the day reading the old files, hoping he might be able to place details of a failed investigation of thirty-three years ago in a new context.

He had told Sundström that he would like to look hard at that aspect of their enquiries to start with, although he didn't know just why. Very likely he simply wanted to begin at the beginning. If it was the beginning. If there really was any connection between the two cases. The files comprised several thousand pages. Kimmo had leafed through the yellowing folders and kept coming upon Ketola's handwriting: illegible notes in the margins. Now and then exclamation marks at certain points that left Kimmo none the wiser.

Meanwhile Sundström had asked about Ketola several times, because he wanted to talk to him, but Ketola had not turned up again and couldn't be reached by telephone that day. Kimmo thought of trying his number again, but something kept him from it.

Instead, he took a folder out of the cardboard carton, sat down at the living-room table and began to read. It was the account of an interview that Ketola had conducted with the missing girl Pia Lehtinen's parents. Yet another and even more meticulous attempt to arrange all the circumstances of her disappearance in a sequence that would make sense.

During this interview the father had broken down. It didn't say so in the report, but it was clear from Ketola's dry phrasing. The mother's replies sounded monotonous and devoid of hope. The interview had taken place in the couple's home about four months after Pia Lehtinen's disappearance. It cast no new light on the investigation.

Kimmo sat up straight. Reading between the lines, he could sense the parents' grief.

Tomorrow he was going to speak to Elina Lehtinen, Pia's mother. He had rung to make an appointment for the morning. The woman had given a calm, controlled, almost absent impression over the phone and said she had been expecting a call. Her phone number and address were still the same as those they had in the old files. At first Kimmo had been surprised to discover that the woman was obviously living in the same house as before; a moment later he thought of himself. He, too, was still living in the same house. Of course. Of course Elina Lehtinen had stayed there.

Her husband, on the other hand, had left, probably because he couldn't bear to live there any longer with that memory. Kimmo Joentaa could understand that too and, indeed, he had concluded as much from the files. After a while they had given a new address for the husband.

Once again, and very slowly, Joentaa read every word of Ketola's interview with Pia Lehtinen's parents, an interview leading nowhere.

Then he turned the page. A piece of paper scribbled in Ketola's indecipherable handwriting, which was hard to read, was stuck to the top of the next page. It was a kind of note about the difference between a missing person inquiry and a murder inquiry, and about the bureaucratic guidelines that Ketola was supposed to follow, on the instructions of the officer in charge of the case. Or something of the kind. Joentaa couldn't make it out. Ketola's handwriting was even more illegible than usual. As if his hand had been shaking while he wrote.

The note bore the date on which Pia Lehtinen, or the remains of Pia Lehtinen, had been found in a lake on the outskirts of Turku, near the place where she had disappeared.

# 5

Elina Lehtinen was standing in her garden, watching the men at their work. They were a few hundred metres away, and a faint twilight that would last until morning had fallen, but she could make out the men easily if she looked across the field.

They wore white overalls and white hoods that hid their faces; they were working carefully and doggedly. The men's second working day here was nearing its close; a little while ago they had switched on searchlights again, giving them some more faint light, and the whole thing looked rather like a scene in a dream.

Elina Lehtinen felt more wide awake than she had been in a long time. She had been perfectly calm when she heard the voices the day before, and had not been surprised when the police car stopped at Pia's cross.

She had looked out of the window to see the two policemen examining the cross and talking to each other. They had stood there for a while, cautiously walking round something, she couldn't see what, because the trees hid her view of it. But the police

143

officers had found something.

One of the pair had gone back to the car and phoned.

Elina Lehtinen had stood by her window, feeling a little nugget of emptiness sink very softly down into her brain; then she had realized, immediately and clearly, that something significant was going on. Something she had been expecting. Something that was bound to happen sooner or later, because she had been waiting for it.

Whatever it was.

She had left the house and, with other onlookers, stood behind a barrier at some distance and watched the men at their work.

She had stayed there until evening began to fall. The other onlookers had come and gone, some had stayed for quite a while, others not so long, she had known some and not others, and at one point she found her neighbour Turre standing beside her.

He and his wife Maria had already been living in the house next door all that time ago, on the day when Pia disappeared, and Elina Lehtinen had looked at Turre and seen the question in his eyes, but Turre did not ask her anything and Elina herself couldn't have answered, for she didn't know what was going on beside Pia's cross; she had not the faintest idea what it was. She knew only that she had been waiting for it.

At some point Turre told her that his wife had fallen out of bed in her care home the night before, and would have to be in hospital for quite a while. Elina had said she was very sorry to hear that.

Then they had stood in silence for a long time looking at the bicycle lying on the path. And the police officers kneeling down carefully beside it, now and then slipping small objects into plastic envelopes.

Later Turre had left without saying anything else. He had just touched her shoulder briefly, a light touch. Elina didn't know if that was by accident or on purpose, but she could feel the touch on her skin as she slowly returned to the house, and she still felt it now. She had only to concentrate on the place that Turre's hand had brushed.

She glanced at Turre's house. There were no lights in the windows. Perhaps he was already asleep, or had gone to visit Maria in hospital.

The men were now packing up their equipment, patiently and with practised movements.

Another searchlight was on. It stood close to a minibus bearing the logo of Finnish state TV. Elina saw a young man with a camera trained on a woman. The woman was holding a microphone and giving the man instructions; she wasn't satisfied; presumably she wanted him to hold the camera in some other way. Or, at least, that was Elina's impression from a distance.

A second man got out of the minibus, and she could even hear what he called to the woman, because all was perfectly still otherwise. A quiet, still evening.

'We're on in twenty seconds!' called the man. The woman with the microphone nodded.

Elina nodded as well, and went indoors to watch the news.

# 6

Timo Korvensuo lay in bed beside Marjatta, concentrating on her quiet, peaceful breathing.

The children were sleeping in the tent.

The four of them had played a board game that evening. Aku had won, not least because Timo Korvensuo let him win, for he himself had had unusual luck throwing the dice all evening, and he kept having to make strategic mistakes to compensate for that luck.

Aku was the only one who hadn't grasped what his father was doing. Marjatta had smiled to herself. Laura had wrinkled her nose, and at the end of the game Aku couldn't contain his delight.

Then Laura had pointed out that Papa had been taking sides anyway, because dear little Aku couldn't lose, and they didn't want him throwing the pieces all over the place and wrecking the board again. But in his moment of triumph Aku had just laughed at that.

It had been a pleasant evening. All through it, second by second, Timo Korvensuo kept thinking what an improbably pleasant evening this was. Otherwise there had been nothing in his mind, just a droning in his head and a flickering in front of his eyes.

First thing after breakfast tomorrow, after a quick goodbye, he would drive to Turku.

# 10 June

# 1

Early in the morning Kimmo Joentaa drove to Lenganiemi. As the ferry made the crossing he stood in the cool breeze with his eyes closed, thinking of Sanna. Without forming any clear picture of her; he just thought of her name.

The ferryman was looking at Joentaa with a sullen or bored expression when he opened his eyes again. The man turned away as their glances met.

The graveyard lay in the morning sunlight. Joentaa was the only visitor. When he came here he sometimes met the pastor, who usually said a friendly hello before disappearing into the red wooden church, but now and then he came over to join him and they stood together by Sanna's grave, exchanging a few words.

Today Joentaa was alone. He watered the grave, looked at the gravestone for a while, the name on it and the figures framing Sanna's life, the wide blue expanse of the sea. Then he knelt down and began talking quietly.

Once, in the first months after Sanna's

death, the pastor had taken him by surprise, suddenly appearing there behind him. Joentaa had risen abruptly to his feet and coughed, hoping the pastor would think he had just been coughing all the time, rather than talking to himself. The pastor had smiled, a gentle, knowing smile — presumptuous, Joentaa had thought at that moment, and ever since he had made sure there was no one near before he began his conversations. Conversations with Sanna. Or perhaps with himself after all, or with the sun, the rain or the snow. It made no difference.

He touched the earth on the grave and talked about all kinds of things, anything that came into his mind. He talked for quite a long time. What he said became more and more meaningless and indiscriminate, more and more rambling and liberating, and sometimes he laughed, knowing that Sanna too would have laughed at what he had just been saying, and in the end he even forgot to wonder if there was anyone close enough to hear him.

He talked until he was drained and exhausted.

Then he returned to his car and drove home on the mainland.

# 2

Timo Korvensuo stopped for a rest halfway to Turku. He sat in the service area drinking coffee. He developed a kind of rhythm between the moment when he put the plastic beaker down and the moment of his next sip, and it soothed him slightly.

He had finally slept after all last night, but it had not been a refreshing sleep. His sleep had been full of dreams, although now he couldn't remember what they were about.

After his first cup of coffee he got himself a second, and began thinking what to do next.

All through his journey he had entertained the idea of turning back immediately. At one point he had actually done it, driving some twenty kilometres back towards his weekend house. He had thought what to say to Marjatta and the children. The client from Turku had called and cancelled their meeting. Just like that. Put it off. Until further notice. Very likely Marjatta and the children wouldn't even ask, they'd just be glad to see him home so soon.

Then he had turned the car and started back along the road to Turku, his foot hard down on the accelerator, closing his eyes now and then and letting his mind wander. For a while he had counted out loud every kilometre he had driven.

Now he was sitting at a table for two in a service station, watching the cars racing by. His thoughts were circling around the fact that he still had a choice: go on to Turku; turn back home.

Or simply stay sitting on this chair, not moving. For an indefinite time. He would carry the cardboard beaker to his mouth at regular intervals, and watch the cars driving back and forth.

Korvensuo smiled a little at his own idea, and a young woman who met his glance at that moment narrowed her eyes, shook her head and turned her back to him.

A little later Korvensuo continued his drive. The sun was dazzling; a hot day lay ahead.

He imagined Laura and Aku diving head first into the clear water, and drove on to Turku at a moderate, regular speed.

# 3

The girl in the photograph was laughing. A peal of laughter, thought Joentaa, those were the words that had occurred to him when he saw the picture of the girl. Pia Lehtinen.

Joentaa stood in front of the photograph and felt a tingling sensation at the idea that it had been hanging here for decades. Just as Sanna's photos would still be in the same place, decades from now.

'That's Pia,' said Elina Lehtinen, who had come to his side. She was carrying a tray with cups, plates and a blueberry cake still steaming from the oven.

'I know,' said Joentaa.

'Of course. You have a photograph in your files,' said Elina Lehtinen.

Joentaa nodded.

'It's incredibly long ago,' she went on, without taking her eyes off the photograph. 'I was thinking about that yesterday, and I was surprised to realize that today Pia would be a woman of forty-six. Hard to imagine.' She looked at him and smiled.

Joentaa nodded again. 'I . . . ' he began.

'Yes?'

'Excuse me, I'm sure this is a strange question, but . . . but do you know what Pia was laughing at so much?'

Elina Lehtinen looked at the picture again and thought for a moment. The photo had been taken in winter; there was snow in the background, but otherwise it showed only Pia's face in close-up.

'No,' said Elina Lehtinen at last. 'No, I'm afraid I don't. I think my husband took it — my former husband — on a skiing holiday. Maybe he wanted to take her by surprise, and she laughed when she saw that, and then he took the photo.'

'Yes,' said Joentaa.

'No one else has ever asked that in all these years,' she said.

'Hm.' Joentaa had another question on the tip of his tongue, but he didn't know how to put it.

'Most people just pass her photo as if they didn't know it was there,' she said. 'Even today. Of course some people don't know who Pia is, but not many. Those are the ones I haven't known long. I don't tell everyone about it straight away, but somehow the conversation always gets around to her.'

Joentaa nodded, and once again felt the impulse to ask his question, but he refrained. He turned away and followed Elina Lehtinen out on to the terrace.

'Home-baked.' She put a slice of cake on his plate.

'Thank you,' said Joentaa.

She sat down and looked at Joentaa enquiringly.

'Well . . . ' said Joentaa.

He was silent for a while and Elina Lehtinen said, 'You're an odd sort of policeman.' For a moment she looked very like her daughter.

'Am I?' Joentaa asked.

'Yes, definitely,' said Elina Lehtinen.

'I . . . I'd like to ask you something, something not at all important. My wife . . . she died two years ago, of cancer, and I'm still living in the house we shared. And her photos, well, there are photographs of her there, and what I want to ask is this . . . not that I know how . . . I have no idea what I really wanted to ask . . . '

He felt the sweat standing out on his forehead and saw Elina Lehtinen calmly returning his gaze. A slender woman with a strikingly round face and laughter lines in the places where her daughter too would have had them.

'Sorry . . . I really don't know what I . . . probably just living up to my reputation.'

'Reputation?'

'For being an odd sort of policeman,' said Kimmo Joentaa.

Elina Lehtinen gave a little laugh. A laugh that Joentaa couldn't interpret.

'I . . . '

'How are the parents managing?' asked Elina Lehtinen.

'The parents?'

'The parents of the missing girl. On TV they just call her Sinikka. It was the same back then, they just called her Pia. But there was much less news about it then. Or else I simply wasn't following it, I don't remember any more. I do recall a colleague of yours very well, another young police officer, very — very committed. He was an odd sort of policeman too.'

'I know the man you mean. We worked together for several years,' said Joentaa.

'Not any more?'

'No, he's retired, since early this year.'

'Of course,' she said. 'It's only in my mind that he's still a young man. Do try the cake.'

Joentaa raised his fork to his mouth.

'Once I really did have a great fit of laughter,' continued Elina Lehtinen and she was laughing again now as she saw Joentaa's face. 'An extraordinary fit of laughter, it's my most vivid memory. On the day my husband left me. He said he was going now, and I started laughing and couldn't stop until that evening, and next day I rang my neighbours' doorbell and they took me to a hospital, and I spent a long time having treatment there. Is the cake all right?'

'It's very good,' said Joentaa.

'My most vivid memory,' she repeated. 'Everything else is almost just a . . . well, a feeling of everything being over. It's sometimes close, sometimes further away. You talk to people, that sometimes helped me. And now it's ages ago, but it's beginning all over again.'

'You mean the missing girl, Sinikka?'

'Yes. It's repeating itself. When I saw the police officers I wasn't surprised. Because I'd always expected it to happen again, somehow. Do you understand?'

Joentaa didn't answer. He didn't know whether he understood or not.

'I always knew that couldn't have been all, because some time everything comes to an end, but this never really did. I'm afraid I can't explain it any better.'

Joentaa nodded. 'Can you think of any possible connection? The missing girl is called Sinikka Vehkasalo. Does the name mean anything to you?'

She shook her head.

'Of course we're looking for some such

connection, with luck someone who lived near you at the time and now lives near the Vehkasalo family.'

'No, the name means nothing to me.'

'We can't assume that there is such a person. There's much to suggest that whoever we're after is not someone from the . . . the victim's immediate environment. But all the same . . . '

'That was just the problem at the time,' she said. 'Your colleague spoke to me about it, I remember that now. I had a feeling he wanted to apologize for not making any progress, he said exactly what you did just now: it was difficult to find out about the murderer because he very likely wasn't someone from our immediate environment.'

'Yes,' said Joentaa.

'And of course there were no clues that were any use, because Pia had been in the water for so long.'

Joentaa nodded.

'What I always kept wondering later, when I was a little further from it, was what goes on inside a person . . . I wanted to know what he looked like, who he was, but most of all I wanted to understand what went on inside him, how it was possible for such a thing to happen at all. Do you understand?'

Joentaa nodded.

'Have you found out anything yet? Back then your colleague was always talking about hoping to bring the enquiries to a successful conclusion. That's the way the police put it, I think.'

'Yes, I mean no, I'm afraid we're only just at the start. It was hardly two days ago. But I'd like to ask you something, I'd like to ask whether, even going against all probability, you would try to think of any possible connections. Any contacts you have, maybe from back then until the present day. Places, localities you visit, then we can compare them with a list made by the Vehkasalos. I know it's a long shot. Oh, and do you have the present address and telephone number of your divorced husband?'

She nodded, stood up and Joentaa saw her searching a drawer in the living room. She came back with a business card.

'It's his private address as well. He was already working from home when it happened. But I'm not sure that the facts are still up to date; he sent me that card by post years ago. We exchange birthday cards now and then. And by the way, we're not divorced, just separated. That mattered to him at the time, and I had no objection.'

'Oh. Sorry.'

She laughed. 'Nothing to apologize for.'

Joentaa read the information on the card, which identified Hannu Lehtinen as representing a well-known insurance company.

'Thank you.' He put the card in his pocket.

His glance fell on a football lying in the middle of the garden. He had been vaguely aware of it all this time, but now he wondered what the ball was doing there.

'My neighbours' grandsons kick a ball around here now and then,' said Elina Lehtinen, who had followed his gaze. 'Because my garden's bigger and I don't mind if my flower beds get knocked about a bit. And because I like to see children playing in the garden.'

She smiled.

Joentaa nodded. 'Thank you. The cake was excellent.' He was going to get to his feet, but sat there for a few more seconds looking at the ball on the lawn.

Then he let Elina Lehtinen lead him through the shade of the living room and the hall to the front door. As he stepped outside, he collided with Ketola.

'Oops!' said Ketola.

'Ouch!' protested Kimmo.

'Watch where you're going!' Ketola's eyes were reddened, and seemed to Joentaa to be unnaturally wide and restless.

'I . . . excuse me, you probably won't

162

remember me,' Ketola said, addressing Elina Lehtinen, as if Joentaa's presence were to be regarded as a matter of no importance.

'I remember you very well,' she answered slowly. 'You're a bit older now. And we were talking about you only a moment ago.'

'Ah. Do you have a little time? This won't take long, just a few minutes.'

'Of course.' With a gesture she invited him in.

'We'll be in touch,' said Ketola to Kimmo Joentaa. He seemed to be in a hurry to get inside the house before Joentaa started asking any questions, but he did turn back for a moment. 'And do you have any news? Can I call you, this evening or tomorrow morning? Is that okay?'

'Of course,' said Joentaa. 'And you should call Sundström as well, he wants to speak to you and rope you in on this case. I told him you'd suggested it yourself.'

'Yes, good, I'm glad. See you, then. I'll call.'

'Two odd police officers,' said Elina Lehtinen, almost imperceptibly wrinkling her brow.

'Hm, well,' Joentaa muttered.

As he got into his car he was thinking that Elina Lehtinen was a nice woman, and Ketola would always be a riddle to him.

163

# 4

Timo Korvensuo reached Turku about midday, but he went on driving. He drove around the city in circles. Again and again. He felt it was important to keep moving. He saw the cathedral towering to the sky from various different angles. When he used to live here it was quite close to the Faculty of Mathematics, and now and then he had gone to sit in the cool of the cathedral for a while, between lectures or in the evening, without thinking of anything much.

He drove around in circles again and again, until in the early afternoon the petrol gauge started blinking red. He made for a petrol station, and then drove straight to his destination.

He knew the way. Along the urban motorway towards Tampere, into the small suburb surrounded by tall trees.

The grass by the roadside was yellow and dry. The supermarket stood where it always had, but the sign over it was a different colour and bore the logo of a well-known chain. There was a kiosk in the adjacent building, which had once been the only bar in the area.

He drove slowly past, his eyes passing over strangers' faces.

The sports field was still there too. The running track looked new; the red of it caught his eye. On the grass, three boys were kicking at a goal. The indoor swimming pool beyond was gone. It didn't exist any more, nothing existed there. All gone, with nothing to replace it. The swimming pool was now an asphalt surface where cars could park.

Korvensuo felt his stomach lurch, and for seconds had a vague sense of relief. He had often been there on winter evenings because Susanna, the girl from the next-door building, used to train in the pool. She always wore a green swimsuit and sometimes smiled at him because they lived in the same housing complex, and he used to lean back at the edge of the pool, feeling the water getting colder round his legs, and staring for all he was worth, as inconspicuously as possible.

He remembered that perfectly. It had been the time when everything began, whatever 'everything' was, although he couldn't pin-point the real beginning, the exact moment in time. There probably wasn't one. No beginning and no end. And no reason. None that anyone could have understood, none that he understood himself. There was nothing of that kind, and the pool where Susanna from

165

the next-door building used to swim was gone as well.

The boys on the football pitch were arguing about the score. Korvensuo got into his car again and let it coast down the slope.

He passed the bus stop.

Then he turned left into the narrow drive and up to the building where he had lived.

Everything he had thought of as he drove from Helsinki was cancelled out. He'd planned to leave the car sooner than this, at a safe distance. Not to arrive until evening, under cover of dark, which anyway would be only a slight twilight. An absence of sunlight, achieved with difficulty and never complete, lasting for several hours.

It was cancelled out; he didn't think of these things any more. He was shaking, but at the same time felt perfectly calm. He didn't see any small red car. Of course not. He got out. The sun warmed him and brought out gooseflesh on his back. The garbage container stood where it had always been, although now there were several of them. For recycling. A middle-aged man in tracksuit bottoms was just putting bottles into the bottle bank. They smashed to pieces: a hollow shattering sound. The man folded up the bag that had held the bottles and passed him without looking up. Korvensuo didn't know him. Of course not.

The man would have been a small child when Korvensuo lived here. And had studied mathematics, for reasons he couldn't put a name to now. Everything was different. An eternity had passed. He turned away his eyes and looked at the playground. Different rides, brightly coloured and new. An engine was humming. Pärssinen was sitting on a bright red mower, cutting the grass.

Korvensuo watched him. It relaxed him. Pärssinen rode regularly up and down the lawn. Carefully, meticulously, he also trimmed the edges of the grass. He was older now. An old man, but he hadn't looked young even then.

Korvensuo wondered whether Pärssinen had chosen that colour. The red of the mower. Very likely these models were always red. He felt the sand trickling through him again. Slowly and steadily. Pärssinen raised his head and lowered it without showing any sign of recognition.

Korvensuo started walking. Metre by metre. He was freezing, and he felt the sand inside him.

'Hello,' he said, when he was close enough, and Pärssinen raised his eyes from the lawn, looking at him questioningly, merely shrugged his shoulders and pointed to his ears, to indicate that he couldn't hear him.

The engine was roaring.

'Hello!' Korvensuo called again.

Pärssinen turned off the engine and said, in the silence, 'Yes, what is it?'

'It's me. We know each other,' said Korvensuo.

'We do?' asked Pärssinen.

Korvensuo nodded.

Pärssinen stared at him. 'Ah. Yes,' he murmured.

Korvensuo was shaking. He had the shivers. And gooseflesh on his back. A hot day. 'Timo,' said Pärssinen and Korvensuo felt himself nodding.

Pärssinen adjusted a few things on the mower and got off. 'It's been a long time,' he said, taking Korvensuo's hand. His own was sweaty and had blisters and weals on it. Korvensuo felt them on his skin.

'Yes,' he said.

'Let's have a drink.' Pärssinen went ahead and Korvensuo followed, thinking he would drive home. At once. To the people who were his life.

'Well, fancy seeing you,' said Pärssinen. He looked almost happy as he opened the door of his apartment. Venetian blinds drawn down. Dappled sunlight on the floor.

'A beer?' Pärssinen asked.

Korvensuo nodded.

Drive away. Just get in the car and drive away, he thought.

'Sit down, do,' called Pärssinen from the kitchen.

Korvensuo sat down in one of the two soft, shabby armchairs where he used to sit all of thirty-three years before. The sofa was also the same, but where the screen used to be there was now a large TV set. A new, expensive model.

'Not bad, eh?' said Pärssinen, following his gaze. Korvensuo nodded.

'Brand new.' Pärssinen handed him one of the bottles. 'Cheers!'

Korvensuo took a sip.

'To our reunion,' said Pärssinen.

Korvensuo looked at the floor. The sense of trickling sand was dying down, his headache had come back. Dappled sunlight. A DVD player and video recorder stood under the TV set; the cases for the discs and cassettes were neatly arranged on a shelf.

'Like to watch a film?' asked Pärssinen.

Korvensuo looked at the bottle in his hand and was surprised, for a moment, to see that he had apparently half finished it already. Then he began to laugh. At least, it sounded like laughter. It broke out of him and lasted only a few seconds. The sand had stopped trickling. He felt nothing except for his headache. 'Sorry,' he said.

Pärssinen was sitting there as relaxed as ever. 'Nothing to apologize for. 'So you don't want to see a film?'

'No,' said Korvensuo. 'That's right, I don't. No, I wanted to ask you something. I'd like to know . . . why?'

Pärssinen put the bottle to his lips and seemed to be waiting for him to ask his question more precisely.

'Why did you do it?' asked Korvensuo.

'Why did I do what?' Pärssinen asked.

'The girl who's gone missing right where we . . . where back then we . . . '

'Oh, you mean that,' said Pärssinen. He seemed to be smiling.

Korvensuo stood up. The bottle felt cold in his hand. Chilled beer. I'll go home now, he thought. 'Why did you do it, you bastard?' he screamed, throwing the bottle at the patch of sunlight in front of his feet. As hard as he could. Then there was silence. The shards of broken glass were lying all over the room. A trickle of beer was making its way towards Pärssinen's shoes. Pärssinen still sat there looking relaxed.

'I didn't do anything,' he said.

Korvensuo stared at him.

'Do sit down again,' said Pärssinen. 'Please.'

Korvensuo sat on the arm of the chair.

'I have nothing to do with it,' Pärssinen continued. 'I heard about it only yesterday evening. By chance. I don't often watch the news . . . I'm not interested in all the crap that happens. It's all just shit, that corrupt stuff.'

'Ah,' said Korvensuo.

'I've got better things to do.' Pärssinen waved the subject away and put the bottle to his mouth again.

Korvensuo thought of Marjatta and the children. Marjatta going for a walk, the children in the rowing boat. Laura rowing, Aku dipping his hand in the water.

'Yes,' he said and saw Pärssinen sitting there in an armchair, relaxed. It hadn't been like that thirty-three years ago. On the day when . . . on that day Pärssinen had seemed distraught, panic-stricken, as he had never seen him before. 'Yes,' he repeated.

'Understand? I have nothing to do with it. You don't either. I'd never have thought of suspecting that you . . . it's just coincidence, that's all.'

'Coincidence?'

'Yes, coincidence. Something happened. We don't know what. We have nothing to do with it. And it's of no interest to us.'

Korvensuo nodded.

'You have nothing to do with it. I have

nothing to do with it. Understand? Timo, our . . . what we did once, it's an eternity ago. Understand?'

Korvensuo nodded. What we did once, he thought.

'After all, it's in the past,' said Pärssinen.

In the past, thought Korvensuo. Past and over. Nothing happened, he thought. Nothing, nothing. Pärssinen smiled and looked friendly. A kindly old caretaker.

Silence reigned for a while. Then Pärssinen said, 'Well, Timo, good to see you again.'

'Yes.'

'I often thought of you . . . back then, the way you went off, that was odd, of course. For a few days I was worried, thought you might maybe go to the police . . . it was like the earth had swallowed you up.'

Korvensuo nodded.

'You always were an oddball,' said Pärssinen, laughing.

Korvensuo nodded to himself again.

'So how are you doing these days? Got a family, that sort of thing?'

Korvensuo tried to meet Pärssinen's glance and saw only eyes looking past him, looking into nothing. Nothing, he thought. Nothing, nothing. Aku is dipping his hand in the water and asking Laura if he can have a go at rowing too.

'I'm going now,' said Korvensuo.

Pärssinen nodded. 'Always on the move, eh?'

Korvensuo started walking.

'Oh, one more thing.' Pärssinen got to his feet and went over to the shelf with the discs and cassettes. Korvensuo stood still. Waited. Don't move, he thought.

'You liked one film specially, your favourite film,' said Pärssinen. 'With the girl you fancied so much. The slim girl with the dark hair, she's doing it with two men in the film and she has kind of a birthmark on her shoulder. Remember?'

Pärssinen went on searching; he wasn't expecting an answer. He found what he was looking for and came towards Korvensuo with a case.

'I managed to transfer it to DVD, simply filmed it again with a new camera. The quality's really good ... particularly the girl. I'll make you a present of it.' Pärssinen smiled and held out the case to him. A neutral white case, with a few letters written on it, denoting some kind of classification known only to Pärssinen. And a date, the date of the year when the film had been made: 1973.

'Here you are,' said Pärssinen.

Korvensuo took the case.

'Drop in any time you like,' said Pärssinen.

Korvensuo walked over the carefully mown lawn to his car. He would call Marjatta, tell her he'd arrived safely. And had a good meeting. About terraced houses. His body was a heavy weight of emptiness, heavy as lead.

He put the DVD case on the passenger seat and started the car.

# 5

Sundström was looking confident. Inclined to make jokes that no one understood. Heinonen was sitting deep in thought, Grönholm was tapping out a monotonous rhythm on the tabletop, and Kari Niemi was telling the core group of the investigating team the results that forensics had come up with. They seemed to lead nowhere.

'There's very little,' he concluded.

Various fingerprints had been found on the bicycle; only one could be identified. Ruth Vehkasalo had touched her daughter's bike.

'The husband was rather annoyed when we asked him and his wife to come in for fingerprinting,' said Heinonen. 'Although we said right away we always do that, it's only so as to compare their prints with those we find. So that we can spare ourselves unnecessary work, but he didn't entirely understand that.'

'I'm afraid I wouldn't either, in his position,' said Grönholm.

'I felt sorry for him,' murmured Heinonen.

'The man's had all he can take,' added Grönholm.

'Kalevi Vehkasalo,' said Sundström. 'Say

the father's been abusing his daughter for years, the daughter grows up to be a big girl, then a bigger girl, and a time comes when she threatens to tell Mama some funny things when she gets a chance. Her father comes home from the office early on the afternoon in question, because his daughter calls him, says she's just quarrelled with Mama again and now she's going to tell her all. Her father's panic-stricken, he sees his daughter on the cycle path, gets out of his car, stops her, they argue for a while, she hits out at him, calls him names, threatens him again with telling her story. The father goes off his head, throttles his daughter . . . '

'That trace of blood,' said Heinonen.

' . . . okay, stabs her with some unknown weapon, probably a mortal injury, puts her in the car, sinks her in water or buries her somewhere.'

'No traces of anything of that kind in Vehkasalo's car,' said Heinonen. 'He was angry with us for checking that too, which I can understand better.'

Sundström nodded.

'There's nothing and no one so far to suggest that Vehkasalo and his daughter . . . had a secret,' said Heinonen carefully.

'And several employees in Vehkasalo's

company confirm that he was there all day,' Grönholm added.

'Which is why that scenario is nonsense,' agreed Sundström. 'Just wanted to run it past myself.'

Joentaa looked at the photograph he was holding. Sinikka Vehkasalo. A serious-looking girl, with hair cut short and tinted black. She was pressing her lips firmly together, but Joentaa thought he could trace a smile. The lurking possibility of a wide, happy smile. In her eyes . . . yes, a hunger for experience. For beautiful things, important things, serious things . . .

Very likely he was making all that up. What does a photograph tell you? And what use would it be even if his impressions were correct?

Joentaa lowered the picture and tried to concentrate on Sundström's curiously ironic remarks. Presumably he was trying to keep them awake. Or keep himself awake. They had finished discussing everything long ago. No suspicious factors in her immediate environment. At least, nothing really tangible.

Outsiders had considered the Vehkasalos the perfect family; the Vehkasalos themselves had made it clear, unasked, that they were having problems with their daughter. That they never met her friends and had no basis in common for conversation these days, that Sinikka had been out all night several times staying with girlfriends, or maybe even boyfriends, but the Vehkasalos knew nothing in more detail, because Sinikka refused to talk about it. It was much like that with many parents and many children.

In an interview with Heinonen and Grönholm, however, Vehkasalo had admitted, or rather had said of his own accord, that he had struck Sinikka twice in the weeks just before her disappearance; then he had begun shedding tears and saying, on record, that he wished he could undo that now, he'd give anything in the world if only he could undo that. Joentaa thought about this statement as he looked at the photograph again. All children wanted to be left alone. At some point, anyway. Wanted to break free of their parents and make their own way. Or so he supposed, although of course he had no idea what it meant to have children, or how to deal with them. Sanna had wanted children, he himself hadn't thought much about it. Later, he had thought, and sometimes said so when they discussed the subject.

Joentaa remembered his own childhood.

Soon after finishing at school he had moved away from Kitee, leaving his mother but at the same time always feeling how much the link with her mattered to him. Knowing that she was there. It seemed to be different in Sinikka's case, at least at the first superficial glance. Why had Sinikka wanted so persistently to get away from her parents? Joentaa stared at the photo as if the girl in it could answer and tell him.

'Everything clear, Kimmo?' asked Sundström.

'Yes, sure,' said Joentaa.

'What does that photo tell you?' Sundström asked.

'Hm . . . what's your impression, everyone?' Joentaa held up the photograph so that they could all see it. None of them said anything for a while.

'In a word,' said Joentaa.

Still silence.

'Likeable . . . I mean, she looks nice,' said Heinonen at last.

Grönholm nodded. 'Mysterious? Kind of as if she'd like to look mysterious.'

'I don't see that at all,' said Sundström. 'No, reserved, sort of shy, but then again no . . . ' He suddenly darted forward, reached for the picture and held it close to his face. 'I think she makes it look as if she'd . . . oh, I don't know.'

'Sad,' Niemi observed.

They all turned to look at him.

'That girl is sad,' said Niemi, with his eternal smile.

# 6

Timo Korvensuo was sitting on a chair in a hotel bedroom, looking out of the window at the city where it lay in the evening sunlight. The window was tilted open and a breeze blew in over his shoulders.

He heard the muted siren of a police car. A little later its blue light flashed near the marketplace. He couldn't see what was going on, but it was almost soundless, just impacts now and then like someone kicking dustbins. Presumably drunks, waking from last night's stupor and rampaging around a little more before going home. Nothing too terrible.

The room was well situated; the sun fell right on his body, warming him. Relaxing him. The shivers were dying down. He had begun shivering so hard as he drove that he could hardly use the gear shift, but it was better now that he was here in this room, looking down on the city. It was going away.

He felt he was getting back a certain amount of control. The glimmerings of a certain order. Reducing things to essentials. A sheet of paper lay on the desk, along with a folder telling guests about the hotel's room service and the price list for the minibar. And the DVD lay there as well. In a white, neutral case.

Nothing, he thought. Nothing at all. In the end there was nothing left but memories, vague notions that might just as well have been fantasies. Or dreams that you had dreamed and then forgotten, seeing them resurface later in a blurred image at a certain and entirely random moment.

Perhaps he had just spoken to Marjatta on the phone. In a firm voice. Telling her all she needed to know and hoping she'd have a nice evening. Perhaps Pia had been lying in that field. Perhaps the girl's voice had begged Pärssinen to stop, a strangely calm voice that came through to him only now and then, because Pärssinen was holding the girl's mouth closed and drowning out her voice with his groans. He thought he could still hear that voice in his ears. He might be wrong. He let himself drift.

Two young women in smart uniforms were standing down at reception, smiling at him in their professional way as he went past. His car was in the underground garage. The laptop was in the boot and weighed light in his hand as he stood beside an old man in the lift.

The DVD was still on the desk when he came back into the room. He inserted it into

182

the computer drive and heard the gentle whirr of technology at work. A window opened. A button to be clicked.

A small, black-haired girl between two men. The picture slightly blurred and wobbling. Korvensuo let the film run as he fetched toilet paper from the bathroom. When he returned, the girl was staring at the camera, and one of the men announced that he was going to come. Timo Korvensuo clutched his crotch and leaned against the desk, groaning quietly.

Later, he sat on the bed for a long time, waiting for the picture he had seen to lose itself again in the void from which it came.

# 7

Kimmo Joentaa read the old files. Pia Lehtinen was found, the number of investigators stepped up. Joentaa read interviews, word by word, forcing himself not to skip anything.

The circle of the victim's relations, friends and acquaintances, people who could be shown to have had the slightest connection with Pia Lehtinen, had been drawn ever wider. Interviews with men already in the files as known sex offenders. These led nowhere. One of the men burst into tears and blurted out that he was sorry for the girl, which made him a suspect until it was established without the slightest doubt that he had been on holiday in Greece on the day of Pia's disappearance.

There had been no useful clues in that old case either: prints on the bicycle that couldn't be matched with any known to the police and the search for a small red car that led nowhere. The boy who had seen it couldn't say what make of car it was.

Hundreds of small red cars were investigated. Hundreds of interrogations leading to dead ends. Reading between the lines, Joentaa sensed the frustration of the detectives of the time. An internal memo finally raised the question of whether the boy could be regarded as a reliable witness and suggested that if the small car did exist it need not necessarily have belonged to the murderer.

Joentaa passed his hands over his face, feeling the weariness that he knew would be gone as soon as he lay down to sleep.

He switched on the TV. On the screen, Ketola was sitting on a chair, leaning forward and talking insistently to the presenter of a talk show.

Joentaa stood there for a few seconds, then sat down on the sofa without taking his eyes off the screen. It was some time before he could concentrate on what Ketola was saying. The presenter, Kai-Petteri Hämäläinen, was nodding the whole time as if he understood it all. Beside Ketola sat Pia's mother, Elina Lehtinen.

It went through Joentaa's mind that half Finland was probably watching. Hämäläinen was the new star among home-grown entertainers. He had originally been a sports commentator, had then successfully moved into light entertainment and had scored a big hit with his new talk show.

Joentaa watched Hämäläinen, Ketola and Elina Lehtinen, and he simply could not focus on the words they were exchanging. Ketola on the screen, Elina Lehtinen; he had been sitting opposite her only that morning. So that was why Ketola had wanted to speak to her, about an appearance on TV at short notice. But what was the purpose of all this?

'Of course he must expect to be caught this time. And I wonder whether he even *wants*, somehow, to be caught,' said Ketola. Hämäläinen nodded. Elina Lehtinen was sitting lost in thought and looked pale, not at all the way she had been that morning in her house.

'I'd say . . . I'd almost like to appeal to the man to take that possibility into account. Just reveal himself, in whatever way he can,' said Ketola. The camera moved close to him until his face was almost filling the screen. He was perspiring, his face looked even craggier and more angular than usual, presumably because of the TV make-up. He was wearing a dark green jacket and appeared both calm and agitated. Joentaa couldn't pin down his mood precisely.

What Ketola was saying sounded as if he'd worked it all out and was trying to give an impression of calm, to speak with composure. But it was as if his own voice were urging him

186

on; he spoke faster and faster, raising his voice more and more, then he slumped when he had followed an idea to its conclusion.

Now and then Hämäläinen turned to Elina Lehtinen, who described, in clear and quiet tones, how she managed to live with her daughter's death. Hämäläinen nodded. Ketola was breathing deeply, looking at the floor, and Joentaa felt Elina Lehtinen's words like snowflakes cooling him for a while, before they began to melt inside his head.

The audience was silent. Hämäläinen became tangled up as he asked his next question. A woman scurried across the picture and mopped the sweat from Ketola's face with a cloth.

The telephone rang. Joentaa went to pick it up without taking his eyes off the screen.

'Switch your TV on,' said Sundström.

'I already have.'

'Then I guess you'll agree with me when I say he's gone right round the bend,' said Sundström.

'What do you mean?'

'What I say. He's interfering massively in our enquiries while they're still in progress, and now he thinks it's his business to offer the murderer good advice.'

Joentaa was trying to listen with half an ear to what Ketola was saying now. He was talking about how he had felt as an investigator during the search for Pia Lehtinen.

'Hello?' asked Sundström.

'Yes. You're right,' said Joentaa.

'What's he after? What does he think he's doing? You know him well, what does he think he's doing?'

'Yes . . . ' said Joentaa.

'Yes what?'

'I think he's . . . well, convinced that the murderer of thirty-three years ago is back. And he wants to lure him out of hiding.'

'Ah.'

'Or that's what I assume, at least. I don't really know either, the programme's still going on.'

'I can see that,' said Sundström and fell silent for a while. They both listened as Elina Lehtinen appealed to the murderer to give himself up.

Joentaa thought that once again, Elina Lehtinen looked very like her daughter at this moment, and Sundström said, 'This programme is a bloody bad joke.'

Hämäläinen was nodding in agreement.

'All we need now is for them to run a number at the bottom of the screen for the murderer to call,' said Sundström.

Hämäläinen was just explaining that it was

sometimes difficult to make a link between items on the show, so this time he wasn't even going to try it; then Ketola and Elina Lehtinen went off and an actor replaced them on the set, a man with a drink problem who nonetheless was getting himself established in Hollywood.

Joentaa stood there with the telephone in his hand and watched the actor, who was doing his best to be both amusing and profound. The audience applauded a short film clip, the actor smiled.

'Right, goodnight, then,' said Sundström and broke the connection before Joentaa could say anything.

# 8

The children were asleep. Probably. At least, all was quiet. The weekend by the lake had tired them out, and now they were asleep and contented, looking forward to the long summer holidays.

Marjatta Korvensuo sat on the sofa with her arms clasped round her knees, thinking of the pale woman on the TV screen.

She had really switched on the Hämäläinen show to relax, but then that woman had been a guest on the show, the mother of the girl who had been killed thirty-three years ago, Pia Lehtinen. She had said things that Marjatta Korvensuo couldn't get out of her head. She wouldn't have been able to repeat a word of it, but the sound of the woman's voice had made a deep impression on her, and so had the silence of the studio audience, the long silences that had followed what she said.

The TV was still on. The late news. The photograph of the missing girl came on screen, and for a few moments pictures of a press conference.

Marjatta felt an impulse to go and look in

on the children, but she made herself stay where she was. The children were asleep in their beds. Briefly, she wondered whether to call Timo again and talk to him for a few minutes about the TV interview she had seen. Timo was a very good listener, and often things looked different to her after he had cast a new light on them in his quiet way.

But Timo was very probably asleep by now.

The President of Finland was still on her state visit to Germany. She was standing in front of a speaker's lectern in a storm of flash photography, smiling.

Marjatta got up and checked once again that the front door was bolted on the inside. She always did that when Timo was away. Then she found herself a blanket and decided to go to sleep on the sofa with the TV still running.

# 9

Timo Korvensuo was sitting on the bed. His eyes were burning; he had to keep opening and closing them quickly, at intervals of a second.

The clock on the television showed nearly one in the morning. There was faint twilight outside the window, a touch of blue and a touch of pink.

He wished for deep, dark winter. And sleep, and a dream. A dream of a deluge washing everything away. This whole mess. All the filth that didn't interest him any more.

He went into the bathroom and checked his eyes in the mirror. They felt reddened, but they didn't look red. They looked the same as usual and the face in the mirror was the face of a man in his mid fifties who had kept his youthful looks.

He went back to bed. He thought of Marjatta and the children. They were home again and asleep. Everything was fine with the exception of the warning lights in Marjatta's car. Marjatta had told him on the phone that they had begun blinking halfway through her drive home from the weekend house. The blinking had worried her, and Korvensuo, who knew a little about these things, was able to reassure her: the lights on the dashboard would probably need attention, but it wasn't urgent.

Earlier in the evening it had occurred to him that this was Sunday, and Marjatta was sure to be watching Hämäläinen's talk show. For Marjatta's sake he had sat beside her on the sofa every Sunday for months, watching that programme. Marjatta would lie with her head on his lap, and he would stroke her back, very gently.

He had thought briefly of switching on the TV in the hotel bedroom. To watch what Marjatta was watching. But he hadn't. He had gone straight to bed and his thoughts had stood still, until after a while it occurred to him that tomorrow he was going to call Marjatta again. Tell her that he would have to postpone coming home, for good reasons.

Pekka was holding the fort at the office.

Marjatta was with the children.

The children were on holiday.

He had wondered for a while what to do tomorrow, without coming to any conclusion.

He sat on the bed. The midnight sun shone outside. A shower started running in the room next door.

He closed his eyes. The pillows felt soft and

cool as his head lay down.

Nothing, he thought. Nothing.

The water in the next room rushed and splashed.

Just before he fell asleep he thought of Pärssinen. Kindly old caretaker.

Then a man moved away from the dark façade of some buildings. He had curly hair, a face like stone, and he was moving fast, moving smoothly forward as if on rails. He was holding a knife and approaching Korvensuo and Marjatta. He was just explaining to Marjatta that this was all a dream when the curly-haired man struck with his knife, and when Marjatta sank into his arms he realized that it was not a dream, because dreams didn't exist.

He woke up.

He sat up in bed. The clock showed five. There was a dull pain behind his forehead and a very distinct thought about Pärssinen.

# 11 JUNE

# 1

Elina Lehtinen woke early in the morning with the image of Pia in her mind. It had filled her dreams, and went away only when she opened her eyes.

She could still feel the TV make-up on her skin, and thought of Ketola. They had talked for a long time, about anything and everything, until late into the night, until they had been the last customers still lingering in the café near the TV studios.

Two old people who had drunk a good deal. They had probably presented an odd picture. At the end of the evening the waiter had even said they suited each other. Elina had giggled, while Ketola stood there with his mouth open.

He was going to get that man, Ketola had said earlier in the evening. The man who did it. That, he said, had been clear to him even on the day of his retirement. It was something he had to do, for reasons he didn't quite know.

Elina Lehtinen had nodded and didn't understand Ketola, but she had known at once that there was a point to it, and she had

197

not for a moment hesitated when at midday, after thirty-three years, he had asked her straight out if they could do an interview on television together. Of course. Hämäläinen. The show that topped the ratings, the one she watched every Sunday. To talk about Pia and answer Hämäläinen's questions.

The idea, Ketola had explained, was to get things moving, to entice the man out of hiding until he made a mistake and then, at that moment, Ketola had said in his calm, cheerful voice, he would get him. Of course, Elina Lehtinen had replied, and she saw her neighbour Turre passing outside. She had wondered how Maria was, his wife who had fallen out of bed in her care home.

During the interview she had felt the spotlights on her skin and Hämäläinen had asked questions, questions he had discussed with them at length before the programme. She must have spoken very slowly, because she had tried every word on her tongue until she knew that it was the absolute truth.

Putting Pia's death into words. For the first time in her life. In conversation with a stranger.

There had been a professionally gentle tone to Hämäläinen's words, a camera-friendly calm in his voice. She didn't blame him for that. Hämäläinen's eyes glided over his questions, Ketola beside her had bowed his head, the spotlights had spread artificial light and she had spoken as if in a trance, feeling that she didn't have the strength — and Hämäläinen didn't have the time — to understand what they were really talking about.

At the close the audience had applauded for a long time, and Ketola, beside her, had been shaking. An actor she liked had come on the programme next, his smile had brushed past her, and once they were off the set Ketola had thanked her and said he wasn't sure if he ought to have asked such a thing of her. He wasn't sure, either, whether anything would come of it, he said, whether it would do any good; then he had invited her to go and have a drink with him.

Curiously, they had not talked much about Pia in the café, or about Sinikka Vehkasalo, nor did they talk about the murderer who had come back after thirty-three years.

Ketola had told her about his son. They had laughed a lot, because the stories about Ketola's son were funny — it was desperate laughter, of course, sad laughter, and when the waiter brought the bill and Ketola was fumbling for money in his jacket pocket, she had noticed that for the first time in her life she was really drunk.

It had felt good, and even going into the bathroom now and throwing up into the the washbasin felt good too.

Oddly enough, as she looked at her vomit in the basin she thought of Hämäläinen, and how she certainly couldn't have appeared on his show in this state, and how even the alcoholic actor had looked perfectly sober as he walked on to the set. Then she wondered whether her neighbour Turre had seen the programme, or Hannu, the ex-husband she wasn't divorced from. And she also reflected that anyway, that had been her first and last such appearance.

# 2

At six o'clock in the morning Timo Korvensuo was sitting in the hotel lobby. A friendly young lady asked if he would like to read the newspaper. He waved the offer aside and watched the waiter setting out the breakfast buffet.

He was turning over in his mind the ideas that had filled it ever since the moment when he woke up.

Pärssinen. Kindly old caretaker. How many people might Pärssinen have raped and murdered?

In all these years.

So many years, he thought. Coming back to find everything the way it used to be. Pärssinen's apartment. The old sofa. Dreams did not exist.

The same friendly lady asked if she could bring him some coffee.

He said no thanks. Good service. A good hotel.

He realized that he was walking over to the reception desk and speaking to the young man there. Yes, he would like to stay another night. A day and a night. The young man looked at a screen and tapped a keyboard.

'No problem, Mr . . . Mr Korvensuo.'

'Thank you.'

He took the top off an egg in the breakfast room. The yolk spread over a roll, and he drank some coffee after all. Ate a yoghurt, stirred a little jam into it.

After a while the staff cleared away the breakfast buffet and removed the tablecloths with a flourish. A little girl of two or three ran around the room and looked at him with wide, curious eyes. Her mother picked her up and apologized.

'That's all right,' he said and made a face. The little girl smiled uncertainly.

He went back to his room. The bed had been made. Nearby a vacuum cleaner was droning in another room, and Pärssinen was crouching in his car removing stains that couldn't be there.

He went down in the lift to the underground garage and got into his car. The road was flooded with sunlight. What a wonderful summer. If it went on like this. Which you could never know. Not with the best will in the world.

He parked on a rise within sight of the grey concrete block. Pärssinen's flat among the trees. The window. The venetian blinds drawn down. The playground. Children. A boy and two girls. The girls were on the slide, the boy on a swing.

Pärssinen was nowhere to be seen.

Get out of the car, walk over at his leisure, say hello to the children, tap on the window, and a stranger would open it and say: Pärssinen? Who's he? Never heard of him.

Aku. Laura.

The girls were sliding, the boy was swinging. Wildly, going higher and higher, until Korvensuo felt sure he would go right over the top of the frame at any moment.

But that was impossible. He'd discovered it himself as a child. However hard you tried, you could never go over the top of a swing frame.

You might fall off, of course, and hurt yourself badly. That had happened to him. His knee had bled, and only years later had a doctor said his trouble in the joint there might well be as a result of the fall.

The boy slowed down, jumped off the swing, uninjured, and pushed one of the girls off the slide. The boy went on the slide, the girls ran to the swings.

Pärssinen came out of doors, stretching. He called out something unintelligible to the children. Korvensuo just heard his voice faintly. Pärssinen jogged along the path and disappeared in the direction of the supermarket.

Wait, he thought. Wait for Pärssinen to come back. Ask a question. Get an answer. We won't be meeting again, he would say as they parted.

He called Marjatta. She was in town with Aku. Aku snatched the mobile and asked if he was on his way home yet.

Aku's voice.

Yes, he thought, and said nothing.

Then he told Marjatta that his business was going to drag on for a while. A day, perhaps two days. He didn't know.

Marjatta asked if he had seen the Hämäläinen show, that woman, the mother of the girl who was killed so long ago and the police officer who had been investigating the case.

No, he said.

Pärssinen came back. He was holding a white plastic bag in each hand. Milk, sugar, eggs. Plum spirit.

Sit with Pärssinen for a while. In the shade. Watch old films.

No, he said, I missed it. What did they say?

She had felt sorry for the woman, Marjatta said.

Aku wanted to go to the cinema. Korvensuo said he hoped they'd have a good time and switched off his mobile. He had the shivers.

Pärssinen had gone indoors and didn't come back. The boy went into the building after a while, no doubt for lunch. The girls rode away on bicycles. Pushing hard on the pedals. Like Pia Lehtinen.

'Ready?' Pärssinen had asked and he had replied, 'What do you mean?'

Timo Korvensuo sat in the car, his hand on the door, ready to get out. Get out and ask Pärssinen one last question. Say goodbye. He opened the door and closed it again. Opened it and closed it once more. Several times he got out and walked a little way. Then he went back to the car, dropped into his seat and looked at the empty scene.

Pia Lehtinen pushing the pedals down vigorously, cycling towards him.

The boy came back and started swinging very high. Braked his impetus, then took off again. Braked and took off again.

Timo Korvensuo got out. He took one step after another. The boy ignored him until he put down his jacket on the grass and sat on the second swing, beside the boy.

'Let's see who can go highest,' said Korvensuo and the boy stared at him.

Korvensuo catapulted himself into the air. A tugging sensation in his stomach. He heard the boy laugh.

Pärssinen's window flew past.

'Come on, push me!' he called.

The boy hesitated for a moment, then started throwing himself against the swing. Korvensuo felt a tingling and a tearing and the possibility of tipping over.

Pia Lehtinen cycled on. He got out of the small red car, watched her go and felt the sun on his forehead.

When the moment came he let go.

The impact felt soft.

'Oh, wow!' said the boy.

Korvensuo took his jacket and crossed the freshly mown lawn towards the trees.

Step by step.

He got into his car and drove away. The pain lingered in his right ankle and his right shoulder. Venetian blinds were down in Pärssinen's window, and the boy was still holding the swing.

# 3

Kimmo had never seen either Sundström or Ketola like this before. Sundström was shouting. After every sentence, something hit the table or the floor. Presumably a file folder or something of that kind, thought Joentaa. Ketola said nothing. Not a word out of him.

Heinonen was staring hard at his computer monitor; Grönholm, unmoved, was eating a breakfast roll. Joentaa tried to hear what Ketola was saying through the closed door of Sundström's office, but there was nothing to hear. The louder Sundström shouted, the more doggedly Ketola preserved his silence.

After a while Ketola came out of the room. He looked almost relaxed. He was smiling. Sundström stood in the background in front of his desk, his face distorted.

'Coming with me, Kimmo?' said Ketola, already out in the corridor. Grönholm raised one eyebrow. Heinonen never took his eyes off his monitor, and Joentaa followed Ketola into the corridor.

They walked along in silence, went down to the ground floor and found a table in the cafeteria. Ketola got himself some coffee. He wasn't smiling any more, and Kimmo had the impression that he was far from relaxed. Rather he seemed tense, edgy, tired.

Ketola stirred his coffee for a while, and Joentaa saw that his hand was shaking. Then he looked up. 'I'm sorry,' he said. 'I ought to have discussed it with you.'

'Yes,' said Joentaa.

'But I'm a private citizen. I can do what I like, or not, as the case may be.'

'Of course.'

'Hämäläinen's editorial team approached me and I said yes.'

Joentaa nodded.

'Because I knew at once it was the right thing. I just knew that,' said Ketola.

'What is the right thing?' asked Joentaa.

'I'd like to ask you something. Something important,' said Ketola. 'Don't you think it's possible, just for once, that I'm on the right track here?'

'What do you mean?' asked Joentaa, although he guessed at Ketola's line of thought.

'That the man has come back . . . that it means something, understand?'

'What exactly *do* you mean?'

'I mean that now we have the chance of . . . I mean that he . . . now that he sees what happens . . . well, perhaps he saw the interview.'

Joentaa nodded.

'And maybe he's started things moving again,' said Ketola. 'As simple as that. They're moving again. After thirty-three years.'

'You're forgetting that we haven't found Sinikka Vehkasalo yet,' said Joentaa.

Ketola stirred his coffee.

'She could be still alive.'

Ketola shook his head.

'Maybe your TV appearance will make him decide to kill Sinikka. Because he's frightened, because he feels threatened.'

'Nonsense,' said Ketola quietly.

'Why is it nonsense?' asked Joentaa.

Ketola looked at him for a long time. 'Because the girl is dead already,' he said at last. 'Easy. We're looking for a murderer, not a kidnapper.'

'But . . .'

'That's it! That's all.' The penetrating, aggressive voice that Joentaa had heard so often. 'I saw what was left of Pia Lehtinen. We don't have to be cautious because of Sinikka Vehkasalo any more.' Ketola had straightened up and was looking Joentaa in the eye. 'Understand?'

Joentaa did not reply.

'What else?' said Ketola, suddenly calm again. 'Have you all been looking for possible parallel cases? Children missing or murdered over the last thirty-three years?'

'Of course. Grönholm and Heinonen are busy on that right now,' said Joentaa.

'Still nothing more positive?'

'They'll be reporting on their findings this afternoon.'

Ketola nodded. 'I know that nothing similar has happened in all these years. At least, not in Turku. I was busy working on that for the first few years; I followed it up. We all followed it up. But after a while of course the case was forgotten. And networking then wasn't what it is today. There weren't computers and all that stuff, and those boxes we did have later on would make you die laughing today. Myself, I was only ever once confronted with anything like it. The girl was even younger and it was cleared up quickly. A family member did it, her stepbrother, to be precise. But there could have been cases in other cities. Cases I never heard of. And above all cases of missing persons, maybe in Turku as well, cases I never set eyes on. After a bit I'd forgotten that one myself.'

Ketola drank some coffee and looked at two uniformed policewomen at the next table. A moment came when the policewomen looked enquiringly at the two of them, and Ketola turned away. He cleared his throat and asked, 'Would you . . . keep me up to date now and then?'

Joentaa said nothing.

'I'll call you. Maybe this evening,' said Ketola.

Joentaa nodded.

'My son, by the way,' said Ketola.

'Your son?'

'His name is Tapani. He's totally crazy. A complete nutcase.'

'What . . . '

'Just wanted to tell you. It suddenly mattered to me.' He finished his coffee in a single draught and stood up. 'Yes, well, I'll call. So long. And if you like . . . some time we could talk too . . . I mean about you. And your . . . about Sanna.'

Joentaa nodded.

'Only if you want to, of course,' said Ketola, and left without looking back.

# 4

Kalevi Vehkasalo watched the pencil as it fell from the desk to the floor. A pleasant moment. A moment in which nothing but a pencil moved and time stood still.

He bent down, picked up the pencil, and when he looked at his screen again there were four new emails.

That's how it was all morning. Every email had a similar text in the Subject line. Problems with the system. A special communications system. The system that he had developed, and its further development ought to have been getting various branches of an international firm of shaver manufacturers on the Internet today. The plan obviously hadn't worked particularly well.

Problems from all over the world because Ville, his closest colleague and best programmer, had failed. He knew that already, because in the morning Ville had come to see him and said that he and Riska and Oksanen had worked all through the weekend, and the time frame was simply too tight.

'It worked okay with France and Italy, but not the rest,' Ville had said.

Kalevi Vehkasalo had nodded and felt that this was, naturally, an impossible conversation, a conversation that just could not be carried on, and he sensed that Ville was thinking just the same and knew that for quite some time they had been exchanging entirely impossible words, words that could not be spoken.

Ville knew what was going on. Ville knew that Vehkasalo's daughter had gone missing, disappeared without trace, murdered by some madman, and Vehkasalo had tried to imagine how Ville and his colleagues had worked for a whole weekend knowing both that the daughter of the owner of this company was a major news item, and that the system for the shaver manufacturers couldn't now be installed in time.

He had nodded, and said that Ville mustn't feel bad about it.

It would all work out.

There were now three more messages on his screen. Most of the Subject lines ended with a question mark. He'd have to come up with an answer. The good thing was that he could say the same to everyone. A minor delay, otherwise all in good order. We're working on it. Will be in touch.

He began typing and felt a rushing sensation like a wave, which was hardly possible in the dry atmosphere of his room. He stood up. Through the window he could see the market square. Through the glazed door he saw his colleagues working on the installation of the system. Their eyes were lowered. At the end of their conversation Ville had asked whether . . . but now he couldn't remember what Ville had said. It had been something to do with Sinikka, and one or two others had mentioned Sinikka as well. He hadn't exchanged a word with most of them.

The wave was in his head. He was standing beside the sea, looking at its blue waters. Hard times, he thought. For the firm. Hard times in general, all things considered.

Ville's eyes met his. Ville turned away at once, and Kalevi Vehkasalo thought that he really did look tense. He had tried to carry out his task all weekend. Until late into the night. Tilting at windmills. Only to be able to give him at least one piece of good news on Monday morning.

They had known each other for years. Vehkasalo had founded the firm, but Ville had been his first employee, contributing much to its success. Thank you, Ville, he thought.

Ville made the thumbs-up sign and seemed to be calling something to him.

Vehkasalo opened the glazed door.

'Poland's on the Net now too,' said Ville.

'Good, good,' said Kalevi Vehkasalo.

He closed the door and pulled down the blinds. Sat at his desk.

He let his head sink to the desktop. The surface was cool. He would talk to Ruth. He would talk to her for a long time. This silence must come to an end. It must all come out. In a minute filled with everything. And then he would understand what had happened. He would go home now, say goodbye to his employees, go home and take Ruth in his arms. He would speak to her. Touch her arm, her shoulder, her hand. They would talk and in the end they would understand everything. And drive off and find Sinikka, wherever she was. Yes, that was what they would do.

Just as soon as he found the strength to raise his head from the top of this desk.

# 5

Timo Korvensuo was driving. Around the city, again and again. Keep moving. In the current of other people. Stopping at lights. Drumming all ten fingers on the steering wheel, impatient, in a hurry, some unknown goal before his eyes.

Once he confused red with green and had to swerve to avoid an open-top car. I had a red light, you bastard, he muttered, before a few minutes later he became aware of his mistake.

After some time he drove into a car park and called Marjatta.

They had been to the cinema, Marjatta said, the film was too violent for an eight-year-old. Aku was in a very good mood.

Korvensuo felt the fabric of his shirt on his skin. Cool and damp. Aku imitated the voice of a witch who had been a major character in the film.

'No harrrm will come to you,' said Aku in the witch's shrill cackle of a voice. 'No harrrm whatsoeverrrr.'

'I'm going to dream of her,' said Marjatta and Aku laughed.

'Listen,' Timo Korvensuo began.

'I liiike little Aaakuuu verrry much,' croaked Aku.

'Did you say something?' asked Marjatta.

'Take the phone away from Aku,' said Korvensuo.

'Papa is afraid of witches,' said Aku.

'Now you've hurt his feelings,' said Marjatta.

'Sorry. Put him on the line again.'

But Aku didn't want to talk any more; he wanted to go and have a pizza.

'What were you going to say?' asked Marjatta.

'I . . . oh, I can't remember. Probably nothing special. Was the witch in the film really so scary?'

'Not just the witch, it was a real chamber of horrors. A fountain running with blood and so forth.'

'Ah,' said Korvensuo.

'What actually is this odd appointment of yours there in Turku?' asked Marjatta.

'Why odd?'

'Do you know yet whether you'll be coming home tomorrow?'

'Yes — or the day after tomorrow at the latest,' Korvensuo promised. 'I want to look at one more property, the kind of thing that might suit the planned estate. The one that's going to be built in Helsinki, I mean. You do understand, don't you?'

'Of course I understand.'

'I'll be back the day after tomorrow at the latest,' Korvensuo promised.

'You neeedn't think youuu'll get awaaay so eeeeasily,' cackled Aku. 'No, no, liiiitle boooy.'

'I'll call again this evening,' said Korvensuo, and for a few moments everything felt normal.

Then he sat in the silence for a long time, thinking of driving home. Giving Marjatta a surprise. And the children. Suddenly appearing in the doorway. Seeing Aku's face as he imitated the witch. Listening to Marjatta's breathing. Lying awake. Sleeping. Dreaming.

He leaned abruptly forward and started the car.

He drove purposefully, for he knew the way.

# 6

They were sitting in the conference room. The same room in which Ketola had sat thirty-three years ago. With the model on wheels.

'I think we have something now,' said Heinonen. He spoke with quiet reserve, as always, but Joentaa detected the excitement in his voice.

'But we don't know if it will get us any further,' said Grönholm.

Then they both fell silent.

'Well, what is it, then?' asked Sundström.

'Marika Paloniemi,' said Heinonen.

'Aha.'

'She disappeared in 1983 and never came back,' said Grönholm. 'In May 1983. She was sixteen at the time.'

'Aha,' said Sundström.

'And in a witness statement there's ... although of course it could be a coincidence ... ' said Heinonen.

'There's what?' asked Sundström.

'A small red car,' said Grönholm.

Silence reigned for a while. Joentaa was thinking of Ruth Vehkasalo. Of the moment when he had looked back at the green house and Ruth Vehkasalo had lowered the venetian blinds.

'What else?' asked Sundström.

'Nothing else,' said Heinonen. 'The witness couldn't say what make of car it was.'

'Go on, go on. Who was the witness? How and where did the girl disappear?'

'After school. In Paimio, an area outside our remit . . . well, I don't mean *our* remit exactly, I mean we were none of us even working here then.'

'Yes, yes, go on,' said Sundström.

'And anyway it was regarded as no more than a Missing Persons case,' Heinonen went on. 'She didn't come home. She always took the bus and walked the few minutes from the bus stop to her home. And on that day . . . ' He looked at the files. 'On 23 May 1983 she didn't come home. As Petri was saying, she never resurfaced again.' He cleared his throat, probably because the lake where Pia Lehtinen had been found occurred to him, and he became aware of the double meaning of the verb he had chosen.

'The small red car? The witness?' asked Sundström.

'Oddly enough there wasn't a very extensive investigation. Because no clues at all had been found and, after all, she was sixteen.

These things happen. Sixteen-year-olds do just walk away,' said Grönholm.

'Was there anything to suggest that?'

'It seemed at least plausible. She lived with her father, her mother had died two years earlier. And her father was away a lot, a rep for . . . ' Grönholm looked down at the papers too. 'A rep for a pharmaceuticals company.'

'And there's been no trace since 1983 of this . . . what was her name?'

'Marika Paloniemi. No, no trace. Disappeared,' said Heinonen. 'And a boy who was at school with her saw the small red car, or said he saw it, but he also mentioned a pale green VW Polo.'

'Ah,' said Sundström.

'He claims to have seen both cars at the bus stop where he and Marika Paloniemi got out. They were parked close together, and apparently there were people sitting in both of them too.'

'And it would have taken the girl some five minutes to walk home from this bus stop?'

Heinonen nodded.

'And she definitely didn't go home?'

'We can't be absolutely sure, because her father wasn't there. It could be that she did go home, and then went out again and never came back,' said Heinonen. 'But when the father got home that evening there was nothing to suggest that she had been there at all. No dirty dishes, for instance. Her father said she never washed the dishes.'

'That's in the files, is it?'

Heinonen nodded. 'Apparently the father could well imagine that she had simply walked out. He probably wasn't particularly distraught.'

'Ah,' said Sundström.

'Mm,' said Heinonen.

'Any indications of that? Had any of her clothes gone? Things that were important to her?'

'It was probably hard to find out, because her father had no real idea of his daughter's possessions. In fact, not much was found in her room, which in one way seems to suggest that she did pack her things and simply left home.'

Silence fell once more.

'Of course a search was made for her, but it led nowhere and it wasn't really, well, intensive,' said Heinonen.

'I see,' said Sundström.

'But, and this is interesting, a list was drawn up,' said Grönholm. 'Seems like they took what her schoolmate said seriously . . . perhaps because it was more or less all they had to go on. Anyway, a list was compiled focusing on the two vehicles he said he'd seen. And here is the list of owners of small red cars in and around Turku.' Grönholm waved several sheets of paper stapled together in the air.

'The boy described the car as bright red, which did reduce the number of vehicles a little, but there were still over five hundred.' Heinonen sat up straight, suddenly speaking louder than before. 'Which is why at the time, and after some toing and froing, they also refrained from questioning the owners of those cars. But we have now established the following: back in 1974 a list in connection with Pia Lehtinen was also compiled. And all the owners of those vehicles were interviewed, but still no result.'

'And now you have compared the 1974 list with the 1983 list, and marked all the vehicles found on both lists,' said Sundström.

Heinonen slumped. 'Exactly.'

'Wonderful. How many are there?'

'Two hundred and three,' said Grönholm. 'But we're interested only in the cars on both lists with the same owner, since we are assuming one and the same murderer, and that leaves us with a hundred and four, and seventy-eight owners of those hundred and four cars are men.'

'Seventy-eight,' murmured Sundström.

'I'm afraid so, and then we have to think that even the cars with women registered as the owners could have had men at the wheel, the owners' sons, for instance.'

'Of course,' murmured Sundström, then he suddenly assumed a confident expression and sat up straight. 'And how many of these seventy-eight or a hundred and four people are still alive?' he asked.

'We haven't got that far yet,' said Grönholm. 'But we're looking into it, and anyway, twenty-three of the seventy-eight men are definitely dead.' He looked triumphantly from one to another of them. 'So, with all due respect to the dead, of course, that does reduce the number of male owners in question to fifty-five.'

'Fifty-five,' said Sundström. 'And there might be one or two others who have passed away by now.'

'Exactly,' said Grönholm. 'We'll have the list up to date by this evening.'

'Good, good,' said Sundström.

'We've already listed the fifty-five.' Heinonen handed out a closely printed sheet of paper to everyone.

'Yes, well,' said Sundström. 'The problem, however, is that we don't know whether Marika Paloniemi was murdered, or whether the red car that her school friend said he saw has any connection whatever with the case, right?'

'Right,' Grönholm agreed.

'And even if there had been a connection, at the moment we're really investigating the case of Sinikka Vehkasolo who's been missing for three days, right?'

'Right,' Grönholm repeated.

Joentaa was only half listening. He was examining the names on the list. Arranged in alphabetical order.

'All the same, we'll follow up that lead,' he heard Sundström saying, and went on scrutinizing the letters making up the names. Oksanen, Orava, Oraniemi, Palolahti, Pärssinen, Peltonen, Seinäjoki, Sihvonen. He stopped at that name. Reijo Sihvonen. No relation, even by marriage. Plenty of other people were called Sihvonen, just like Sanna. In the background he heard chairs being pushed back.

He must call Sanna's parents. Merja and Jussi Sihvonen. He kept putting the phone call off, day after day, week after week, and it was a long time since they had called him.

He must call his mother as well. She kept writing letters, she must be writing every other week, although he never answered.

'We'll have to take it further,' Sundström had just said.

Joentaa nodded. 'I think so too,' he said and looked up.

The others had already left.

# 7

Timo Korvensuo knew the way. Which wasn't really possible. It couldn't be possible. He thought about that as he drove. He was waiting for the moment when he would have to ask someone for directions, but that moment never came, and Korvensuo wouldn't have known how to put his question either.

He knew the way. It was as simple as that. Driving like a sleepwalker. Dreams did not exist. The cross looked small and spindly. The field was full of yellow flowers. Yellow as it had been at the time. Identical. He drove past it. Not slowly, not fast.

He saw no police officers. No one at all. Houses in the distance, half hidden beyond the field. He turned, drove back, stopped at the roadside and got out of the car.

He crossed the road. The bicycle path ran into the trees. He stood in their shade. Scraps of paper lay on the ground, the remains of police barrier tape. There were flowers left beside the cross.

Pia Lehtinen, he read. The lettering was large by comparison with the small size of the cross. And they were carefully applied to the wood, in white paint. The yellow field beyond. Murdered 1974. Those words were in rather smaller lettering. Aku imitating a witch. Laura. She was going to be fourteen in July. How time flies, thought Korvensuo. Pärssinen a kindly old caretaker. Laura's birthday was on 19 July. He had straightened the handlebars of the bike.

'A sad story,' said a voice beside him.

He turned and saw a woman and a man, out walking. The woman was very small, white-haired, and the man said again, quietly and looking at the cross, 'A sad story. And now the same thing has happened again.'

'Are you from the police?' asked the woman.

'I . . . no, no,' Korvensuo replied.

'The police came here, but yesterday evening they dismantled all their equipment and went away,' said the man and the woman nodded.

'Yes, I . . . I'd heard about it,' said Korvensuo. 'It's on the news a lot.'

'They've even been filming here over the last few days,' said the man. 'Always with the police in their white outfits in the background, and the field. We could even see our house.'

Korvensuo nodded.

'We know Pia's mother slightly . . . Elina.

We live in the same road,' said the woman.

'But at the other end of it,' added the man. 'The other end of the same road.'

Korvensuo nodded again.

'Yes,' said the woman.

'Well, goodbye,' said the man.

Korvensuo watched them walk away.

The couple went along the bicycle path and turned off into the wood.

He was alone again.

Red, he thought. Not a trace of red.

His silver car stood in the sunlight. He went back to it and got in. A wave of heat, then the shivers. His headache was back. He took two tablets and called the enquiry service. Elina Lehtinen in Turku, he said, and was given a phone number and an address.

He started the car, drove it slowly to the far end of the field, and stood in the road leading to the residential district. He switched off the engine and sat there in the silence.

Two girls came cycling towards him. They rode past him, hands free, and turned off on the bicycle path that Pia Lehtinen had once used. Timo Korvensuo saw them cycling past the cross without slackening speed, and called Marjatta's mobile just to hear her voice.

# 8

Hannu Lehtinen spoke fast and at the same time thoughtfully. In well-polished sentences. He had retired from work some years earlier, but the address on the visiting card that Elina Lehtinen had given Joentaa was correct.

They sat on the terrace, which led to a small garden that looked almost manicured. Identical colours. All the plants flowering at the same height. No sign of any football.

'Forty years,' he said, and Joentaa looked enquiringly at him. 'I worked forty years for Ventiga,' Hannu Lehtinen explained and handed him a card.

Joentaa took it, although he had already been given the same card by Elina Lehtinen.

'There was a big retirement party. I sometimes go back to visit my colleagues at the firm.'

Joentaa nodded.

'We eat in the canteen together,' he said, 'and they always tell me things aren't what they used to be now I'm not there any more. But of course, you haven't come to hear about that.'

'No, well, I . . . '

'I know why you're here. The girl who disappeared. I saw it on the news.'

'Yes. I've already talked to your wife about it,' said Joentaa.

'Elina — how is she?' He looked straight at Joentaa and seemed to feel this was a perfectly normal question.

'I'm afraid I can't really judge that,' said Joentaa.

'No, of course not. Forgive me.'

'However, I think that she . . . I thought she was a remarkable woman.' Joentaa was surprised by his own words.

Lehtinen stared at him for a while, then nodded almost imperceptibly and said, 'I'll call Elina some time soon.'

'Yes. I'm here to ask you whether you think there's a possible connection,' said Joentaa.

'Connection?'

'The girl's name is Sinikka Vehkasalo. Does that mean anything to you? We're looking for some kind of connection.'

'Connection?' Lehtinen repeated.

'Between Sinikka Vehkasalo and your daughter Pia. There are thirty-three years between the two incidents, but as we see it there has to be a connection.'

Lehtinen thought about that for a while. 'Why?' he finally enquired.

'What do you think?' asked Joentaa. 'What

did you think when you first heard about it?'

'When I heard about what?'

'The girl's disappearance. At the very place where your own daughter went missing in the past.'

Lehtinen looked at him and seemed to be seeing past him at the same time. 'Nothing at all.'

'Nothing at all?'

'No.'

'But you must . . . maybe we're talking at cross purposes.'

'No,' said Hannu Lehtinen. He got to his feet. 'I'd like you to leave now.'

'I . . . listen, we could perhaps be looking for the man who killed your daughter.'

'I'd like you to leave,' Lehtinen repeated.

Joentaa rose to his feet. As he walked out, his legs were shaking.

'I don't know anyone called Vehkasalo,' Lehtinen added as they reached the door. 'And I can't talk about the rest of it. I ask you to understand that.'

Joentaa nodded and Hannu Lehtinen closed the door.

# 9

Timo Korvensuo went to the cinema. He saw the film that Marjatta and Aku had seen.

It was cool and dark, and the pain was beginning to wear off. His head felt light. The cinema was almost empty, just a few young people sitting in the front row, laughing at moments that Korvensuo didn't find funny.

He sat in the back row, and thought that he was seeing the same images as Marjatta and Aku.

Marjatta had been surprised when he called her again just now, and had given an uncertain laugh when he said he only wanted to hear her voice.

The witch really did cackle like Aku's imitation.

He had stood for a while within sight of the house where Elina Lehtinen lived. He had not seen Elina Lehtinen herself, but there had been an old man watering flowers in the garden of the house next door and, unless he was mistaken, the old man had been weeping and shaking his head, and watering the flowers.

Timo Korvensuo had looked from the man

233

to the house where Elina Lehtinen lived and back again, and after a while the man put down his watering can, went over to the house and rang Elina Lehtinen's bell.

The man had waited with his head bowed, and a woman opened the door. A slender woman with a strikingly round face. She took the weeping man in her arms and closed the door, and Timo Korvensuo went to the cinema.

On the screen he saw the fountain running with blood that Marjatta had mentioned. The young people in the front row laughed. The witch spoke with Aku's tone of voice, he had broken off his mathematical studies early, there was an empty lemonade bottle lying on the seat beside him.

The film ended happily, with the death of the witch.

As Timo Korvensuo drove around the city again the evening sun was shining, and his headache returned.

# 10

Kalevi Vehkasalo had put words together. Even whole sentences. He had sat in his office, watching Ville and the rest of them working, and wondered what he would say to Ruth, what they would talk about that evening when he came home. He had thought so many thoughts, all to do with Sinikka.

For instance, he had decided to thank Ruth again, with all his heart, for going through with her wish for children in spite of his initial opposition, because Sinikka had been the best thing ever to happen to him.

Even if he hadn't always shown it. Even if Sinikka certainly hadn't known it, but it was the truth, and if he could never tell Sinikka herself again, at least he would tell Ruth.

He had gone home that evening and when he tried to kiss Ruth's cheek she had flinched.

Then he had said there was chaos at the firm, sheer chaos, but it was all going to be sorted out.

Then he had sat opposite Ruth and felt there was no more to say.

Ruth had peeled and eaten an apple.

After a while she had gone over to the TV

set and switched on the news. She had knelt on the ground in front of the set, and he had sat at the table and thought that he wanted to put his arms round Ruth, but he hadn't been able to move.

They had waited together.

After a few minutes Sinikka's photo came up on the screen. From the start, she was at the centre of the programme, presumably because there weren't any fresh headlines.

Ruth had turned off the TV again and looked at him with an expression that he had never seen before, and he hadn't been able to hold her gaze. She had said she was going to lie down and he had nodded, but all the same he had got to his feet and held her close.

'I'd like us to face this together,' he had said, trying to meet her eyes, and Ruth had removed herself from his embrace and gone out without another word.

Kalevi Vehkasalo hoped she was asleep.

That was the only thing to do. Sleep for a long time, sleep until it was all over. He didn't know how much time had passed since Ruth left the room. Presumably hours. Or minutes. He had no idea. He just knew that he wanted to sleep. Until the moment when it would be possible to breathe again. Breathe out and breathe in.

He switched on the television set once

more and read the brief report on teletext. His glance lingered on the name. Sinikka. His daughter was called Sinikka too. He heard water running. Ruth was awake.

He stood there motionless for some time, as if he could create a silence that would let Ruth get some rest at last.

He went downstairs to Sinikka's room. He stood in the doorway for a while, staring into the darkness. Then he switched on the light. For the first time it struck him as a beautiful, warm light.

Raising his eyes to the lamp, he saw that it had been carefully shaded with paper and fabric of different colours. Sinikka had made her own lampshade and her own light, and he admired it. He decided to tell her so at the first opportunity.

'I would like us to separate,' said Ruth, behind him. He hadn't heard her coming. He turned round and saw her standing in the doorway.

'I thought you were asleep,' he said.

'Sinikka was all that still kept us together,' said Ruth. 'Or isn't that how you see it?'

He saw her pale face. He felt dizzy. He stood opposite her and saw a beautiful woman, and Ruth came up to him and started hitting out. He waited, motionless. Ruth flung her arms round him and pulled him down on to Sinikka's mattress. The pillow was soft. Ruth lay on top of him; he felt her tears on his cheeks and his tongue.

After a while Ruth got up, went over to the little stereo system and switched on some music. 'The last thing Sinikka listened to,' she said.

He nodded. He didn't know the song. There were no lyrics, it was a tune played on two acoustic guitars. He liked it, and was surprised that Sinikka had liked it too.

Ruth had closed her eyes. He let his head rest on her shoulder, and only now did he remember that he had shouted at Sinikka. When he last saw her. Only a few days ago. Sinikka had preserved an iron silence and gone to her room when he had finished shouting. There had been fury in the last glance she gave him. He couldn't remember what it had all been about.

He would ask Ruth later, as soon as she opened her eyes again.

# 11

Timo Korvensuo was driving. Keep moving.
Round and round the city. He couldn't
decide whether to go back to the hotel. Eat
supper. Watch old films. Or go and see
Pärssinen. Ask one last question. Sit on the
swings, swinging over the top of the frame.
Stand up and laugh with the boy. Laugh his
head off. Say goodbye. To the boy and to
Pärssinen.

Finally he drove back to Naantali, parked
at the same place as before, where the field
ended and the estate of small houses began.
There was a light on in Elina Lehtinen's
window. The field lay pale in the midnight
sun. He called Marjatta to tell her that he had
seen the film. Marjatta didn't know what he
was talking about.

'The witch talks just like Aku,' he told her.

'You've been to the cinema?' asked
Marjatta.

'I mean Aku talks like the witch. He
imitated her very well. Tell him I said so.'

'I thought you were meeting your client
about those terraced houses,' said Marjatta.

'I did. But I had some spare time first.'

'Will you be home tomorrow?' asked Marjatta.

'Yes. Or the day after tomorrow at the latest.'

Marjatta did not reply to that.

'I miss you all,' he said.

'We miss you too.'

'Tell Aku what I said about the witch. I mean that he imitated her well. He'll like to hear that.'

'I'll tell him,' said Marjatta.

'And give them both my love, of course.'

'Will do.'

'Sleep well.'

'You too.'

He opened the window on the driver's side and heard voices. One agitated male voice, one calm, quieter female voice. The voice of Elina Lehtinen, Pia Lehtinen's mother.

Elina Lehtinen and her visitor were sitting in the garden. He heard their voices, but he couldn't make out what they were saying. He just heard the peaceful calm of Elina Lehtinen's voice.

His mobile signalled an incoming text message. Aku was pleased, wrote Marjatta.

He put the mobile down on the passenger seat and listened as the man, Elina Lehtinen's visitor, uttered suppressed cries. Elina Lehtinen said nothing for a while, then he heard her quiet voice again. Pia had tried to cry out too. Lying under Pärssinen. He had seen only her legs. And her arms. And the bicycle.

He had sat in the car while Pärssinen sank the body in the lake. He had watched him through the windscreen.

Through his windscreen now, he saw a man coming out of Elina Lehtinen's house. The man's head was still bowed.

Elina Lehtinen watched him go until he had disappeared into the house next door to hers. A small, slender woman. She closed the door.

Another text message from Marjatta. Aku is wide awake, she wrote, badgering her about the witch, but when you're away I can't sleep anyway.

He turned off his mobile, started the car and drove. Around the city. Several times he was about to follow the sign pointing to the city centre, towards the hotel, but then he went on driving round in circles, until finally, with the last of his strength, he found a car park, put his head on the steering wheel and was asleep within seconds.

# 12

Kimmo Joentaa looked at the stack of paper on the table in front of him. All the information gathered in the last few days by some forty officers investigating the case.

He passed his hand over the sheets of paper. Hundreds of them, crammed with writing. He thought of the others now sitting at home reading them too. Heinonen, Grönholm, Sundström.

He concentrated on statements concerning Sinikka Vehkasalo. He read, picked up the photo and imagined himself slowly becoming able to see through those eyes as he examined marginal notes.

He didn't know why he was doing that, it made no sense, because very probably Sinikka Vehkasalo had been the victim of a criminal whose actions were subject to chance and instinct, and had nothing at all to do with the girl Sinikka Vehkasalo herself. All the same, he was concentrating just now, for reasons he couldn't explain, on the factors that made Sinikka begin to take shape as he read between the lines.

Most of the interviews ended nowhere.

Dealt with and summed up in well-rehearsed phrases that were meant to show accuracy and efficiency, and in reality were always just beside the mark. Or, at least, that was his impression.

Interviews with boys and girls at her school. She didn't seem to have any close girlfriends, but most of them had liked Sinikka. She had always known everything but never put up her hand in class because she didn't like to show off, said one of the boys who had been interviewed, in a throwaway comment.

One of the girls mentioned a birthday party when Sinikka suddenly disappeared. She had come back hours later, lost in thought, smiling in a mysterious way, and wouldn't answer when asked where she had been.

Magdalena, the girl who had originally been going to volleyball training with her, said she had been very surprised when Sinikka didn't turn up. She had always been there. And if, for once, she was unable to keep a date she would certainly have said so. Magdalena had tried to reach Sinikka several times on the day she went missing, but her mobile had been turned off.

Joentaa nodded. They had found Sinikka's mobile in her room at home. Sinikka had obviously forgotten it when she went to volleyball.

There had been three messages from Magdalena in her voicemail, never listened to, and seven from Ruth Vehkasalo. Where was she, Ruth Vehkasalo had asked. At first sounding cross, shouting now and then, and finally, late in the evening, just before her husband Kalevi had recognized his daughter's bicycle on TV, she had begged Sinikka very quietly please to get in touch, because she was beginning to worry.

Recently, Sinikka Vehkasalo had been elected Years Seven to Ten delegate at school. She had won against another girl, a considerably older candidate, and that had attracted some attention. She hadn't told her parents about her election.

A male teacher described Sinikka as a brilliant personality; a female colleague of his called her inconspicuous and silent. Joentaa highlighted these remarks, although they were just marginal notes, random assessments of her character.

It was really all about something else. About Sinikka's body and where it was. And her murderer. And about the fact that, three days after Sinikka's disappearance, they still had not the slightest idea of what had happened. The search for Sinikka's body now involved more than a hundred police officers and volunteers, and two dozen divers.

Joentaa looked at the time. Three minutes after midnight. He hadn't called Sanna's parents. He hadn't called his mother Anita. Tomorrow.

Someone rang the bell. Joentaa knew who it was. He went to open the door, thinking of another man who had come to his house on another night, in winter two years ago. He opened the door.

'Hello,' said Ketola. 'I thought you'd still be up.'

'That's right.'

Ketola came in and said, 'By the way, it's my birthday.'

'Oh.'

'Since a few minutes ago.'

'Many happy returns,' said Joentaa.

'Thanks,' said Ketola and went into the living room, swaying slightly.

'Sit down.'

'Thanks.' Ketola looked at the stack of notes and asked, 'Champagne on ice?'

'What?'

'That was a joke.'

'No, no, in fact I do have some in the cellar,' said Joentaa. 'It's been there for some time, but . . . well, not champagne, of course, just sparkling wine.'

Ketola stared at him and Kimmo went down to the cellar to fetch the ancient bottle of sparkling wine. Bought by Sanna for reasons that never materialized. He opened the bottle in the kitchen. The cork hit Ketola, who happened to be standing in the doorway at the wrong time.

'Ouch,' said Ketola.

'Sorry.'

'Never joke with Kimmo Joentaa. For a moment I forgot that iron rule.' Ketola rubbed his forehead.

Joentaa poured the sparkling wine into two glasses that he and Sanna had bought together. 'Cheers,' he said, handing Ketola a glass.

'Thank you,' said Ketola.

'Are you all right?'

'What?'

Joentaa pointed to Ketola's forehead.

'Oh, not so bad.' Ketola was standing uncertainly in front of the sofa. 'Well, cheers,' he said, clinking glasses with Joentaa.

'And happy birthday again,' murmured Joentaa.

The sparkling wine was warmish, had an odd aftertaste and fizzed like mineral water.

'Delicious.' Ketola drained his glass and sank into the sofa.

'Do you like the glasses?'

'Nice, very nice,' said Ketola.

'Sanna had set her heart on them. As far as

I'm concerned, to be honest, one glass is much the same as another.'

'No, no, these are really beautiful,' said Ketola. 'Reading, I see?' He indicated the stack of paper. Joentaa nodded. 'Anything new?'

'Not much. Possibly another case involving a small red car. In May 1983. It could get us a little further on, but of course it has nothing directly to do with Sinikka Vehkasalo.'

'A murdered girl? In 1983?'

'Missing. Missing to this day,' said Joentaa. Ketola nodded.

Joentaa refilled their glasses. 'We're really just clutching at straws with this one,' he said, 'But we don't have much else.'

Ketola nodded. His glance fell on the cardboard carton standing next to the table. The old files that Joentaa had cleared away for the time being. Ketola's files.

Ketola picked out one of the yellowed folders and leafed through it. After a while he smiled as he read. Then he closed the folder and put it down carefully on the table. He said nothing for some time, then he remarked, 'Interesting, all the same.'

'What's interesting?' asked Joentaa.

'This carton standing here. These files lying around. With you. Who'd have thought this carton would ever leave Päivi's room in the basement again? What was that boy's name?'

'Hm?'

'The boy who took us down to the basement. On my last day at work.'

'Oh yes. Antti.'

'That was it.'

'The lumber room?'

'Exactly. Who'd have thought this cardboard box would ever make it from there to your living room?'

'Well . . . '

'At least for a few days,' said Ketola and Joentaa wondered briefly what he meant by that. 'Nice lad, anyway.'

'What?'

'Nice lad, that Antti from archives. Is he still with you?'

'Oh yes. He has a permanent appointment now. He and Päivi are always in fits of laughter when I'm in there. They get on fine,' said Joentaa.

Ketola nodded. 'And how about you?' he asked after a while.

'Me?'

'How are you getting on?'

'How am I getting on?'

Ketola looked at him for a bit, his eyes fixed calmly on Joentaa. Joentaa met his gaze and thought that they had never looked into one another's eyes like this. Then he turned away, drank some wine and refilled his glass.

Ketola was smiling when he looked up again. 'You're a funny one, Kimmo,' he said. 'I really do like you.'

'Funny?'

'I can't think of a better way to put it. Thank you for the bubbly.' Ketola put down his glass and stood up.

'Stay a bit longer.'

Ketola stopped in front of the photographs. 'Sanna?' he asked, pointing to the photo of Sanna knocking the biscuit out of her mother's hand.

'Yes,' said Joentaa.

Ketola looked at the photograph. He stood in front of it for several minutes. Then he nodded firmly, as if he had understood something, and left.

# 12 June

# 1

It was a cool morning. Timo Korvensuo felt a brief, sharp stabbing in his back when he woke up. His left arm was hanging through the steering wheel and it was a few seconds before he could move it. His arm no longer felt like part of his body.

He waited for a while, looking through the windscreen at the car park, while the pain crept into his arm and from there through his body.

Then he sat up straight and thought of another morning many years ago, when he and some friends had been sitting beside a camp-fire in a wood. All night long. After a while some of them had gone to sleep, others had stared at the flickering flames in silence, and he had risen to his feet, murmured a goodbye and walked away.

He had made his way through the bushes and trees until he finally found the path through the wood; then he had gone the wrong way and he could no longer find his bicycle. He had a cut that stung on one arm, and with every breath he took he sensed smoke in his lungs.

He had walked through the wood for hours, and the whole place had looked exactly the same: trees, paths with other paths branching off from them.

When he finally did find his bike it was considerably warmer, and the sun was shining. The others' bikes were not there any more.

As he cycled home, he had felt annoyed with himself the whole time for leaving earlier than the others, only to get home later than they did. They must have wondered why his bike was still there. Or maybe not. Very likely they had hardly registered it. He hadn't mentioned the incident to anyone afterwards. That night had left them all exhausted.

It had been in the holidays. They had talked all night, eaten meat, drunk beer and spirits, and talked. Talked and talked, and he couldn't remember a single word of it, only how tired he had been in the morning, and the vague fear he had felt as he walked the same paths through the same wood again and again.

He drove to the hotel. He parked the car in the underground garage and took the lift straight up to the fifth floor. He didn't meet anyone.

His room was empty. His laptop was humming on the table. The DVD case lay beside it. He took off his jacket and hung it over the chair. The clock on the TV set said five thirty in the morning.

The bed was freshly made up and chilly. He lay on his back and thought about breakfast. In an hour's time he would go down and eat something. He felt hungry. Very hungry.

He really liked the idea of that wonderful breakfast, fresh yoghurt with strawberries, scrambled egg with ham, salmon with horseradish and strong, sweet coffee. He was ravenous, and in an hour's time he could satisfy his hunger.

His left arm still felt like a foreign body lying beside him. He watched the numbers on the TV clock moving on, and counted along with them quietly.

Never before had he looked forward so much to eating. A man in a neighbouring room had a bad coughing fit. For a while the man fell silent, only to go on coughing worse than ever. Timo Korvensuo could hear the mucus coming up.

He counted the minutes and sensed that something was happening. Something important.

He didn't know what it was, but anyway it was important, and everything felt very light.

# 2

Joentaa woke up and reached for Sanna's hand, thinking that she was lying beside him. For a moment he was annoyed, and wondered where she could have gone so early in the morning. Then he sat up. Sunlight was flooding through the picture window. The lake was flat calm. He was lying on the living room sofa. He had gone to sleep over the files he was studying, and now they lay scattered on the table and floor.

After Ketola had left, he had leafed through them for hours, imagining that he might come upon some crucial point if he only read attentively enough. He had fought his weariness, and after a while had begun picking up a new file every five minutes in the hope that the next moment, any time now, a key word would leap to his attention. The idea wouldn't let go of him. The idea of having seen and failed to understand something important. Presumably as the result of his exhaustion and his odd midnight conversation with Ketola.

Finally he had concentrated entirely on the list drawn up by Heinonen and Grönholm.

The fifty-five names had been whittled down to forty-eight by the evening. Seven more had passed away, as Sundström had put it, so they were left with forty-eight living men who had in common the fact that they had lived from 1974 to 1983 in Turku and the surrounding area, and had owned small red cars.

He looked at the closely printed page and wondered how they were ever going to get anywhere this way. A murder thirty-three years ago and a girl missing for twenty-four years. Vague indications of small red cars, leading to the compilation of a list of names decades later. Random names on a sheet of paper. That was all the list was, but last night he had suddenly felt quite sure that the list contained an answer. He had studied the names, addresses and telephone numbers until the letters began to dance before his eyes. And he had obviously fallen asleep over them. He couldn't remember.

He quickly showered and got dressed. As he drove to the city centre he was thinking of the moment in the morning when he had thought Sanna was lying beside him, and he had only to put out his hands to touch her. A moment that left behind a complete void and total clarity, a moment such as he had known often in the past, during the first months after Sanna's death. Sometimes he would go around the house for minutes on end after waking, looking for Sanna and thinking that her death was the last of his dreams the night before.

In the office he sat at his computer and looked at the picture on the screen saver. The red church with the water in the background, taken on a hazy day like the day of her funeral. Ketola had narrowed his eyes when he first saw it, and for a moment Kimmo had thought he ought to say something to justify himself. He hadn't, because there was nothing to say. He had scanned it in and put it on the screen, and not thought for a second of anything else. He had chosen this picture because there was no other picture he could have chosen. That was his answer to the unspoken question in Ketola's eyes.

He thought of Ketola. He had come to work for years with a queasy feeling because he knew he would need strength to avoid Ketola's piercing gaze. He had always admired Grönholm, who seemed to bear Ketola's outbursts of rage with perfect equanimity, and of course Kari Niemi, who had a winning smile ready for Ketola even in his craziest moods.

Ketola's swivel chair was still there. No one used it, no one even thought of removing it from the office. Sundström had brought his own chair with him and moved into an office of his own in the room next door. At this moment he strode vigorously out of it.

'Kimmo, good to see you,' he said, waving some sheets of paper in the air. 'I'd like us to work through this during the morning. Conference at fourteen hundred hours,' he added.

Joentaa took the list and once again saw the names he had been studying all night. 'Right,' he said.

'I know it's vague. More than vague, so it ought not to take up too much of our time, but I don't want to find out later that the murderer really was on this list.'

Joentaa nodded.

'Heinonen and Grönholm have provisionally filtered out forty-eight names. That makes twelve for each of us. I've circled who checks up on which of these people. Phone or go to see them, I don't mind which. We just want all of us to be able to say something about them at two this afternoon.'

Joentaa nodded again and glanced at the names. Oraniemi, Palolahti, Pärssinen, Peltonen, Seinäjoki, Sihvonen. Must call Sanna's parents.

'Niemi sent through to say the blood group matches. The blood we found therefore more than likely comes from Sinikka Vehkasalo.'

Kimmo nodded. That was no surprise. He sat up straight and looked at the names that Sundström had assigned to him. 'I'll get going right away,' he said.

'Wonderful,' said Sundström. 'We'll look pretty silly if we can't find this joker.'

Joentaa looked enquiringly at him.

'The wanker. The arsehole. The bloody murderer,' Sundström said, clarifying his meaning. 'Coffee for me — tea for you?' he asked.

'Yes, please,' said Joentaa.

# 3

Timo Korvensuo was sitting in the breakfast room. His ravenous hunger had gone away, leaving him with a queasy sensation. But he ate all the same. Cornflakes. It was a long time since he'd eaten cornflakes. With cold milk.

The little girl was running about again and looked at him with curiosity. He shovelled cornflakes into his open mouth and rolled his eyes. Milk ran down his chin into the collar of his shirt. The little girl laughed.

Then he took the lift up to his room, went in and packed his things.

The young woman at reception wished him a safe journey home.

His car was in the underground garage. He put his travelling bag and the laptop in the boot. The machine ate his parking ticket, the barrier rose and as he drove he wondered how it actually functioned. What kind of mechanism was at work, what did the link between feeding in the parking ticket and the raising of the barrier consist of? It was probably very simple. A simple mechanism. A simple but good idea. There were bunches of flowers at the foot of the cross. He turned right at the far end of the field and brought the car to a halt at the roadside.

He thought of Aku. The way Aku had looked at him that night by the lake. It wasn't long ago. Aku had felt sick because he'd eaten too much ice cream. Or maybe not too much, maybe he'd eaten it too fast. Stuffed it all down his throat in too much of a hurry. That was something Aku would have to learn. The more he thought about it, the more important it seemed to him. He'd talk to Marjatta about that as soon as he had a chance.

He sat there for a while. Then he put his mobile on the passenger seat and got out of the car. He walked towards the house through a great surge of warm air.

The curtains were drawn in the house next door; it looked deserted. Korvensuo thought of the tall, stooping man who had been to see Elina Lehtinen yesterday evening.

He felt sweat on his throat and forehead as he pressed the bell. Nothing. Nothing at all. Nothing whatsoever. He hummed a little tune. Elina Lehtinen stood there facing him. A few metres away. She stood in the doorway and looked at him, a question in her eyes, and Timo Korvensuo thought that it was all over.

At last.

He pushed open the garden gate and went towards Elina Lehtinen, and he heard her saying something, heard the sound of her voice.

'I'm sorry to bother you,' he said.

'Yes?' asked Elina Lehtinen.

'I'm sorry to bother you,' Korvensuo repeated.

Elina Lehtinen waited.

'I . . . do you know if the house next door . . . do you happen to know if by any chance it's for sale?'

Elina Lehtinen's eyes followed his glance at the property next door. 'No, it isn't,' she said.

'I was just thinking it looks empty,' said Korvensuo.

'No,' said Elina Lehtinen.

Korvensuo nodded. 'That's a pity. I was thinking . . . you see, I'm looking for a house in this area for my family and me . . . '

The tall, stooping man came out of the house next door. He did not seem to notice them, although he was hardly twenty metres away. He got into his car and drove off, looking straight ahead. Korvensuo watched him drive away, and Elina Lehtinen said, 'Would you like a cup of tea?'

'Oh . . . yes . . . yes, that would be very nice. Thank you,' he said.

Elina Lehtinen smiled.

He followed her into the shade of the house. She went to make tea, and he looked out at her little garden. There was a football on the lawn, and Laura was rowing and Aku was dipping one hand in the water. He could feel it. What a strange sensation. It was cold and tingled on his skin.

He turned and looked into the smiling eyes of Pia Lehtinen. She was laughing out loud. Just a little louder and he would be able to hear it.

'We can go out on to the terrace if you like,' said Elina Lehtinen.

'That would be good,' said Korvensuo.

Elina Lehtinen poured tea into two cups.

'Your daughter?' asked Korvensuo.

Nothing, nothing at all. All energy.

'I mean, in the photo hanging in your living room.'

'Yes,' said Elina Lehtinen.

Korvensuo nodded. 'I . . . I have two children myself.'

Elina Lehtinen handed him a plate with a slice of cake on it. Blueberry cake.

'She looks . . . nice,' said Korvensuo.

Elina Lehtinen helped herself to a slice of cake as well.

'Mine are eight and thirteen. A boy and a girl.'

Elina Lehtinen did not reply.

'Aku and Laura,' said Korvensuo.

Elina Lehtinen still did not reply.

'And . . . what is your daughter's name?'

'Pia.'

'Pia. A lovely name.'

He raised the fork to his mouth, and Aku felt a cool tingling on his skin.

'So you're looking for a house in this area?' asked Elina Lehtinen.

'Yes, that's right. We . . . I'm having a change of career. Do you know if there's a property for sale anywhere near here?'

'I'm afraid not, but I can ask around for you, if you like.'

'Yes, thank you very much. That would be nice of you. Although in fact . . . '

Elina looked at him with a question in her eyes.

'I'm an estate agent. So I can look into it myself. I came here on impulse, because I thought the house next door was empty. But all the same, it would be really kind of you to ask around.'

Elina Lehtinen said nothing.

'This cake is very good,' he said.

Elina Lehtinen raised her cup to her mouth, and Aku stood up and dived head first into the water.

'Here,' he said, handing her his business

card. 'Just in case anything turns up. It would be really good; I like it here. I'm sure my wife and children would like it as well.'

Elina Lehtinen looked at the business card.

'Does . . . does your daughter . . . I was just thinking, maybe my son is about the same age as your daughter's children . . . '

'My daughter has no children.'

He nodded.

'She is dead,' said Elina Lehtinen, and Marjatta called to Aku not to swim too far out.

'Oh, I'm very sorry,' he said.

Elina Lehtinen nodded. 'It was very long ago,' she said.

'All the same, I'm sorry. I didn't mean to . . . '

Elina Lehtinen nodded.

'I really am sorry,' he said and got to his feet. The flickering in front of his eyes wore off when he stepped into the shadow of the house.

Aku came up to the surface, and Pia laughed without a sound.

'Well, you have my card,' he said when they were at the door. He felt her hand in his.

He walked away and Elina Lehtinen closed the door. He heard the latch engage, and Aku came up to the surface breathing deeply in and deeply out, because he had

266

been holding his breath for so long.

Timo Korvensuo got into his car. He imagined driving home, and instead he drove along a road where he had not been for a long time, yet he knew it.

# 4

The building at numbers 86–90 Korval-ankatu was a concrete colossus, a rectangular series of flats surrounded by an unusually well-mown area of lawn.

Tuomas Heinonen stood looking at it for a while, wondering whether, during a hot summer like this, he had ever seen such a large, well-tended expanse of turf. The sprinkler system was throwing out jets of water in all directions.

The building must contain dozens of flats, but there was no one in sight. Classical music drifted out of an open window, and a boy was sitting on a swing in the playground. A man with a large beer belly was taking a few rapid steps forward and a few rapid steps back near the refuse containers. Forward and back. Heinonen assumed this was some kind of game that only the man himself, in his drink-sodden brain, understood.

The flat he was looking for was on the ground floor. Venetian blinds were drawn down. Heinonen entered the shade of the stairwell and rang the doorbell belonging to Pärssinen. Olavi Pärssinen. One of the last names on the list that Sundström had given him that morning.

While he waited, he thought about what Sundström really wanted to hear later. That they had spoken to the men, that they now knew what makes of car they had been driving in the years 1974 to 1983 and that none of them had confessed to killing Pia Lehtinen, let alone Marika Paloniemi, still less Sinikka Vehkasalo.

He pressed the doorbell a second time, and rubbed his face and eyes while he waited. Obviously Olavi Pärssinen wasn't at home. Why should he be?

'You were looking for me?'

He turned and saw the face of a sunburnt old man carrying a box of tools.

'Olavi Pärssinen?' asked Heinonen.

'That's me,' said the man.

'My name is Heinonen.' He showed the man his ID. 'We need a little information from you to help us in our enquiries in the case of a missing person.'

'Oh,' said Pärssinen.

'Yes.'

'Right, well, if I can help you.' Pärssinen looked him in the face. Heinonen waited a few seconds, trying to form an impression. The man's expression seemed relaxed and a little absent.

'Shall we go inside?' asked Pärssinen.

Heinonen nodded, and Pärssinen opened the door. 'This way,' he said and Heinonen entered a sparsely furnished living room entirely in the shade.

'A beer?' asked Pärssinen.

'No, thank you,' said Heinonen.

Pärssinen smiled, disappeared into the kitchen and came back with a biscuit tin, which he opened and placed on the table.

'Help yourself, they're excellent,' he said, taking a chocolate biscuit. 'I usually drink plum spirit with them, but you're on duty, so . . . ' Pärssinen raised his hands, fending off the mere idea, and smiled. Heinonen nodded.

'But do have a biscuit. Like I said, they're really good. And please sit down.'

Pärssinen indicated the sofa.

'Thank you,' said Heinonen. He sat down and took one of the biscuits. The chocolate flavour was unusually strong and instantly made him feel rather sick. Plum spirit with it! Cheers, thought Heinonen. The man opposite him looked as relaxed as ever. The flat was meticulously tidy. A huge silver flat-screen TV set stood against the wall, with DVD cases carefully arranged on the shelves beside it, all of them white. There was a fresh, lemony smell, as if someone had only just been cleaning the place thoroughly.

'Right,' said Pärssinen.

'We need information about a small red car for our enquiries,' said Heinonen. 'You owned such a small car from 1974 to 1983, is that correct?'

'A red Ford, yes,' said Pärssinen. 'In fact I had it rather longer . . . it finally gave up the ghost in the mid eighties. And I'd bought it in 1972. But that's . . . '

'Yes?' asked Heinonen.

Pärssinen helped himself to another biscuit and said, 'But that's very long ago.' He seemed to be thinking. Heinonen waited. 'Very long ago,' Pärssinen repeated. 'I have a Golf now. That's red too. What's it all about, then?'

'What do you think?' asked Heinonen.

'I've no idea.'

'You'll have heard about the case of the missing girl. The bicycle in a field in Naantali?'

'No,' said Pärssinen.

No, thought Heinonen. Not a muscle moved in the man's face when he said that.

'Don't you watch the news from time to time?'

'No,' said Pärssinen.

No, thought Heinonen. No. An old man. A strong, sunburnt old man with a few bats in the belfry.

'I'm the caretaker here,' Pärssinen explained. 'I have been for over thirty years.'

Heinonen nodded.

'Help yourself.' Pärssinen pointed to the biscuit tin.

'No, thank you,' said Heinonen. 'Can you tell me what you were doing last Friday? Between twelve noon and eleven in the evening, in as much detail as possible?'

'Of course,' said Pärssinen.

Of course, thought Heinonen, and Pärssinen took a notebook out of a drawer. 'In the morning I mowed the grass. From ten till twelve thirty. It's a large surface, you see. Takes a long time. I like it to look nice. Then I oiled the hinges of the swing, because old Mrs Kononen in number 89 was complaining they squealed. That old bag, oh, my goodness!' He chuckled to himself and shook his head, presumably at the thought of old Mrs Kononen. 'At one o'clock I went to Virpi Jokinen in number 90 to repair her TV.' He looked up and smiled. 'I don't have to do that, of course, but I do it all the same. I like to do it. And in return she gave me lunch, it was black pudding with potatoes and mushroom sauce, my favourite. Yes . . . I noted down that I stayed at her place until three thirty. She was telling me about Mikko, that's her grandson, and he's just about to

272

start studying. At least, he wants to start studying, but he's failed his exam and now they don't know what to do . . . his parents, I mean. He wants to study medicine and I said what a good thing he failed the exam, then, because who really wants to go around cutting people up and stitching them together again?' He looked up and seemed to be waiting for Heinonen to agree. 'Then . . . then I had a little nap, and in the evening . . . '

'May I see?' asked Heinonen.

'Here you are.' Pärssinen handed him the notebook. Carefully formed letters. Neat handwriting, rather stiff, like a primary school-child's. Sure enough, no gaps in the record.

'I've been doing that for a long time,' said Pärssinen. 'Years and years. I don't mean like a diary, for God's sake, no, just so as I know where I've been and what I've done.'

Heinonen nodded. 'Thank you.' He rose to his feet. 'If I have any more questions I'll phone. I can reach you here, I suppose?'

'Of course,' said Pärssinen. 'What do you think would become of this place if I wasn't around?' He smiled again, his glance still rather absent. Heart trouble, thought Heinonen. Or a slight stroke. Something of the kind, he didn't know much about these things. Surprising that the man was still able to work.

'Well, then . . . ' said Pärssinen.

'Right, thank you. Goodbye.' Heinonen, as he went out of the door, toyed briefly with the idea of visiting Virpi Jokinen at number 90, but decided not to. For one thing he had only twenty minutes before the meeting at two.

The dark green expanse of turf lay there in the midday sun like an optical illusion.

Before he drove away, Tuomas Heinonen also opened a notebook. He put a special mark against the name of Pärssinen, one he had not put by any of the other names. Slowly and carefully, almost in the style of that strange old caretaker himself, he traced a question mark.

# 5

Pärssinen sat in the dark, relishing the sweet, fruity flavour on his tongue.

The chocolate biscuits were only half as good without plum schnapps, he had explained that clearly and distinctly, but you could understand that a policeman on duty had to turn down the offer. Particularly as this one was the very correct sort. He'd seen that at first glance.

He topped up his glass and let his eyes wander over the flickering images. One of his favourite films at present. One of those he really knew by heart. Every movement, however small, every facial expression. Every change, however slight. Every barely perceptible twitch of the little bodies. Five men and two girls. He thought of the young policeman.

A policeman had come to the door of his flat only once before, in all these years. Because he had been careful. He had never lost control again, but once, that first time, he *had* lost control and Timo had gone off, simply disappeared, and a few weeks later there had been a policeman at his door.

That time, too, it had been about a missing girl. Back then, he didn't know why any more, he had soiled himself during the interview. He had felt the soft shit trickling gently down his thighs. He had crossed his legs and told the police officer everything he wanted to know, and that time it had also been about his car, his little red Ford that had done him good service for years.

When the policeman had left that first time he had gone straight to bed, trembling all over, and next morning he had got up in the firm belief that he was done for. But the policeman had never come back, and everything went on as usual.

Then, yesterday, Timo had come back after all these years, and he had been glad to see him.

And now another police officer had come to his door and it hadn't meant anything.

Today, when he thought of what had happened in the past, he couldn't remember any details. Not with the best will in the world. He just felt something warm, a kind of warm wave pouring over him and burying everything that had once been.

The girls were kneeling in front of the men with their heads bowed. The scene was coming to an end. He could already feel the urgent pain between his legs and the beginnings of release. After a while he straightened up, with difficulty. He was feeling exhausted and a little dizzy.

He would have liked to go on sitting there, but he had to move the sprinkler. And then he would water the new bed beside the car park, or nothing would ever come of it.

Two fifteen.

Water flowers by car park.

He noted it down for his records before he went out.

# 6

Elina Lehtinen stood there in the silence, and through her open window watched the wind blowing over the field.

She was thinking of Turre. And Maria. Maria had died in the care home. She had not recovered from her fall. Her body had become smaller and thinner within a few days, then she had died.

That was how Turre had described it the evening before. They had sat out on the terrace and Turre had been in tears, and Elina had talked, although she hadn't known what to say.

Maria and Turre. They had never had children. They had been fond of Pia. They had always given Pia a present on her birthday, and every time Turre's and Maria's present had been one of those that Pia liked best.

That was very long ago, but Elina Lehtinen remembered how Pia's eyes used to shine on her birthday. And she remembered a young, strong Turre bringing Pia her present as soon as she came home from school. And Maria standing beside Turre and insisting that Pia

278

must unpack the present at once, because she wanted to see her delight.

Then months of helpless silence, because there was nothing left to say after Pia's death. At most they might say the wrong thing.

Then years of quiet, careful remarks feeling their way around the gap that could never be filled.

Then, at some point, an easy and natural tone in their voices. And Maria looking at the photograph in the living room and saying how she missed Pia. She smiled as she said it, and they stood together in silence for some time in front of the photo.

Then came the years in which Maria began to drift away from reality and Turre lost all his strength. The day when Turre called, looked out at the snow-covered garden and said that Maria would soon be living in a care home, and Pia had not stopped smiling in her photograph on the wall.

The sports car had shone like silver, brighter than the sun. She had seen the man coming towards her house and had gone step by step to open the door.

She tried to feel something and thought of Maria. Of their last meeting. Maria had rung the bell and slapped Elina's face with the flat of her hand before Elina understood what was happening. Turre took floozies to bed with him, she said. Any number of floozies. Floozies. She remembered Maria's voice and it had not been Maria's voice any more, nor had it been Maria's eyes looking at her.

A few days later Turre and Maria had gone to the care home, and Elina regularly visited Maria there, but she had never come home again.

She was waiting to feel something, but she felt nothing. She only thought of Maria and that she was dead, and two names were wandering through her mind, two names of people she didn't know. Perhaps that. A vague sense of sadness.

She had already forgotten what the man looked like. A silver sports car, brighter than the sun. And a business card. It lay smooth and cool in her hand.

She made herself go to the telephone and dial a number. The voice that answered sounded more familiar than she had expected.

'Happy birthday,' she said.

'Oh . . . you know.'

'You'd had a few too many and let it slip about your birthday.'

'Ah,' said Ketola. 'Well, thank you.'

'You were right,' she said.

'I was right?'

'He came here.'

Ketola said nothing.

'I know his name,' she went on.

Still Ketola said nothing. A few seconds passed.

'I'll come right over to you,' said Ketola. Now there was a strange and agitated tone in his voice.

Two names. Of people she didn't know.

'His children are called Aku and Laura,' she said and hung up.

# 7

Aku was dipping one hand in the water.

Laura was lying in the sun.

Pia was laughing soundlessly.

I know this place, Pärssinen had said. Had braked the car sharply, jumped out, opened the boot. He himself had stayed sitting in the car, watching Pärssinen and thinking of nothing in particular, only that it was a beautiful lake and Pärssinen was disturbing its peace.

He remembered that now. It was not so long ago. What were thirty-three years?

At that time all had been still here; he had heard just that one sound. The sound that Pärssinen made dragging the lifeless body over the sand and stones towards the water.

Timo Korvensuo got out of his car. He stretched and looked up at the sky for a while. His legs were giving way. He waited until he could stand on them, then went to the bank, crouched down and held one hand in the water.

Like Aku. He sensed what Aku was feeling. Now, at this moment, and it felt easy. Even easier than this morning.

Elina Lehtinen was a nice woman. A clever woman. He liked her.

A woman with a strong will to live and a quiet pain in her eyes that he had absorbed until his whole body was permeated by it.

He straightened up and took his mobile out of his trouser pocket. He tapped in the number. Marjatta's voice sounded close and distinct. He turned, suddenly thinking that she must be standing behind him, but there was only his car, its silver paint slowly beginning to soften under the weight of the sun.

'How are you all doing?' he heard himself asking.

'Fine. How about you?'

'I'm fine too.'

'Of course we miss you a bit. Was that what you wanted to hear?'

Marjatta laughed. Marjatta's clear, genuine laughter.

'No, no,' he said.

'It's true, all the same,' said Marjatta. 'Aku keeps asking about you.'

'Yes . . .'

'And I slept badly. It seems I somehow miss your snoring.'

She laughed again.

'I . . .'

'Where are you now? Is there any progress

with this business?'

'I'm beside the lake,' he said.

'The lake.'

'Yes, beside the lake. Rather a beautiful lake.'

'What sort of lake? I thought you were looking at the site for that development?'

'Yes, yes . . . I'll have to say goodbye now. Tell Aku and Laura . . . '

'When will you be coming home?'

'Soon. Today.'

'Good. Pekka was asking after you as well.'

'He'll manage,' he said. 'Tell Aku and Laura that . . . that they're the best kids in the world.'

'Well, they'll be glad to hear that. See you this evening, then. We'll look forward to it.'

Marjatta had broken the connection.

He crouched down, switched off the mobile, put it down and dipped his hands in the water again. He let them rest on the cool, smooth stones on the bed of the lake.

At that time all had been still; today he could hear distant voices. That was the only difference. On the other side of the lake there was a couple. Teenagers, if he could judge that from this distance. When he arrived they had been tucking into the contents of a picnic basket, but now they seemed to be quarrelling. He could hear the girl's shrill voice and the boy's calmer but irritated tones.

How stupid people were. Enjoying a picnic by the lake and spoiling it all by starting to quarrel. Probably for no good reason. He almost felt an impulse to swim over to them and explain that they were making a mistake. Someone would have to tell them that in good time.

Marjatta. Aku. Laura. Elina. He would introduce them all to each other. Of course. No reason not to. Aku and Laura would like Elina, and Elina would have a family after all. They really would move to somewhere near her.

That was why he had left his business card with her. To start the process. Only now did he become aware how simple it all was. That was why he felt so light, so liberated. Even this morning, directly after waking, he had felt that lightness.

He would reopen his firm in Turku and they would live very close to Elina Lehtinen, in a house that she had recommended to them. Elina would help them with the move, and they would sit on the packing cases and eat blueberry cake, and Elina would tell them about Pia.

He heard laughter, a cackle of silly laughter, then, after a while, another sound. A kind of sigh. Unnaturally loud, uttered in a high voice. Right beside him.

He turned, but there was no one there. A deserted lake, a real insiders' tip known only to a few. Pärssinen and the couple on the far bank.

An unnaturally loud note, uttered in a high-pitched tone, right beside him, over him, in him, around him.

He felt his lips still quivering slightly. Then they came to rest and the note died away above the water.

# 8

Elina Lehtinen looked different. Ketola couldn't work out just what the change in her was, he simply noticed it through the blur of his own excitement.

They were sitting in the kitchen. The business card lay on the table and Elina Lehtinen was calmly looking deep into his eyes as he asked her whether she could be mistaken.

'No,' was all she said.

Ketola picked up the business card again, turned it this way and that. This way and that. Timo Korvensuo, Estate Agent, Helsinki.

'It was what he wanted,' said Elina Lehtinen.

Ketola looked up with a question in his eyes.

'He wanted to reveal himself. He wanted me to know his name.'

'He can't know that you saw through him.'

'Yes, he can.'

'He just found a pretext for speaking to you. He didn't admit it . . . '

'Yes, he did. Not directly, but . . . in another way.'

Ketola nodded, although he didn't understand. He understood nothing at all, but nor did that seem to him necessary. What was the use of all that understanding?

'He wanted me to know everything. Or at least, a part of him wanted that,' she said.

Ketola had an answer on the tip of his tongue, but he bit it back. He lowered his gaze to the card again, trying to concentrate on what to do now, but somehow he couldn't manage it.

He was excited and at the same time very calm, and somewhere between those two sensations he must have lost the ability to think clearly. He felt the card in his hand. This was not how he had imagined it. Well, he had not imagined it at all.

He thought of a bicycle in a field on a TV screen and an unusually cool day in spring. A day a few months back. He thought of the rain pattering down on the awning over his terrace that day. It had been a strange day, and again something strange had happened. Something really remarkable.

A man looked in and gave Elina Lehtinen his business card. Address. Telephone numbers: landline, mobile. Email address. Korvensuo, Estate Agent.

He felt the card in his hand, and didn't know what to do with it. All he had been able to think of since Elina's phone call was that it had actually happened. And that it was impossible.

He heard rain pattering on the awning, saw the cloudless summer's day through the window and abruptly straightened up.

'Your telephone?'

'Out in the hall,' said Elina.

He nodded, went into the hall, picked up the phone and dialled. He didn't know what he was going to say; he just knew that he mustn't waste another second wondering about it. Now he must get it right and do it well. Better than anything he had ever done.

It was a recorded reply. The voice sounded pleasant, likeable. Reserved but self-confident. Modest but self-assured. Younger than the man described by Elina Lehtinen. Timo Korvensuo's mailbox could not be reached at the moment, but he would call back.

Ketola dialled another number. No stopping to think, he told himself. Joentaa answered just before Ketola was about to give up.

'Kimmo. Listen to this.'

'Just a moment. We're in a meeting right now. Can I call you back?'

'No. It's important. Go out of the room, we have to speak.'

Kimmo seemed to be hesitating briefly.

Finally he repeated, 'Just a moment,' and Ketola heard his footsteps and Sundström's voice in the background. A door closing.

'Right, I'm out in the corridor. What is it?' asked Kimmo.

'He's been here. At Elina Lehtinen's.'

Kimmo said nothing.

'Did you get that? He actually came here. He left his business card with her. Address, phone numbers, the lot.'

Kimmo remained silent and Ketola thought, once again, that this man could sometimes drive him mad. With all the urgency of which he was capable he said, 'Elina is sure of what she says. He told her some kind of story, about wanting to live in that area, and maybe she could help him and so forth, but Elina is sure, do you understand?'

'Yes,' said Joentaa.

'I'm sure too. His name is Timo Korvensuo.'

'Timo Korvensuo,' Joentaa repeated.

'That's right. We've got him. Now we just have to find him.'

'I see,' said Kimmo with infuriating slowness, and Ketola was about to make a remark about Kimmo Joentaa's phlegmatic nature, but he thought it inappropriate just now.

'You see. That's great. We must get going.'

'Where to?'

'Well, his place. To Timo Korvensuo, resident in Helsinki. He has a wife and two children. I must take a look at this. At first I thought of calling his home, but that's no use, his wife won't understand what it's about.'

'She won't understand if you ring her doorbell either.'

'Never mind, that's what I have to do now. I have to follow my instinct at this point. That's a good idea, right? You've always been keen on following your instincts. And you must come along. I need you because you're a member of the investigating team. I'm sure you can see that.'

Once again Joentaa said nothing for a while. Ketola forced himself to wait.

'I'll have a word with Sundström,' said Joentaa at last.

'Do that. Tell him Ketola has one of his crazy ideas and you want to watch him to make sure he doesn't do anything stupid.'

'That's exactly what I'm planning on doing,' said Joentaa.

'Ah.'

'I'll be at Elina Lehtinen's in half an hour,' and Joentaa broke the connection.

Ketola took a deep breath and heard Elina's voice behind him.

'Do you know what I think?' she asked.

He shook his head.

'I think that man . . . Korvensuo . . . I think I know why he came,' said Elina.

'Yes?' asked Ketola.

Elina looked out of the window and did not seem to be speaking to anyone in particular when she quietly went on in a soft voice, 'He wanted to tell me he was sorry.'

# 9

Ketola rushed out of the house, even before Kimmo Joentaa had a chance to press the bell, and insisted on taking the wheel. 'I know how you feel, Kimmo, but we have to move fast now.'

Joentaa sat in the passenger seat and took the business card Ketola handed him before noisily starting the car. As Ketola drove off, Joentaa saw Elina Lehtinen through her kitchen window and waved to her, but she probably didn't see him. Ketola drove at excessive speed the whole way, and Joentaa looked out of the window, thought of the name on the business card and wondered what to make of it.

During the discussion following Ketola's call Sundström, as was only to be expected, had been sceptical, and Joentaa himself was not sure what to think of all this. He had originally meant to talk to Elina Lehtinen about the man who had visited her, but it was too late for that.

'You can set your mind at rest, it's him,' said Ketola. 'The name on the card is the name we want, and the man we're after goes with the name.'

'Maybe,' said Kimmo.

'Elina isn't mistaken,' Ketola insisted.

'Did she say anything else? How exactly did their conversation go?'

'His pretext was that he was looking for a house in that neighbourhood. He was thinking of moving there with his family. After a while he suddenly began asking questions about Pia. Then he told her about his own children. Aku and Laura.'

Kimmo nodded.

'But it's like this: Elina noticed at once . . . even before he'd said a single word, she knew who she had before her.' Ketola was careering along the road at a crazy speed and turned to look at him. 'She sensed it, do you understand? She saw the man standing at her garden gate and she knew who it was.'

Kimmo nodded and for the time being took over Ketola's job of watching the traffic.

'Because she was expecting him,' said Ketola. 'Because she's been waiting for this for years and now it's happened.' Ketola turned back to look at the road and added, 'A seventh sense. You're keen on that sort of thing, you ought to like the idea.'

'Sixth,' said Joentaa.

'What?'

'I believe it's called a sixth sense.'

'Ah.'

'At least, I think so.'

'Could be.'

Ketola joined the motorway, which lay wide and empty ahead of them.

Joentaa felt a vague weariness. The names Aku and Laura passed through his thoughts, and at the moment when his eyes were almost closing he wondered what cloud Sanna would be sitting on when the day was as cloudless as this.

He felt himself slump and didn't know where he was when Ketola shook him.

'Wake up, friend, we're nearly there.'

After a few moments memory and consciousness returned. 'Fine,' he murmured.

'Nearly there,' Ketola repeated.

'Good, good,' muttered Kimmo.

Ketola drew up outside a house that Joentaa liked at first sight.

'Number 24. This is it,' said Ketola.

A pale green clapboard house. Like the Vehkasalos' home. A pale green clapboard house surrounded by a dark green garden that appeared both wild and well tended. The house stood on a rise, with a view of the city baking in the sun some distance away. A little boy was kicking a red ball against the garage wall.

'Nice place,' said Ketola, about to get out.

'Wait a minute.' Joentaa still felt slightly

dazed. 'How long was I asleep?'

'Almost the whole way,' said Ketola.

'Give me a moment to wake up properly.' He tried to tense his muscles and massaged his scalp.

'Okay?' asked Ketola.

The boy was practising headers now, and Joentaa said, 'I'd like to conduct the interview, if you don't mind. And if we realize that we're on the wrong track, we'll call it off quickly and leave.'

Ketola looked at him for a while, then said, 'Of course. That's how we'll do it.'

Joentaa nodded. They got out. Ketola strode ahead as fast as if he planned to shake Kimmo off over the last few metres. Tense, edgy, and at the same time calm and controlled. Ketola had often been like that in the deciding phases of a case.

The boy was immersed so deeply in his game that he didn't even notice their arrival.

The woman who opened the door was smiling, and obviously expected to see someone else. 'Oh,' she said.

'Good day, Mrs . . . Korvensuo?' said Joentaa.

'Yes, do excuse me, I thought my son . . . what can I . . . what did you want?'

'Mrs Korvensuo, my name is Kimmo Joentaa, I am an officer in the Turku police,

and this is Antsi Ketola, a . . . a colleague.'
He showed Marjatta Korvensuo his ID and
saw the inevitable shadow pass over her face.

'It's nothing to do with . . . with Timo, is it?
My husband is in Turku at the moment.'

'No, no,' said Joentaa. 'Please, there's
nothing for you to worry about, we're here
because we're making enquiries into the
. . . the case of a missing person and we'd just
like a little information. As I said, it's nothing
that need trouble you . . . ' Joentaa fell silent
and thought he ought to have prepared
himself better for this interview.

'Yes. Well, you'd better come in,' said
Marjatta Korvensuo.

'Thank you.'

They sat in the living room. He noticed the
uncertainty and sudden tension in Marjatta
Korvensuo's eyes, and sensed Ketola's
uneasiness as he sat beside him, jiggling his
foot up and down. At regular intervals the
ball crashed against the garage door.

'Mrs Korvensuo, this is in fact about your
husband Timo Korvensuo . . . but not in any
way that need trouble you. We would simply
like to ask a few questions that may clear
things up quickly.'

'Yes, well, go on,' said Marjatta Korvensuo.

'You said that your husband is in Turku at
the moment?'

'Yes, he's meeting a business partner. My husband is an estate agent.'

'Right. This business partner . . . do you have an address or a phone number for him? Or for the hotel where your husband is staying?'

'No,' said Marjatta Korvensuo. 'I'm sorry, he didn't tell me the man's name.'

Ketola had abruptly risen to his feet. 'Excuse me, may I use your loo?' he asked.

'Of course. Just to the left of the front door,' said Marjatta Korvensuo. Joentaa saw Ketola striding out into the hall and turned back to Marjatta Korvensuo, who went on, 'Timo called from the hotel. I must have stored the number.' She picked up the telephone lying on the low glass-topped table in front of her. 'Yes, here we are. This is it.'

Joentaa took the telephone. 'Do you have a pen?'

'Of course.' She stood up, left the room and came back in a moment with a ballpoint. Upstairs, Joentaa could hear music and girls laughing. The ball thumped against the garage wall.

'Thank you.' Joentaa noted down the phone number of the hotel on the business card.

'That . . . that's Timo's business card,' said Marjatta Korvensuo.

'Er, yes,' said Joentaa.

'Where did you find it? What exactly is going on?'

'We — well, it's hard to explain. The card came up in the course of our enquiries, so to speak, but there's really no cause for concern. It's merely a matter of clearing everything up.'

She sat down again, and Joentaa wondered why he was talking all this strange stuff and why he was so intent on not worrying Marjatta Korvensuo. He tried to concentrate on his questions. 'Your husband,' he began. 'Do you know whether he ever lived in Turku, quite a long time ago? In the seventies?'

'Yes, he did,' she said at once and Joentaa felt a pang in his stomach. Although all that naturally proved nothing. He thought of the boy practising headers outside. Aku.

'He did,' she repeated. 'In fact, he studied there. Mathematics. But then he dropped out of his studies and moved to Helsinki. Which was a good thing, or we would probably never have met.' She smiled briefly. 'Why is that important?'

'Do you happen to know the exact date? When precisely that was?'

She thought about it for a moment. 'He's never talked much about it. Very little, actually. And it's ages ago now. He must have moved to Helsinki about . . . yes, he moved in 1974, so he must have left Turku the same year.'

Joentaa lowered his eyes to the business card, and thought of Ketola's old files and the date Marjatta Korvensuo had just mentioned: 1974. On every single page of the files, only the days and months before that year varied, until a time came when 1974 gave way to 1975. That proved nothing, he thought again; then he noticed that the ball had stopped hitting the garage door, and a boy rushed into the room.

'Oh,' he said tonelessly, when he met Joentaa's eyes.

'Hello,' said Joentaa, anxious to seem friendly and normal.

'Hello,' replied the boy.

'This is Mr Joentaa,' said Marjatta Korvensuo.

The boy nodded and looked relaxed again, with his mind on other things, as he turned and went out of the room.

Upstairs, the girls were laughing.

Joentaa heard water rushing and was about to ask a question when he saw a change in Marjatta Korvensuo's face. She was suddenly attentive to something.

'Aku!' she called.

'What?' Aku called back.

'Where are you?'

'In the loo, Mama!' replied Aku, irritated.

There was a short pause. Then she asked Joentaa quietly, 'So where is your colleague?'

A few seconds passed. Then Joentaa stood up and went out into the hall. One flight of stairs led up, another down, just like the stairs in the Vehkasalos' house. Upstairs the girls were still laughing. He went down. In the Vehkasalos' house, Sinikka's room was on the lower ground floor. A washing machine was running. The basement corridor was dominated by huge bookshelves, which reminded him of the garden outside. The books were all over the place, yet somehow there was a system to it. He heard a familiar sound, one that always reminded him of the red wooden church. The hum of a computer. Ketola was sitting in the shadows. Leaning forward, chin propped on his hands, he was looking at the flickering monitor. He seemed to have calmed down. Joentaa stood in the doorway.

'This must be Papa's study,' said Ketola.

Joentaa entered the room, which was meticulously neat and tidy. Unlike the garden. Unlike the bookshelves. The room seemed to consist of a profusion of perfect right angles.

'It was very simple,' said Ketola. 'Even for a layman like me. Evidently Papa's study is out

301

of bounds to the rest of the family.'

Joentaa stopped behind Ketola.

'How about a little slide show?' said Ketola. 'My son Tapani showed me how you do it recently. He may be crazy, but he's good with computers.'

Ketola clicked, and the images began to take shape before Joentaa's eyes. Very slowly, then in rapid succession. He heard Ketola's voice as if in the distance.

'The computer is stuffed with them. Amazing,' said Ketola.

'This is outrageous,' said Marjatta Korvensuo, behind Joentaa's back. He turned and saw her standing in the doorway. He would have moved towards her, but his legs didn't obey, and she quickly came closer. He leaned over Ketola and tried to switch the computer off.

'Keep your hands off that,' said Marjatta Korvensuo. 'This is quite enough. Outrageous.'

Then she was beside them.

Ketola sat there motionless and relaxed, and didn't even raise his head, as if he hadn't noticed Marjatta Korvensuo at all.

'What . . . ?' said Marjatta Korvensuo.

'Please turn that computer off,' said Joentaa, but Ketola didn't move.

'What's that?' asked Marjatta Korvensuo.

There was a long silence.

Then Ketola said suddenly, 'We must go.' He halted the succession of images, turned off the computer and rose to his feet. 'No one is to touch this thing,' he told Marjatta Korvensuo. 'Is that understood?'

She did not react.

'We must go, Kimmo,' Ketola said again, but Kimmo remained fixed to the spot.

'Mrs Korvensuo, do you know where your husband is? Have you spoken on the phone? Did he say anything that could get our enquiries any further?' asked Ketola.

'He . . . he's in Turku,' she said, without taking her eyes off the computer screen. 'You know that.'

'Where in Turku? Where exactly is he?'

'By the lake,' she said.

'By the lake?' Ketola's voice almost cracked.

'He was beside a lake. I don't know which lake.'

'I do,' said Ketola. 'Come on, Kimmo.'

Ketola walked out. Joentaa stayed where he was beside Marjatta Korvensuo, following her eyes to the blank screen.

'Will you come on, damn it?' shouted Ketola from above.

Joentaa started moving, but then he turned back to Marjatta Korvensuo and said, without thinking, 'I'd like . . . when all this is cleared up, when there's more time, I'd like to come back here, and then we can talk.'

He didn't know why he had said that.

Awkwardly, he held out his hand.

She nodded.

'We'll send someone who — I'll make sure someone comes who you can talk to. We have people trained for that,' he added.

She nodded again.

He moved away, and sensed that the picture of the woman standing in front of the blank screen was imprinting itself on his memory.

Ketola was already in the car, drumming his fingers on the steering wheel.

The boy had gone back to kicking his ball against the garage door. 'Goodbye, Mr Joentaa,' he called as Kimmo got into the car.

# 10

Ketola sat back in a remarkably relaxed, casual attitude as he drove well above the speed limit, while Kimmo Joentaa called Sundström. Sundström reacted with surprise but also with composure, his mind going straight to the point. 'Rather a lot of coincidences, admittedly,' he said after thinking for a few seconds.

'Well, naturally none of this is proof of anything,' said Joentaa.

'No, indeed,' Sundström agreed. 'But I'm prepared to take it seriously now. There's Elina Lehtinen's impression of him, and the man has child porn on his hard disk, and he was living in Turku in 1974 and moved away in the same year . . . So Ketola thinks the man's gone to the lake where the body of Pia Lehtinen was found?'

'Yes. Maybe.'

'But we've searched that one. He's more likely to be at the lake where he sank Sinikka Vehkasalo's body . . . and we don't know what lake that is yet.'

'Ketola is sure he's by the lake where Pia Lehtinen's body was found.'

'Ah. Why?'

Joentaa glanced sideways at Ketola. 'I don't know,' he admitted.

'Well, okay, since that's the only lake we can connect with the case at all, we'll drive out there,' said Sundström.

'Could you phone Helsinki and make sure someone's with Marjatta Korvensuo? A psychologist, I mean. Someone good at dealing really well with a situation like this,' said Joentaa.

'Sure. I'll do that. What's the address?'

Joentaa gave it to him. 'And of course someone must secure the computer immediately. We probably left in too much of a hurry.'

'Of course. Right, then I'll set off to pick up our murderer. Tell me the name again, please.'

'Timo Korvensuo.'

'Timo . . . Korvensuo. Right.'

'I'll call the hotel where Korvensuo has been staying. If he happens to be there I'll let you know.'

'Fine. See you later.'

Joentaa rang the number of the hotel and found that Korvensuo had checked out that morning. No, there were no records of calls or other messages from any kind of business partner for their guest Timo Korvensuo.

Joentaa thanked them, finished the call, dialled another number and passed the information on to Heinonen. Sundström and Grönholm were already on their way to the lake.

Joentaa leaned back a little, but then sat upright again next moment and thought that all this was moving very fast. Maybe too fast.

Perhaps Korvensuo was calling his wife at this very moment. Then he'd realize what had happened. If she would speak to him. But she wouldn't pick up the phone, surely. It was unthinkable that she would pick up the phone if the display showed the number of her husband's mobile. She wouldn't be able to speak to him now, she wouldn't be able to speak to anyone, too much had turned upside down in too short a time.

Joentaa glanced sideways at Ketola and wondered whether he was thinking similar thoughts. It didn't look like it. Ketola's eyes were firmly on the road, and he was almost lying back in his seat, as if planning to drop off to sleep any moment now while doing 200 kpm.

'All clear?' asked Joentaa.

'Sure,' said Ketola.

'Sundström is on his way to the lake,' said Joentaa.

'I heard.'

'Do you think . . . are you sure? About Korvensuo?'

'Perfectly sure.'

Joentaa nodded. 'And what, in your opinion, is he doing beside that lake?'

Ketola glanced at him. 'He . . . ' he began, then fell silent for a while before starting again. 'Yes, good question. I'd say . . . '

Joentaa waited, but Ketola's eyes were on the road again and he seemed to have forgotten that Joentaa had asked him a question at all.

Heinonen called and said all was going to plan in Helsinki. Their colleagues there were on their way.

'Thanks,' said Joentaa. He closed his eyes, and saw Marjatta Korvensuo at the moment when she had opened the door to them. The boy kicking the ball against the garage door.

'About your question, Kimmo,' said Ketola into the silence.

Joentaa opened his eyes, but once again Ketola did not answer it. Instead, he began to laugh.

First chuckling quietly.

Then roaring with wild laughter.

'I don't know!' he suddenly cried, began laughing again, and repeated that remark at regular intervals.

'I haven't the faintest idea! I just don't

know! Please don't ask me. Ask me another! Something easier!' he kept shouting.

And all the time he laughed, pausing for a moment only now and then to wipe the tears of laughter from his eyes.

# 11

Matti Ylönen tasted peppermint, and yet again he felt an impulse to punch Outi hard in the face.

Which of course he wasn't about to do, because men don't hit women, it simply isn't done, although he had been getting more and more inclined to entertain powerful doubts of the good sense of this fundamental rule, particularly recently, more particularly when he and Outi were together, for example like now.

Outi was sitting on the towel, calmly consuming the contents of the picnic basket, which he had put together with some care, and burying her face in a fashion magazine, while complaints and insults issued freely from her mouth.

So he was a weed and useless in bed, was he? Not that Outi was in any position to judge, since she kept putting him off until later in that respect. Furthermore, he was a figure of fun, or then again a stupid arsehole, her girlfriends had probably been right to say nothing would come of their relationship, all she was saying was, it had lasted nearly six weeks now, so maybe it was past its best.

That was how she put it, past its best after six weeks, and right at that moment Matti Ylönen felt so too, he had to agree with her wholeheartedly there, and when Outi also stuffed the last chewy sweet into her mouth without even offering it to him, he realized that the time had now come, he was about to punch her this minute; then, at that very moment, the relationship would indeed be past its best, the whole thing would be over, and to his entire satisfaction at that.

He spat out his now tasteless chewing gum, took a step her way, felt the anger gathering in his arm, in his fist, and Outi raised her head and for the first time in a long while looked him straight in the face and said, 'You stay away from me, you sod.'

He took another step her way and was just deciding not to punch her but to start by slapping her face good and hard, when a sound stopped him in his tracks.

A sound that he couldn't identify, because he had never heard anything like it before.

A long-drawn-out whistling. It began quietly, it grew louder, it ebbed again and then grew louder once more.

He saw Outi's mouth drop open. She looked up, because she seemed to suppose that the sound came from the sky, and he thought he had gone too far, some awful retribution was about to descend upon him, although he hadn't even touched her yet.

Now the sound was very high and very shrill, and when Outi got up and came to stand beside him, when she even took his hand, he realized that the sound was the scream being uttered by the man on the opposite bank of the lake.

The man was walking. No, he was running. He ran round his car, a silver sports model at which Matti Ylönen had earlier been gazing, fascinated, whereupon Outi had said that men who defined themselves through cars were just ridiculous, and if memory served him right, that exchange of words about the silly sports car had started the whole silly quarrel in the first place, and now the man on the opposite bank of the lake was running round his car. He slipped, he got to his feet, he ran again and let out a scream that seemed to go on for ever, and to Matti Ylönen it didn't sound particularly human.

He felt the firm pressure of Outi's hand in his.

They stood in silence as the man ran faster and faster, and the scream turned into a kind of hysterical native-American howl, and when the unknown man finally, as if guided by sudden inspiration, got into his car and roared the engine, drove away over the landing stage and catapulted himself and his car into the lake in a high arching flight, it occurred to Matti Ylönen, oddly enough, that he and Outi were going to live together.

It was as simple as that.

They belonged with each other.

Whether she wanted that just now or not.

The car sank into the churned-up water surprisingly fast, then all was calm except for the echo of the scream, and Outi leaned her head on his shoulder.

# 12

Laura was lying in the sun.
Aku was diving.
Pia was laughing soundlessly.
Don't breathe, said Marjatta.
He didn't want to breathe.

# 13

Aku was running. He kept turning round, because he was sure they would follow him, Laura at least would have to run after him to fetch him back, or anyway ask what he thought he was doing, but no one came. There were strange men in the house, some of them had smiled at him while he tried to find out why they were there. After a while the men began avoiding his gaze and looked as if they didn't even notice his presence.

Laura had been hovering on the edge of the group, smiling uncertainly. Her girlfriend had gone home. The strange men had carried his father's computer out of the house.

His mother had been sitting on the sofa with one of the men beside her. She hadn't spoken, not a single word; she had just been nodding as she listened to the man, who spoke in a quiet, gentle voice, and Aku had gone out without saying goodbye.

He was standing at the bus stop. He could see the house, the window of his room on the top floor. The bus came. He got in, and had just enough money for a ticket to the city centre. He sat in the back row and watched the suburbs flying past.

He wondered what the men wanted the computer for. Especially because easily the best computer in the whole house was in his own room.

He got out in the inner city, and just walked around for a while, because he had no money left, not even enough for a single scoop of ice cream. Then he sat down by the harbour and watched the ferries gliding over the water. Next week they were going to Tallinn on the ferry. He was looking forward to that.

When he got home there was only one of the cars left outside the house. Laura opened the door. Her face looked white and stony. The man and his mother were sitting on the sofa. The man was still talking, his mother was nodding. As if only a few minutes had passed. No one asked where he had been.

He ran up to his room, flung the door open and saw his computer standing on the table. For a few moments he was relieved. So they'd left his considerably better computer here.

He sat down on the bed and began looking at a comic. He hummed a tune to himself.

Now and then he looked out of the window to see if the car was still there. The car that belonged to the man who was sitting beside his mother in the living room.

# 14

Even from a distance, Joentaa could see the car sticking up above the water, Sundström and Grönholm and the divers, and members of the salvage team. A boy and a girl were hanging around on the outskirts of the group, talking to Tuomas Heinonen. Niemi and his colleagues were scattered over the entire area, in white overalls. The body was in the driving seat of the car, slumped over the steering wheel. The car was just being pulled out with heavy lifting gear.

Ketola parked carefully beside the police cars and looked at the scene without saying a word. His eyes were reddened; he had been laughing until just before they arrived. Laughing and laughing and laughing, until the moment when he braked sharply and turned into the woodland path leading to the lake.

'That's it,' he said after a while, and fell silent again, as if all had now been said.

Joentaa got out and went over to Sundström and Grönholm. His glance kept going to the crumpled body on the driver's seat. He thought of the boy kicking his football against the garage door. Again and again. Again and again. He thought of Sanna. He saw nothing, only the wreck of a sports car. He thought of Sanna's name.

'That's it,' said Sundström too when Joentaa was beside him.

Joentaa nodded.

'The car is registered in the name of Timo Korvensuo. Astonishing. I'll admit I'm prepared to congratulate Ketola. When I get a chance. All we need now is the girl's body,' said Sundström.

'What exactly happened?' asked Joentaa.

'The man screeched like a lunatic, got into his car and drove straight into the water, just like that.'

Joentaa looked at him, intrigued.

'I didn't see it myself. That couple over there did.'

Joentaa followed Sundström's eyes and saw the two teenagers standing with Heinonen.

'Of course they're pretty upset, but they'll get over it,' said Sundström.

Behind them, two more vehicles came to a noisy halt. One was a TV outside broadcasts van.

Nurmela, the chief of police, got out of the other. He walked over to them at a rapid but well-controlled pace, waving before he reached them. 'A television team from YLE.

For the news. I'll give them a short statement and then they'll be off again. So they told me.'

Sundström nodded.

'Good work,' said Nurmela, looking in turn at Sundström, Grönholm and Joentaa, and clapping Joentaa on the back before walking away towards the TV van. Joentaa watched him go and felt, with some reluctance, that the praise pleased him. Even though he had nothing at all to do with it and there was not the slightest reason to be pleased.

'I'm an arsehole,' said Joentaa.

Sundström and Grönholm looked at him, taken aback.

'What?' asked Sundström.

'I said I'm an arsehole,' Joentaa repeated.

'Oh, really?' said Sundström.

'And I wish I knew what those bastards are doing here.'

'Er . . . ' said Sundström.

'How come Nurmela is giving an interview for the news when we know absolutely nothing? Like, for instance, why Korvensuo drove into the lake?'

'Guilty conscience?' suggested Grönholm.

'Guilty conscience. After thirty-three years. And before that he just quickly does away with another girl in the same spot. Then he

319

suddenly starts bothering about his conscience. Or what?'

'Exactly,' said Sundström, unmoved.

'I'm not convinced,' said Joentaa.

'Kimmo, calm down, do. You've had a
strenuous drive. Don't upset yourself. If
Nurmela is going to talk nonsense, that's his
problem. It makes no difference.'

'It does make a difference. The wife of the
man who was driving that car is sitting at
home in Helsinki. And Nurmela is shooting
off his stupid mouth with the wreck of the car
as a backdrop.'

'They won't show the body. Not on
prime-time television.'

'That's not the point, you idiot!'

'I beg your pardon?' said Sundström.

'For God's sake!' Joentaa turned and
walked away, without knowing where he
intended to go. He himself was surprised by
his fury. Presumably Ketola's fits of laughter
had got on his nerves. Why was he always the
one who let these things get to him? Why was
he always the one who was supposed to keep
calm?

He stood there undecidedly for a while,
then went purposefully towards Kari Niemi,
who was issuing instructions to his colleagues
and, of course, gave him an easy smile as he
approached.

'Hi, Kimmo,' he said.

That was all, but it was enough to restore a little of Joentaa's sense of balance.

Niemi went on talking to his team, and Joentaa looked at the boy and the girl standing sheepishly beside Heinonen.

Further away something attracted Joentaa's attention, although for a moment he couldn't see what it was. A car was beginning to move away. His own police car. Ketola was driving it off along the woodland path. Without any frantic haste, perfectly calm again now. Times when Ketola calmed down had always had something final about them. Joentaa watched the car moving away, and told himself that something had come to an end.

Nurmela had finished giving his interview and waved to him.

Again and again, thought Joentaa. Again and again. A ball, a red ball. And a garage door. Again and again, never stopping.

His legs gave way. He sat on the ground, cross-legged, and watched the members of the salvage team hauling the silver sports car up on land, little by little, metre by metre.

# 15

Tapani came that evening. To wish him a happy birthday. He handed him a cake. A chocolate cake with kiwi fruit and raspberries.

'Thank you,' said Ketola and for a while he looked at the raspberries, which appeared to be arranged in numerals or letters that he couldn't work out.

'AK,' explained Tapani after a while. 'Antsi Ketola. The birthday boy's name.'

'Oh, I see,' said Ketola.

'Makes sense, doesn't it?'

'Absolutely,' Ketola answered, realized that they were still standing in the doorway and asked Tapani in.

They sat in the living room, both of them eating slices of Tapani's cake.

'I made it myself,' said Tapani.

'It's very good,' Ketola said.

The TV was on. Ketola had switched it on as soon as he got home and had watched every news bulletin since. The reporting was all over the shop. The presumed murderer had presumably committed suicide. His name was Timo K., a Helsinki resident. Timo K. was dead and it was Antsi K.'s birthday.

Ketola was too tired to laugh at that, although he had a vague idea that it was funny.

It all seemed very far away. The drive to Helsinki. The car in the lake, the dead body in the driver's seat. Kimmo. Kimmo, sitting beside him in silence. Nurmela in jacket and tie, at over thirty degrees in the shade. And Nurmela hadn't even been sweating.

All of it could have been an eternity away. The sequence of events was getting muddled up. Now Tapani was here; this was the present. Tapani eating his cake, taking small bites, and in the background, one after the other, pictures of Pia Lehtinen and Sinikka Vehkasalo coming up on the TV screen, and Ketola was thinking of a misty, very cool day in spring, a few months ago, but it seemed a long way off. He thought of the rain, of the sound of raindrops pattering down on the awning, of a very distinct emptiness in his brain. What surprising importance that distant day had now acquired.

He felt a longing. A particularly annoying longing, because he couldn't put a name to it, he couldn't assign it any content, he only felt that it was of huge extent and seemed to be sinking deeper into him by the minute.

'By the way, I brought you a present too,' said Tapani.

Ketola looked at his son.

'It's outside. Well hidden, of course.'

'Yes. Of course. I'm delighted,' said Ketola.

'Come on.'

Ketola followed Tapani, who opened the door and turned into the garden as if he knew where he was going. 'Look,' he said, producing his present from behind a bush.

'A bicycle,' said Ketola.

'That's right.'

It was on the tip of Ketola's tongue to ask how he had been able to pay for the bicycle, but he bit back the question.

'And seeing you already have a bicycle, you could lend me your new one now and then,' said Tapani.

'Of course,' Ketola agreed.

The daughter of the family next door was diving into the swimming pool. Her parents were sitting on the terrace. Ketola got the impression that they were looking at him and would have liked to ask him any number of questions. About the case on the news. Did he know any more about it? Of course they were interested, and he'd been in the police for a long time.

'Sure. I'll lend you the bike any time,' said Ketola. 'And thank you very much. I . . . well, I always find it hard to show it, but I'm glad to see you here. I really am very glad.'

Tapani looked at him and nodded, but he didn't seem to grasp what Ketola was trying to tell him.

'Do you understand?' asked Ketola.

Tapani nodded again.

They stood there for a while in silence. Then Tapani said, 'Will you lend it to me?'

'Hm?'

'The bike. Will you lend it to me?'

'Yes, sure. I just said so.'

'I mean now. I have to leave. I have to go into the woods. I must stop those people doing anything stupid.'

Ketola felt a pang and thought how pointless it was. What a pointless surge of emotion. 'Yes, sure,' he said.

'Thanks.' Tapani swung himself on to the bicycle, pedalled hard to give himself a good start, then cycled smoothly away, holding himself very upright and going goodness knew where.

# 16

Kimmo Joentaa was sitting on the landing stage. In the decrepit rocking chair where Sanna used to sit, wrapped in blankets, during the last months of her life.

As soon as he got back Kimmo had gone down to the lake and he had taken the rocking chair out of the shed where it had spent the last two years.

He looked at the calm surface of the water and thought of that other lake, the silver sports car, the crumpled body in the driver's seat.

He remembered the day when he and Sanna had bought the rocking chair cheap at a furnishing centre. Soon after they met and just before they moved in together.

Sanna had carried the chair to the car like a trophy and put it in the boot, just as Ketola had stowed the model on wheels into the boot of his car. In the driving snow. Not so very long ago.

The rocking chair was damp, and rotting away in places. It had been kept in the dry, Sanna always used to put it away in the shed when there was rain or snow, but all the same the chair got splashed with water every time Sanna had jumped up, gone to the end of the landing stage and dived head first into the water. That was earlier, not in the months before her death, because at that point Sanna had no longer been strong enough to swim.

Some time, thought Kimmo, some time, just when he least expected it, this chair would collapse under his weight, and if Sanna could see that she would be sure to laugh when she saw him lying on the landing stage, with the broken arm of the chair in his hand.

He closed his eyes and spent a little while trying to put his thoughts in order, but it couldn't be done, it was totally impossible, and he let them drift.

He saw blurred, flickering images and heard words that had been spoken. Today or many years ago. Or maybe only now, at this moment, in his imagination.

Sanna, wrapped in blankets. Sundström, who could always put everything in a nutshell. In clear, comprehensible terms. In the brightly lit conference room. In the room where Ketola, an eternity ago, had investigated the disappearance of Pia Lehtinen. Ketola sitting in the shadows, chin propped on his hands, in front of a computer screen. In a strange house, in a room full of perfect right angles. The members of the salvage team calmly going about their work. Pulling the car out metre by metre. Elina Lehtinen in the garden of her house. Blueberry cake and tea in white cups. Pia, laughing out loud in a photograph, and Sinikka looking gravely into the camera. Niemi had said Sinikka looked sad. Just sad. A boy calling to him, a red football. And a business card. Timo Korvensuo, Estate Agent. A number under Timo Korvensuo, Estate Agent, that could no longer be reached. But there was the woman who had opened the door to them, expecting to see her son. Aku. Goodbye, Mr Joentaa. A number that he would not be dialling. And the vague feeling of having seen something. At a time that he couldn't specify any more closely. Without a doubt, something of minor significance.

They had sat in the conference room, and Sundström had been integrating the estate agent Timo Korvensuo into the general context of their enquiries, expressing it all in short, clear sentences, when the call from their Helsinki colleagues came through. The thought of the annoyance on Sundström's face almost made Kimmo laugh. Sundström, who had been in full swing, was suddenly stopped short in his tracks.

The times didn't match. It was as simple as that. Timo Korvensuo had driven to Turku on

Sunday. On Friday, at the time of Sinikka Vehkasalo's disappearance, he had still been in Helsinki. His colleagues at the estate agency confirmed that. His wife Marjatta also confirmed it. So did Heinonen's enquiries at the Turku hotel.

'Which doesn't have to mean anything,' Sundström had said, after thinking for a while. 'Of course he could have been in Turku at midday on Friday and back in Helsinki in the evening. That's no problem.'

'But if I understood it correctly,' Heinonen had objected, 'Korvensuo's colleagues said he spent all Friday at meetings in Helsinki.'

'Hm, yes . . . we'll have to check that,' Sundström had said, adding that he would drive to Helsinki first thing tomorrow. And Kimmo was to go with him.

He thought of Marjatta Korvensuo. So he would be seeing her tomorrow. And the boy, Aku. And the daughter, Laura. He'd see how they were. Get an impression. He would sit opposite Marjatta Korvensuo. They'd be sitting opposite each other tomorrow, just as they had this afternoon. He would have an opportunity of beginning from the beginning again, talking to her once more. But what about?

He opened his eyes and saw the white, calm expanse of water. The pale midnight sun persisted in shining. Somewhere, tucked away in a blind spot, the idea of something he had seen but not taken in was waiting for him.

He tried to approach that idea and saw himself, Ketola and Antti from Archives running through heavy, driving snow.

Antti now had a permanent appointment and seemed very happy working in Archives with Päivi Holmquist. Kimmo was really pleased for him.

Päivi Holmquist's lumber room.

Ketola's old files.

Ketola's handwriting. On the day when Pia Lehtinen's body had been found. Ketola's hand had been shaking as he wrote a note on a piece of paper. A note in the old files.

Kalevi Vehkasalo. Sinikka's father. His hand had been shaking too as he sat beside his wife on the sofa, asking her to keep calm.

Tomorrow Heinonen and Grönholm would speak to Sinikka's parents. They would try to establish some connection between a dead estate agent and their daughter. Although it couldn't have been Korvensuo who crossed Sinikka's path last Friday. Or presumably not.

He thought of Sinikka. Of her face in the photo. Of the message Ruth Vehkasalo had left in her mailbox. Always the same message. Would Sinikka call? Please. In the end Sinikka's mother had been shouting, almost weeping, with a premonition of disaster, even though she hadn't yet known that Sinikka's bicycle had been found.

Ruth Vehkasalo's message had not left the house, because Sinikka's mobile was still in her room. So why . . . why hadn't Sinikka taken her mobile when she went to training? He would have to ask the Vehkasalos whether their daughter was forgetful; then he began drifting into sleep . . . Sundström would be at his door in a few hours' time.

Sundström wanted to make an early start and had suggested picking up Joentaa at home. He didn't know how late it was now, but the early start could be only a few hours away. He had the impression that the midnight sun was merging already, almost imperceptibly, into the morning twilight. Yet he felt that he didn't want to fall asleep . . .

He sat up very suddenly.

He thought of the model on wheels. In the driving snow. And months later in Ketola's house. On the living room table. Ketola had laughed . . . incredulously . . . had simply not been able to understand it. That was how he had felt himself, but all the same there was something he had seen, something of very minor significance. One of the investigators had conducted an interview, one of the less important interviews . . .

He got up and went back to the house. Something that had briefly met his eyes . . . a passage that he had merely skimmed, because it was not of great importance and he had been too tired to concentrate on it properly. A conversation, only recently . . . He opened the front door and went into the living room, where the files lay scattered untidily around. He was looking for a statement about Sinikka, something that had struck him because it was odd. Not important, but odd.

He leafed and leafed through the files, and couldn't find the wretched page. He sat down and forced himself to look through folder after folder calmly. Very calmly.

Relax, Kimmo, Sanna had liked to say, although she herself had been capable of considerably more alarming outbursts of rage than he was.

Here was the text he had been looking for. Tuomas Heinonen had written it and it wasn't a formal record, just a summary of several interviews conducted by Heinonen that had brought up more or less important questions, matters that might still be explained. A girlfriend talking about a birthday party . . . Joentaa read the statement, then read it again, and again, and the longer he read it the less he understood what could be so important about it. He had been wrong, it must be something else, it wasn't about this text after all.

He turned it over and saw a note in Heinonen's very clear writing, so different from Ketola's scribble. Clear and distinct, a word and a number.

Joentaa tore out the page, read the word and the number, and had no idea what they meant.

He sat there without moving for several minutes.

Then he stood up and left the house.

He didn't understand it, he didn't understand anything any more, but he felt an unspecified fear.

And a very specific hope.

# 17

'Come in, Kimmo,' said Ketola.

He didn't seem surprised to see Kimmo, although it was nearly three in the morning. The buildings on both sides of the street might have been dead when Kimmo was driving through the city.

He followed Ketola into his living room. The terrace door was open.

'I'm sitting outside. It's a warm evening,' said Ketola, looking straight at him as if to make sure that Joentaa agreed.

Joentaa nodded.

They sat on garden chairs, there on the threshold between night and morning, and said nothing.

Ketola had one hand on the model, which was now back on its wheels again. The field, the road, the avenue of trees, the bicycle, the red car.

On the table stood a chocolate cake decorated with kiwi fruit and raspberries.

'Would you like a piece?' asked Ketola.

'No, thanks,' said Joentaa and after a moment's hesitation he leaned over the table, because the way the raspberries were arranged had caught his eye.

'A and K,' said Ketola. 'Antsi Ketola. The birthday boy's name.'

'I see.'

'My son baked it,' said Ketola.

Their conversation lapsed again and Joentaa waited to feel the impulse to express what he hadn't yet thought out fully.

Ketola seemed happy with the silence.

'Sinikka Vehkasalo,' said Kimmo.

Ketola looked up. 'Sinikka Vehkasalo,' he repeated.

'She went to a birthday party. A few months ago. A girlfriend said something about it and Heinonen — well, you know Heinonen — in his thorough way he noted down the place where that party was given. The address, although it didn't seem to be of any importance.'

'Ah, yes, Heinonen . . . ' said Ketola.

'Number 20 Oravankatu. That's the house right next door to here. Those are your neighbours.'

'Hm, yes,' said Ketola.

There was a long silence.

'Sinikka suddenly left the party,' Joentaa finally said. 'After a while she came back and she seemed different. As if something significant had happened. But she didn't tell even her girlfriends what it was. She kept it to herself, like an important secret.'

'Well . . . ' said Ketola.

'She was here. With you. Why? What happened that day?' asked Joentaa.

'Nothing,' said Ketola.

'Nothing?'

Ketola nodded.

'Was she here?' asked Joentaa.

'Yes. Of course.'

Of course, thought Joentaa. Of course. 'Why?' he asked.

'Ask me another,' said Ketola. 'Something easier.'

'Why?' Joentaa repeated.

'I don't really know why.'

Joentaa waited.

'I was sitting on the terrace. Same as now. The girls were running about in the garden, even jumping into the swimming pool, though it was very cold. And then it started raining. They all went indoors except for Sinikka. Sinikka climbed the fence and joined me here on the terrace.'

'Why?' asked Joentaa.

'I don't really know why. She knew that I'd been in the police. I expect her friend, my neighbours' daughter, had told her. She was probably a bit curious. And she asked why I was sad.'

'What?'

'Funny, isn't it? I thought so myself. A girl of Pia Lehtinen's age climbs the fence and asks me pointless questions . . . '

'And then?'

'Then what?'

'What happened after that?'

'I sat here in my chair, much as I'm sitting here now, and I probably stared at her as if she were a ghost. And she began to laugh.'

Joentaa thought of the photograph. The girl's serious features and how he had thought he could detect loud, hearty laughter lurking beneath them.

'Yes,' said Ketola. 'She . . . she said she'd been watching me and wondering all the time what was the matter with me, and then I began telling her all about it.'

'All about it?' asked Joentaa.

'Everything, from the moment when I thought of Pia Lehtinen. On my last day at work, you remember. Everything that had been going through my head since then. All about Pia. Everything I could remember. Everything I'd thought about during the months after . . . after my retirement. I had plenty of time to rack my brains over it. I guess that was about the longest monologue I ever delivered in my life.'

Ketola stopped.

'And?' Joentaa asked.

'She sat there listening. She was surprisingly calm. I talked and talked, and after a while I had the feeling that nothing I had ever said before was sinking in so . . . so directly. It's hard to describe. I had this sense that she was actually absorbing it all, understanding the whole thing, without once interrupting me or asking a question. And then, at the end . . . '

Joentaa waited.

'At the end she pointed to the model and said, as if it was quite natural, that she knew the place. The place where the cross stands, she always passed it on her way to volleyball training. And then . . . we neither of us said anything for a long time. I couldn't think of anything else to say. Then she suddenly said I had to find the man who killed Pia Lehtinen . . . '

Ketola fell silent again.

'And after that?' asked Joentaa.

'After that I thought: either this is just childish and I'm sitting opposite a precocious girl talking nonsense at random, or I'm dreaming, or I've gone crazy, or all at once . . . good heavens, how would I know?'

Ketola got up, stood there for a minute, and cut himself a piece of cake as if he had just been waiting for the moment when he could do that. 'Want some too?' he asked.

Joentaa did not react, and Ketola was not to be deterred. 'It's really good, come on,' he said, cutting another piece.

Joentaa took the plate that Ketola handed him, bit into the soft chocolate icing and thought he felt just as Ketola had on the occasion he described. Soon Sundström would be standing at his door, waking him up.

'It had been raining hard,' said Ketola, wiping his mouth. He seemed relaxed now, as if he were over the worst of it. 'I keep hearing the rain pattering down on the awning when I think back to that day. I said it was too late, it was many years in the past, something like that, and she . . . Sinikka . . . she said well then, it just had to happen again.'

'Had to happen again?'

'Yes. It had to happen again, at the same place and in exactly the same way. Then the murderer of thirty-three years ago would come back, because it would never leave him in peace.'

'And you went along with this?'

'Of course not. I thought it was the silliest idea I'd heard in a long time.'

'But . . . '

'She said she was going to do it. She said she had so often got off her bike when she came to that cross, wondering who Pia was, and now she knew and she was going to do something about it. She would be the girl who disappeared. Her parents were sodding well getting on her wick anyway, excuse the expression but that's how she put it, and she didn't really get on with the people at school either, so anyway she felt like disappearing for a while, as long as necessary. Good, isn't it?'

'What?'

'The cake,' said Ketola.

'Ah.'

'Yes, well, of course I thought: she's just showing off. Well, I probably didn't think anything. The girl left. She did say I'd have to wait a little while, because she wanted to go up into the next year at school, so the whole thing would have to wait until the holidays. Then she left.'

'Go on,' said Kimmo, when Ketola leaned back again.

'I stayed sitting out here on the terrace for quite a long time. That evening I put the model away down in my basement. In my own lumber room. In the furthest corner.'

Ketola raised his eyes and looked Joentaa in the face for the first time since the beginning of this torrent of words.

Joentaa avoided looking back. 'What else?' he asked.

'Nothing else,' said Ketola.

'Nothing else.' He looked at Ketola and felt like laughing. Laughing out loud. Instead, he stood up and went over to the model standing on its worn wheels beside Ketola.

'What do you mean . . . ' he began, but then he heard a rushing sound in his ears, a sound drowning out his own words, and he swung his leg back and kicked the model as hard as he could. It hit the terrace door, came off its wheels and fell into a flower bed. 'What do you mean, nothing else?' shouted Joentaa. 'What's that supposed to mean?'

Ketola looked at the model in the flower bed.

'Where's Sinikka Vehkasalo?' shouted Joentaa.

'I've no idea.'

'Sinikka Vehkasalo . . . is alive,' said Joentaa.

'Of course she's alive,' said Ketola.

Of course . . .

'She simply did what she said she was going to do. I couldn't grasp it myself. I thought it out this way and that, wondered how I ought to react, then I decided to give her a fair chance.'

'A what?'

'Well, I did my best to carry on with what she'd begun. Like the TV interview with Elina. All the time I was trying to . . . to hint all of you in the right direction.'

'Hint us in the right direction?'

'Yes. I mean, I knew Sinikka was alive, that's why I wanted you to concentrate on Pia, so that you'd really look into that old case again.'

'Are you out of your mind?'

'What?'

'I said, are you out of your mind?' Joentaa repeated.

Ketola did not reply.

'How could you face Sinikka's parents knowing that their daughter is still alive?'

'It wasn't easy for me. You know that. I'm . . . it tormented me. Don't you remember, when we went to see the parents together . . .?'

'Yes. I do remember.'

'I thought it over for a very long time, and I was on the point of telling the whole story on the very first day, but then . . . well, something kept me from doing it. It's hard to explain why. I probably made a mistake.'

'Yes. That is perfectly possible.'

'But look at what's happened. That's the crazy part of it. Sinikka was right. That's the craziest part of the whole business!'

Joentaa nodded.

'It's over, Kimmo,' said Ketola.

Joentaa nodded.

'The girl, Sinikka . . . she'll come back.'

Joentaa nodded.

'Soon,' said Ketola.

'Sure,' said Joentaa, suddenly feeling very light-headed and very tired. 'Sure,' he said again.

Then he went over to the flower bed, bent down, picked up the model and anchored it back on its wheeled base. He stood it beside Ketola.

'Thanks,' said Ketola.

Joentaa sat down. 'Sure,' he said again.

He was a little cold, and remembered a night when he had not slept at all and a morning by the sea. In a Dutch seaside resort, he had forgotten its name. Sanna had been lying on the sand beside him asleep, and her little snores had risen above the sound of the waves breaking.

'Sundström will wring my neck,' said Ketola. 'But don't worry, I'll speak to him. We'll put this behind us. I'll take the consequences if there are any.'

'Yes, fine,' murmured Joentaa. He was hardly listening. He was thinking of Sanna. Of the moment when her pulse had stopped. He had felt it fail against his fingers. The moment marking Sanna's death. He had sat up night after night to be with her at that one second.

He thought of Sinikka Vehkasalo and tried

to imagine a day when Sanna would be standing at the door, telling him that it hadn't been like that at all.

He sought Ketola's eyes, but he couldn't meet them.

Soon, Ketola had said.

The word echoed in his thoughts as they sat there together, staring straight ahead.

# 13 June

# 1

Sundström called just after six in the morning. 'I'm here outside your house. Where are you?' he asked.

'Out,' said Joentaa.

'I beg your pardon?'

'It's not developing at all as we expected,' said Joentaa.

'What?'

'I'm just leaving here. I'll be with you in half an hour, and then we can talk.'

'Where are you, then? Hello?'

'See you soon.' Joentaa cut the connection and rose laboriously to his feet.

'Sundström?' asked Ketola.

Kimmo nodded. 'We were going to drive to Helsinki. Well . . . we'll be in touch.'

'We'll be in touch,' Ketola agreed.

Joentaa walked over the lawn that swallowed up his footsteps, feeling weightless. As he drove, he thought vaguely about what he ought to tell Sundström. Probably nothing at all. He would tell him that he had to sleep for a couple of hours, then they'd see.

He drove the long way round.

Silence lay over the pale green clapboard house.

He didn't know what he would tell them. All he knew was that he had to speak to Sinikka's parents. At once.

He was about to get out of the car when he saw the girl in the rear-view mirror. Some way off. She was walking very slowly but easily, almost with a spring in her step. Her head was bent, and she seemed to be concentrating on counting her own footsteps.

She came closer. Now Joentaa saw the backpack over her shoulders, and the sleeping bag and mat under her arm. For a moment he wondered why her parents hadn't noticed that these items were missing. But if he had assessed Sinikka correctly, she would have bought them new and hidden them well while she waited for the right time.

She had been well prepared for this . . . this venture.

She stopped outside the pale green house. After a while she sat down on the bottom step of the flight up to the front door.

She seemed to be waiting. For her parents to wake up. Or for the impulse to ring the bell herself. Or for something quite different.

Joentaa too waited for a while, but then he turned the car and drove towards a day that looked like being as summery as the day before.

# 2

Ruth Vehkasalo lay awake. Kalevi hadn't fallen asleep until morning either. His face looked relaxed, but at the same time marked by pain.

Ruth Vehkasalo turned over and lay on her back. She was relieved to be alone at last. Really alone at last. She had pretended to be asleep during the night, so as not to have to talk to Kalevi. Because she simply had not felt strong enough to exchange another word with him.

Kalevi had paced restlessly round the house. He lay down in bed, jumped up again a few minutes later, left the room, came back again, went out and came back once more. Then he had sat upright in bed, breathing in and out very deliberately and with great concentration, leaning over her from time to time to reassure himself that she was asleep. He had caressed her shoulder very gently for a while, and he never stopped concentrating on the regularity of her breathing.

The TV news had shown a lake that evening, and the car of a man who had died in that lake, in that car. Ruth Vehkasalo had knelt down in front of the TV set, Kalevi had sat on the sofa, leaning forward and murmuring words that made no sense. About how he was going to murder that bastard. A man who was no longer alive and whom they didn't know from Adam. Not even his name.

After a while Kalevi had stopped cursing this unknown, nameless man and had called the police to find out more news. But there was no more news. Or at least, they hadn't told him anything more.

Then he had sat down on the edge of the sofa again and started talking about Sinikka. Had simply started and didn't stop talking about Sinikka, digging up memories from the deepest crannies of his mind, speaking in a voice that seemed to come from a distance, from another room, and she had concentrated on not listening.

She had waited for the torrent of words to ebb away.

A quiz show had begun on television, and Kalevi had brought up films from the lower ground floor and connected the camera to the video recorder, taking no notice of her protests.

'Let's just try it,' he had said. 'If it's no good we'll simply stop. But I think it will do us good,' he had added, red in the face as he sometimes was when he ate too fast, or came

351

back from jogging on a Sunday.

The on-screen quiz had given way to a wintry Alpine panorama.

'Austria,' said Kalevi. 'Four . . . no, five years ago. In winter. As we can see. Sinikka was having her first skiing lessons.'

She had seen Sinikka skiing down a slope. Towards the camera and past it. At high speed. Doing the snowplough. Unsteady on her legs, but confident.

'You remember,' Kalevi had said, winding forward as if he had to find something in particular, but there hadn't been anything specific, just his compulsion to bring Sinikka to life on a screen.

'Kalevi,' she had said, but it was no use talking to Kalevi, he was aimlessly winding the film forwards and backwards, and saying constantly, 'Just a minute. I'll soon find it. Wait.'

After a while she had got up and gone to bed. She had taken two of the tablets that the doctor had prescribed for her. Sinikka's voice could be heard downstairs. And Kalevi's. And her own. A little tinny, but distinctly audible.

She had sat there in bed.

Later Kalevi had come in, taking off only his jacket and trousers, and lay down beside her. 'I'm sorry,' he had said. 'I was probably a bit hysterical.'

'You don't have to apologize,' she had said.

Then they had lain side by side waiting for sleep, which finally came for Kalevi, if not for her. Although she had taken two of those tablets that were supposed to be so strong, and later on two more.

She looked at Kalevi, saw his face marked by pain and exhaustion. Even in sleep he still looked exhausted.

She got up, taking care not to wake him, and went down to the kitchen. She boiled water. She felt thirsty and wanted some tea. Camomile tea. When you were ill camomile tea was soothing, so her mother had taught her. She had died a few years earlier. Ruth Vehkasalo was relieved to think that her mother didn't have to know about what was going on now. The water came to the boil. She chose a large white cup. She sat down at the kitchen table. The steam from the hot water rose to her face. She would have to wait a few minutes before she could drink the tea.

She looked out of the window.

Sinikka was sitting on the steps outside. Not really Sinikka, of course. She had just briefly had the impression that she was looking at Sinikka. It was because of those tablets. So they did have some effect after all, even if not the intended one.

She went over to the window and looked

more closely at the girl. She was looking at the road, and Ruth Vehkasalo hoped she wouldn't turn round, because then of course she would notice her curious glances. The girl did look very like Sinikka. She even had the same short hairstyle, the boyish cut that had annoyed Kalevi. The two of them had had an almighty battle over it, and she herself had even taken Kalevi's side in the end. Although it was an attractive style. What Kalevi had said wasn't true . . . that she wouldn't be recognized as a girl any more, she'd be taken for a boy, and was that what she wanted? What nonsense. Ruth Vehkasalo had seen at once that it was a girl sitting on the steps in front of their house. In spite of the short hair.

The girl had a sleeping bag with her. And a backpack over her shoulder. And a rolled-up mat lying on the ground beside her. That was why it wasn't Sinikka, because Sinikka didn't own those things. And anyway, it couldn't be Sinikka.

She would have to send the girl away. It wasn't right for a girl who looked like Sinikka to be sitting there. Of course the girl couldn't help it, but it was too painful for her to bear, it was just too much. She would tell the girl to go away, she would very calmly just ask the girl please to go.

She went across the hall to the front door

and felt something in her throat, a sense of constriction that made breathing difficult. She opened the door and was going to close it again at once, because she couldn't breathe and she was afraid she couldn't speak.

The girl turned and said, 'I'm back, Mama.'

The hairstyle, she thought. A lovely hairstyle. The pain in her throat seemed to be spreading. Up into her cheeks, down into her chest. She walked backwards. Step by step. She was already in the front hall again and the girl was coming towards her, looking unsure of herself.

'Mama?'

She groped for the banisters. That was better. She could hold on to them. She heard Kalevi's voice. Upstairs. He was standing in the stairwell, at the top of the stairs.

'What is it?' he asked.

She felt something gathering in her throat. It was insisting on breaking out. And she felt something else, she felt everything fizzling out into nothing within seconds. That wasn't bad, quite the contrary. She clung to the banisters and thought that for those things, those things from the past, they had Kalevi's camera and photo albums to look at. When there was a good moment, in fact, they must do that, but only when there was a good moment and it could be some time in coming, she would have to tell Kalevi so. Kalevi, who was just coming downstairs looking at her enquiringly, uneasily.

Kalevi came down, step after step, then he saw the girl in the doorway and stopped.

And stood there.

'Sinikka,' he said.

She heard the name, she felt it sinking in. And now she also felt the scream in her throat slowly moving upwards, and that too would pass over.

Kalevi was beside her. She felt his tears on the palms of her hands and a scream in her throat, and she saw Sinikka standing in the doorway, both strange and close.

Everything else would have to wait, because life, real life, had only just begun.

# 3

Sundström couldn't grasp it. Simply could not grasp it, although Kimmo Joentaa had felt his account of the situation was accurate. He had put it into simple, cogent words. But Sundström said nothing; then, after a long pause, he asked, 'So if I understand you correctly, that means that Sinikka Vehkasalo . . . that possibly . . . she may still be alive?'

They were sitting in Joentaa's kitchen with the morning sunlight flooding through the window.

'No, no,' said Joentaa.

'She isn't?' said Sundström, sounding almost relieved. 'Then I misunderstood.'

'No, what I mean is she's definitely alive. I've seen her.'

Sundström stared at him and waited.

'She's back. She was sitting outside her parents' house when I drove away,' said Joentaa.

'When? When did you drive away?'

'She's back. I saw her outside her parents' house twenty minutes ago,' said Joentaa and when Sundström still went on staring at him

357

with a question in his eyes, he repeated it: 'She's back.'

Sundström stayed in his upright position for a few seconds, then slumped and said in a toneless voice, 'Well, well. Amazing.'

'Ketola says it was her own idea.'

Sundström nodded, but he still didn't seem to understand. 'That means, if I understand you, that Ketola knows Sinikka Vehkasalo . . . '

'No, he doesn't really know her. She visited him. She was at his neighbours', their daughter was having a birthday party. And Ketola was sitting on his terrace and that model was on the terrace as well.'

'What model? You keep on talking about this stupid model . . . '

'The model made at the time of Pia Lehtinen's death, a kind of scene-of-crime sketch. I told you how Ketola took it away on his last day at work. We'd been looking for it down in Archives.'

'Yes, yes, all right.' Sundström fell silent again, stared at a point on the wall and seemed to be busy assembling the pieces of the puzzle into a whole. 'Well, well,' he murmured. 'That would mean . . . correct me if I'm on the wrong track now, but that means that the girl was playing a kind of . . . well, a practical joke.' Sundström's glance moved away from the wall and met Joentaa's eyes. There was even a touch of amusement in his expression. Sundström was fond of jokes.

'No, I wouldn't call it a joke. She . . . I suspect she saw it as an adventure. I don't know exactly what was going on inside her,' said Joentaa.

'A strong wish to torment her parents?' Now Sundström was grinning.

Joentaa did not reply, thinking that he understood that aspect of the case less than anything else about it.

'That must be it. The girl must be out of her mind. Totally deranged!' cried Sundström, and now he appeared almost happy.

Joentaa thought of Sinikka. Of the way she had been sitting on the steps in front of the house. He wondered if she was still sitting there, or whether she had . . .

'And you're out of your mind too, if I may say so. You just drove away without speaking to her! That girl has been the subject of an expensive investigation, am I right?'

Joentaa nodded.

Sundström nodded too.

'I wanted to let her get home first,' said Joentaa.

'Yes,' said Sundström. 'Yes, who wouldn't understand that? Presumably, at this very moment, the daughter is running a kitchen knife into her mother's breast, in return the father is throttling his daughter to death, and now he's sitting quietly with his two dead women in his house until we finally put in an appearance.'

'I don't think so,' said Joentaa.

'How nice,' said Sundström. He was silent for a while, then continued, 'All the same, we'll have to speak to her.'

'Of course,' said Joentaa.

Yet again Sundström seemed remarkably cheerful as he said, 'What an enormous . . . enormous shambles.'

'What do you mean?'

'What do I mean? I mean we've made ourselves appear ridiculous.'

'No one's looked ridiculous.'

'Searching for a girl who wasn't even missing.'

'But she was missing.'

'You know what I'm getting at. No, really, now I'm doubly, trebly curious about that . . . peculiar young person.'

'We ought to take this slowly,' said Joentaa.

Sundström was going to say something, but then he stopped and just nodded. 'Luckily Nurmela's the one responsible for contact with the press. Don't worry, he'll show it all as a great success. And ultimately, well, it doesn't matter. The main thing is that the girl is back and the old case . . . well, the really crazy part is that her extraordinary idea even, in a certain way, worked.'

Joentaa nodded and thought that Ketola had put it in just the same way.

'What a weird thing,' murmured Sundström.

Joentaa thought of the woman who had opened the door to them. Of the business card. Of the boy with the football outside the garage.

'Her parents will be beating the living daylights out of that young lady,' said Sundström.

He thought of Sanna on the landing stage in the rocking chair, wrapped in blankets.

'Beating the living daylights out of her,' Sundström repeated.

'They'll be glad to have her back,' said Joentaa.

# 4

Sinikka was small and slender. A slender little figure, making her purposeful way through the woods a few metres ahead of them, while Kimmo concentrated on the feeling he had had when he was walking over the lawn in Ketola's garden early that morning.

A feeling that did him good, one he wanted to hold on to, a sense of lightness.

A sense of being slightly out of this world, hovering a little way above the ground.

It was pleasantly cool in the shade of the trees. At first joggers and cyclists had come towards them, casting curious glances. By now the paths were narrower, and Sinikka went on and on as if she were never going to stop again.

Nurmela kept up with her, even overtook her now and then, although he didn't know the way. Sundström strolled along beside Kimmo like someone out for a casual walk.

Joentaa thought of the conversation they had had that morning in the conference room. Sundström had explained the changed situation to the others. The message had been slow to make its way into their heads. Then

362

Grönholm, who liked to talk a lot at the top of his voice, had lapsed into deep silence where he sat. Quiet Heinonen had uttered curses in loud, clear tones. Kari Niemi had leaned back against the wall, smiling. Nurmela had looked at Sundström as if, by means of an intensive stare, he could cancel out what had just been said. But Sundström hadn't let that shake him and ended his account of the latest incidents with the remark, 'I'd say that girl has a sense of humour.'

Then they went to see the Vehkasalos. Sinikka's father opened the door. In his pyjamas, with reddened eyes. Ruth Vehkasalo had been sitting beside Sinikka in the kitchen, an arm round her shoulders. There was a bowl of oatflakes and milk on the table in front of Sinikka.

Nurmela tried to find words. The others said nothing.

'Sinikka is back,' Kalevi Vehkasalo finally said.

Ruth Vehkasalo had been shedding silent tears.

'In the woods,' Sinikka said when Nurmela asked where she had spent the last few days.

In the woods they were now walking through.

'Are we nearly there?' asked Nurmela yet

again. Sinikka nodded and walked on and on, until Joentaa thought that they would never arrive. Then after all Sinikka stopped, and seemed to be surprised that her companions were surprised.

She pointed up. Nurmela breathed out as if he had been making a strenuous effort. After a few seconds of surprise, Sundström began chuckling quietly.

They stood there for a while, craning their necks and looking up at the tree house under the clear sky.

'I didn't build it myself,' said Sinikka. 'I just found it here. Last summer.'

'Well, well,' said Nurmela.

'I knew at once that was how to do it. No one ever comes this way.'

'I can well imagine it,' said Nurmela.

'Crazy,' said Sundström.

Sinikka clambered up.

Nurmela took a jump, slipped and fell to the ground. 'Not for me,' he muttered, straightening his jacket.

'Who are you telling?' said Sundström.

Joentaa himself made several false starts before hauling himself up to the tree house. Then he was sitting beside Sinikka. He felt dizzy. He saw the things that Sinikka showed him through a blur. A bag of provisions. Mainly cans. A small rectangular radio.

'The reception was quite good,' she said as he stared at the radio.

The tree house seemed stable and had a surprising amount of room in it. Sinikka's left hand was bandaged with a thick layer of sticking plaster.

'Your injury? Did you do it yourself?' asked Joentaa.

Sinikka nodded. 'Well, the blood was important, wasn't it?'

'I suppose so,' replied Joentaa, thinking of what Ketola had said. A silly idea; the silliest idea he'd ever heard of.

'Did you really think that this . . . that all this would work?'

She looked at him for a long time. Then she shrugged her shoulders and said, 'I hadn't the faintest.'

'How long would you have stayed here? If . . . if your plan hadn't worked?'

'I don't know,' she said. 'As long as possible.'

'What I don't understand — and you must have thought of this — is . . . well, about your parents, and of course your friends as well. You must have thought how they'd be feeling.'

Once again she looked at him for a long time.

'Everything okay up there?' called Sundström from below.

Joentaa leaned forward and saw the other two standing side by side on the ground. Nurmela was nursing his arm and swearing quietly. Presumably he'd hurt himself in his run-up to the tree.

'We're coming right down,' Joentaa called back.

He got no answer to his question from Sinikka. Perhaps there wasn't one. Or at least, not one that he would have understood.

They went back the same way as they had come. This time Nurmela and Sundström went ahead. Nurmela was talking to Sundström, planning the next few hours. He held his arm at a right angle as if it were broken, and talked on and on, although in a calm, self-controlled voice. Whether you liked Nurmela or not — and he could certainly pull out the emotional stops, as he was doing now with that arm — no one could say he didn't keep a cool head in awkward situations.

Sinikka walked beside Kimmo, listening attentively to the two men ahead of them. Joentaa got the impression that only now, in the minutes during which she heard Nurmela and Sundström in animated discussion, was some idea of the consequences of what she had done dawning on her.

They drove back in silence. Nurmela was

scribbling notes in a small book, and he pointed out in passing, just in case they were anxious about it, that he had only wrenched his arm.

'Don't worry, we aren't anxious,' said Sundström.

Outside the pale green house, Ruth Vehkasalo was waiting for her daughter to return.

# 5

Nurmela dealt with the exigencies of the day in commanding fashion and with alarming efficiency.

He had a conversation with Sinikka's parents in which he gently pointed out that it wasn't over yet. He told them that inevitably Sinikka was going to be at the centre of public interest, and the question of the consequences still had to be cleared up. After all, Sinikka had started off an expensive investigation. Kalevi Vehkasalo thanked him and said no more, but Joentaa thought he heard the words that were on the tip of his tongue, and his wife's tongue too: they none of them needed to worry about that, not at all, not today or at any time in the near future.

Then Nurmela coordinated the break-up of the groups of investigating officers. He seemed to enjoy restoring order. In the corridors and the canteen, after that, a mood that was difficult to define but seemed almost relaxed prevailed. Some people were amused, some acted as if they were amused. Others didn't understand what exactly had happened, others again freely expressed their disapproval, in the same way as Tuomas Heinonen that morning. Not much work was done, simply because the case that had been occupying at least the officers on the third floor of the police building had burst like a soap bubble.

Nurmela did not seem to be disturbed by the chaos following the restoration of normal order. He held his arm away from his body for all to see, thus appearing to be borne up on wings of inspiration. In Joentaa's opinion, he took that feeling with him to the press conference that he staged with Sundström's support, and with an eye on the right quarters, as a perfect mixture of objectivity, serious concern and smug satisfaction. Questions about details were blocked with the indication that it was still too early to go into that.

Nurmela went to hospital to have his arm X-rayed.

A TV team from the public broadcaster YLE parked a transmission van outside the police building and issued hourly bulletins on the news. A small commercial station in Turku even built an improvised studio.

Tuomas Heinonen and Petri Grönholm communicated with officials in Turku and their colleagues in Helsinki to gain a more precise picture of the dead man in the lake,

Timo Korvensuo. The last meeting of the day was devoted to his person, and at the beginning of his remarks Petri Grönholm, himself very likely light-headed with the absurdities of the last few hours, said something that stuck in Kimmo Joentaa's memory. 'Somehow it's kind of funny, but while Sinikka Vehkasalo in the flesh has come back to us, our estate agent seems to have been, in a way, entirely extinguished. At least so far as his life and activities in Turku are concerned.'

'Meaning?' asked Sundström.

'I've had several telephone conversations, and I have to say, well, it's turning out difficult to form any idea of him. He seems to have been very much a loner. When he was living in Turku. And would you believe it, there was a fire at City Hall. The register of residents went up in flames. In 1985. No computer data available.'

'Oh.'

'So we don't even know where Korvensuo was living. As long as no friend or fellow student of his can tell us anything, all we know is that he was studying mathematics. And chemistry and physics as subsidiary subjects.'

'Excellent combination,' said Sundström.

'And the university did have an address,

370

but it was his parents' home address in Tampere. When Korvensuo registered he probably didn't have a place of his own yet in Turku, so he gave that address. And he never corrected it.'

'I get the idea,' said Sundström.

'The parents are both dead. No brothers or sisters . . . and considering the state of affairs, none of that really matters,' said Grönholm. 'Sinikka is back, and as for the girl who went missing in the mid eighties . . . '

'Marika Paloniemi,' said Joentaa.

'That was it. Any connection between Korvensuo and her disappearance seems fanciful, in view of the new situation. Korvensuo had been living in Helsinki for a long time then. And incidentally, he never had a small red car after 1982. That's according to his wife, who knew him from then on. She says her husband didn't like the colour red. Which does not suggest that he ever had a red car.'

Or maybe he did have a red car and never wanted to be reminded of it again, thought Joentaa.

He saw Marjatta Korvensuo again in his mind's eye. The living room where they had sat on white sofas. The bright entrance hall. The sparsely furnished room in the basement, all right angles. Ketola in front of the

371

screen, now switched off. Nothing in that house had been red.

'It's quite possible that this small red car never existed. Either in connection with Pia Lehtinen or with anyone else,' said Sundström. 'Just a false trail.'

Grönholm nodded. 'Incidentally, the wife is twelve years younger than Korvensuo. When they met in 1982 he was twenty-nine and she was only seventeen,' he said. 'He obviously kept silent as the grave about his days in Turku. His wife knows almost nothing about that time.'

'Of course our colleagues in Helsinki are seeing if they can connect Korvensuo with any unsolved cases. They're only just beginning, but nothing so far,' said Heinonen.

'Right,' said Sundström, nodding.

The rest kept quiet.

'How . . . how is his wife?' asked Joentaa.

Heinonen shook his head. 'I don't know.'

Nor did Grönholm. 'We've only spoken to our colleagues, not to the wife herself.'

'About the files on Korvensuo's computer. The thing is stuffed with child porn: photos and clips. What you might call bursting at the seams with them,' said Heinonen.

'Charming,' said Sundström. 'Then if I may sum up: we have a missing girl who has come home safe and sound. We have a case thirty years old . . . '

'Thirty-three,' said Joentaa.

'A case thirty-three years old of a murdered girl which was cleared up yesterday, in view of the fact that the presumed murderer drowned himself and his showy car in the lake where he sank his victim back in the past. Right?'

'That's it,' Grönholm agreed.

'We have a Helsinki estate agent, name of Timo Korvensuo, as the sole tangible object of this . . . er, absurd investigation. Korvensuo, who goes off two days after the disappearance of Sinikka Vehkasalo, pretending he has a business engagement, to seek out Pia Lehtinen's mother, give her his business card and take his own life. Belated remorse. Or whatever. Is that it?'

No one replied. No one contradicted him.

'Okay,' said Sundström. 'Great. Speaking for myself, my head is spinning.' He turned away and had almost crossed the room when he turned once more.

'And by the way, you'd better start thinking up ideas,' he said. 'Ideas for ways to bring tears to Nurmela's eyes, I mean. Because of the usual present given to sufferers in such cases. He called me half an hour ago. His wrist is broken. In a very complicated way, like he emphasized. Surprise result of the X-ray examination.'

# 6

A quarter to six.

Mow the grass behind number 86.

He wrote it down in his notebook before going out.

A hot sun was shining down. Old Mrs Kononen from number 89 was putting out the washing on her balcony, and ostentatiously looked away when she saw him.

Even though he'd oiled the squeaking hinges of the swings long ago. Not a sound to be heard when the children went on the swings. Like the little boy just now, who shouted that he was just going over the top of the frame.

'Any moment now! Watch out!' shouted the boy, and he swung higher and higher, and Pärssinen felt as if the boy would crash to the ground on the seat of his trousers any moment, and took a few steps back, ready to catch him.

But the boy lost impetus and beamed at him, and Pärssinen returned the smile and thought that it must be a lot of fun playing on the swings. Not for him now, though. Not at his age.

He went to the shed and pushed the lawnmower out. He sat on it, started the engine and rode round to the other side, to the back of building 86. He began circling round the grass area that, he knew, it would take him half an hour to cut. Tomorrow it would be the turn of numbers 87 and 88. And the day after that numbers 89 and 90. And next week he would mow the big expanse of turf surrounding the playground. He liked the loud roar of the engine, the effortless power with which it drowned out all other sounds.

He waved to Virpi Jokinen, passing with her two little dogs, and thought of Timo, who had come back. He wondered how Timo was. It had been an odd meeting between them a few days ago. How long ago exactly? He'd written it down in his notebook.

He liked Timo. Always had, even at the time when he'd been so worried, after Timo's disappearance and after the bad thing that had . . . had happened to him and Timo.

He wondered whether Timo knew that. Knew that he really liked him, even liked him a lot, or whether Timo maybe saw him in quite the wrong light.

He had a feeling that this time Timo

wouldn't come back, and he felt sad. But maybe he was wrong, because only a few days ago he would never in his wildest dreams have expected to see Timo again, which meant that Timo might surprise him by coming to his door some other day. Some time or other.

Soothed by this idea, he turned off the engine and surveyed the regularly mown grass. It looked lovely. He liked it.

The boy was swinging himself up to the sky as he pushed the mower into the shed.

'Careful,' called Pärssinen, but the boy didn't seem to hear him, or simply didn't want good advice.

He's right, thought Pärssinen, he himself hated good advice, and now here he was beginning to hand it out. He really must be getting old.

He went over to the new flower bed at the side of the car park and moved the sprinkler from right to left. The plants were in bloom already.

When he went back to the building old Mrs Kononen called to say he'd done a good job. The swing wasn't squealing any more.

'Thanks,' he called back. 'Thanks.'

Then he went into the stairwell.

He looked at the time.

Six fifteen.

Sprinkler by the car park moved, he thought.

And thanks from old Mrs Kononen.

He smiled as he entered the darkness of his flat.

# Acknowledgements

My thanks to Niina and Venla, Georg and Wolfgang, Esther and my parents.

We do hope that you have enjoyed reading
this large print book.

Did you know that all of our titles
are available for purchase?

We publish a wide range of high quality
large print books including:
**Romances, Mysteries, Classics**
**General Fiction**
**Non Fiction and Westerns**

Special interest titles available in
large print are:
**The Little Oxford Dictionary**
**Music Book**
**Song Book**
**Hymn Book**
**Service Book**

Also available from us courtesy of Oxford
University Press:
**Young Readers' Dictionary**
**(large print edition)**
**Young Readers' Thesaurus**
**(large print edition)**

For further information or a free
brochure, please contact us at:
**Ulverscroft Large Print Books Ltd.,**
**The Green, Bradgate Road, Anstey,**
**Leicester, LE7 7FU, England.**
**Tel:** (00 44) **0116 236 4325**
**Fax:** (00 44) **0116 234 0205**

*Other titles published by*
*The House of Ulverscroft:*

## INTO DARKNESS

### Jonathan Lewis

Lying facedown in Docklands mud, saintly Sir Tommy Best, Britain's best-loved entertainer and tireless charity benefactor, is found dead. His guide-dog, Suzy, is found cowering a mile away. With no clues or witnesses to the killing, the case is assigned to the brilliant DCI Ned Bale. But police dog-handler Kate baker, believes that Suzy holds the secret of her master's fate. The public turns the wharf into a shrine and the tabloids bay for blood. meanwhile, the police suspecting that Sir Tommy wasn't all he seemed, must retrace, step by painstaking step, his last walk into darkness . . .

# BLOOD IN GRANDPONT

## Peter Tickler

When a woman is stabbed to death in an Oxford car park, a revealing photograph on her mobile points towards a crime of sexual passion or revenge. But as DI Holden and her team investigate further, it seems that things might not be as clear cut as they first appeared. Then another body is found in the Guardian-reading, Labour-voting area of Oxford known as Grandpont, adding a whole new dimension to the case. Now, as the complications pile up in Holden's professional and personal life, finding the killer becomes more than a matter of life and death . . .

# ALL THAT FOLLOWS

## Jim Crace

Leonard Lessing is a jazzman taking a break. His glory days behind him, his body letting him down, he relives old gigs and feeds his media addiction during solitary days at home. Increasingly estranged from his wife Francine, who is herself mourning the sudden absence of her only daughter, Leonard has found his own safe, suburban groove. But then a news bulletin comes that threatens to change everything. A gunman has seized hostages a short drive from Lennie's house. His face leaps out of the evening news — and out of Leonard's own past . . . Leonard has a choice to make.

# THE KILLING CLUB

## Angela Dracup

Christian Hartwell's scarred corpse is found at the foot of Fellbeck Crag in Yorkshire. Was his death a suicide — or something more sinister? DCI Ed Swift and DI Cat Fallon question Ruth Hartwell, the victim's adoptive mother, who is unable to shed light on her son's final days. Whilst her daughter Harriet has a strange, unrelated tale to tell Swift . . . Then a man calling himself Mac the Knife threatens Ruth and her family. Swift knows that it's vital for him to find the truth and fast — yet he will risk not only his job but also his life . . .

# CRACKS

## Sheila Kohler

A beautiful schoolgirl mysteriously disappears into the South African veldt. Forty years later, ten members of the missing girl's swimming team gather at their old boarding school for a reunion, and look back to the long, dry weeks leading to Fiamma's disappearance. As teenage memories and emotions resurface, the women relive the horror of a long-buried secret, which hides the tribalism of adolescence — and the violence that lies in the heart of even the most innocent . . .